Patricia Cornwell's most recent number one bestsellers include *Book of the Dead*, *Predator*, *Trace* and *Portrait of a Killer: Jack the Ripper – Case Closed*. Her earlier work includes *Postmortem* – the only novel to win the Edgar, Creasey, Anthony and Macavity awards, and the French Prix du Roman d'Aventure in a single year – and *Cruel and Unusual*, which won Britain's prestigious Gold Dagger Award for best crime novel of 1993. Her fictional chief medical examiner, Dr Kay Scarpetta, won the 1999 Sherlock Award for best detective created by an American author.

Visit her website at www.patriciacornwell.com

Also by Patricia Cornwell

PATRICIA CORNWELL OMNIBUS

AT RISK

THE FRONT

SPHERE

This omnibus edition first published in Great Britain in 2008 by Sphere

Copyright © Cornwell Enterprises, Inc 2008

Previously published separately:
At Risk first published in the US in 2006 by G.P. Putnam's Sons, a member of
Penguin Group (USA) Inc.
First published in Great Britain in 2006 by Time Warner Books
Paperback edition published in 2007 by Sphere
Copyright © CEI Enterprises, Inc 2006
Originally published in serial form in the *New York Times Magazine*
The Front first published in the US in 2008 by G.P. Putnam's Sons, a member of
Penguin Group (USA) Inc.
First published in Great Britain in 2008 by Little, Brown
Copyright © Cornwell Enterprises, Inc 2008

A CIP catalogue record for this book
is available from the British Library.

ISBN 978-1-84744-290-1

Papers used by Sphere are natural, renewable and recyclable
products made from wood grown in sustainable forests and certified
in accordance with the rules of the Forest Stewardship Council.

Mixed Sources
Product group from well-managed
forests and other controlled sources
www.fsc.org   Cert no. SGS-COC-004081
© 1996 Forest Stewardship Council

FSC

Typeset in Caslon by M Rules
Printed and bound in Great Britain by
Clays Ltd, St Ives plc

Sphere
An imprint of
Little, Brown Book Group
100 Victoria Embankment
London EC4Y 0DY

An Hachette Livre UK Company
www.hachettelivre.co.uk

www.littlebrown.co.uk

AT RISK

To
Dr. Joel J. Kassimir,
a true artist

1

AN AUTUMN STORM has pounded Cambridge all day and is set to play a violent encore into the night. Lightning sears and thunder startles as Winston Garano ("Win" or "Geronimo" most people call him) strides through the dusk along the eastern border of Harvard Yard.

He has no umbrella. He has no jacket. His Hugo Boss suit and dark hair are dripping wet and pressed flat against him, his Prada shoes soaked and filthy from a false step out of the taxi into a puddle. Of course, the damn taxi driver let him out at the wrong damn address, not at 20 Quincy Street in front of the Harvard Faculty Club but at the Fogg Art Museum, and that was Win's miscalculation, really. When he got into the taxi at Logan International Airport, he happened to tell the driver, *Harvard Faculty Club, it's near the Fogg,* thought maybe if he referenced both he might sound like someone who went to Harvard or collects fine art instead of what he is, an investigator with the Massachusetts State Police who applied to Harvard seventeen years ago and didn't get in.

Big raindrops feel like irritable fingers tapping the top of his head and he is overcome by anxiety as he stands on the old red-brick walk in the midst of the old red-brick Yard, looking up and down Quincy Street, watching people spew past in cars and on bicycles, a few on foot and hunched under umbrellas. Privileged people move through the rain and mist, belonging here and knowing they do and where they are going.

"Excuse me," Win says to a guy in a black windbreaker and baggy, faded jeans. "Your Mensa question for the day."

"Huh?" He scowls, having just crossed the wet one-way street, a soggy satchel dripping from his back.

"Where's the faculty club?"

"Right there," he replies with unnecessary snottiness, probably because if Win were a faculty member or anyone important, obviously he would know where the faculty club is.

He heads toward a handsome Georgian Revival building with a gray slate roof, the brick patio blossoming with wet, white umbrellas. Lighted windows are warm in the gathering darkness, and the quiet splashing of a fountain blends with the sounds of the rain as he follows slick cobblestones to the front door, running his fingers through his wet hair. Inside, he looks around as if he's just entered a crime scene, taking in his surroundings, making judgments about what must have been a parlor for some wealthy aristocrat more than a century ago. He surveys mahogany paneling, Persian rugs, brass chandeliers, Victorian theater broadsheets, oil portraits and polished old stairs that lead somewhere he'll probably never go.

He takes a seat on a stiff antique sofa, a grandfather clock reminding him that he is exactly on time and that District Attorney Monique Lamont ("Money La-Mount," as he calls her), the woman who basically runs his life, is nowhere in sight. In Massachusetts, the DAs have jurisdiction over all homicides and have their own state police investigative service assigned to them, and what that means is that Lamont can bring anybody she wants into her personal squad, meaning she can also get rid of anybody she wants. He belongs to her and she has her ways of reminding him of that.

This is the latest, the worst of all her political maneuvering, and in some instances shortsighted reasoning, or what he sometimes views as her fantasies, all of it radiating from her insatiable ambition and need to control. She suddenly decides to send him way down South to Knoxville, Tennessee, to attend the National Forensic Academy, saying that when he returns he will enlighten his colleagues about the latest innovations in crime scene investigation, show them how to do it right, exactly right. Show them how to ensure that no criminal investigation *will ever, and I mean ever, be compromised by the mishandling of evidence or the absence of procedures and analyses that should have been done,* she said. He doesn't understand it. The Massachusetts State Police has CSIs. Why not send one of them? She wouldn't listen. She wouldn't explain.

Win looks down at the soggy shoes he bought for twenty-two dollars at the vintage clothing shop called Hand-Me-Ups. He notices the beginning of dried water spots on the gray suit he got for a hundred and twenty dollars at the same shop where he's gotten quite a lot of designer clothing dirt cheap because everything is used, cast off by rich people who easily tire of things or are infirm or dead. He waits and worries, wondering what is so important that Lamont has summoned him all the way up here from Knoxville. Roy, her wimpish, supercilious press secretary, called him this morning, yanked him out of class, told him to be on the next flight to Boston.

Right this minute? Why? Win protested.

Because she said so, Roy replied.

INSIDE THE HIGH-RISE, precast Cambridge District Court building, Monique Lamont emerges from the private powder room inside her large private office. Unlike many DAs and others who wade in the world of criminal justice, she doesn't collect police caps and patches or foreign uniforms and weapons or framed photographs of famed law enforcement officials. Those who give her such mementos do so only once, because she doesn't hesitate to give them back or away. She happens to like glass.

Art glass, stained glass, Venetian glass, new glass, old glass. When sunlight fills her office, it turns into a prismatic fire, flashing, winking, glowing, sparkling in a spectrum of colors, distracting people, amazing them. She welcomes distracted, amazed people to her rainbow, then introduces them to the nasty storm that preceded it.

"Hell no," she picks up where she left off as she sits down at her expansive glass desk, a see-through desk that doesn't deter her in the least from wearing short skirts. "Another damn educational video on drunk driving is not going to happen. Does anybody besides me think outside the box?"

"Last week in Tewksbury, an entire family was killed by a drunk driver," Roy says from a sofa catty-corner to the desk, looking at her legs when he assumes she doesn't notice. "That's far more relevant to citizens than some old murder case from some provincial Southern city nobody around here cares . . ."

"Roy." Lamont crosses her legs and watches him watching her. "Do you have a mother?"

"Come on, Monique."

"Of course you have a mother." She gets up, starts pacing, wishes the sun was out.

She hates rain.

"How would you like it, Roy, if your ninety-pound elderly mother were beaten savagely in her own home and left to die alone?"

"Oh, come on, Monique. That's not the point. We should be focusing on a Massachusetts unsolved homicide, not one in Hickville. How many times do we have to go through this?"

"You're foolish, Roy. We send in one of our finest and solve it and get—"

"I know, I know. Huge national attention."

"The sure, strong hand reaching down to help those less fortunate, less, well . . . less everything. We get the old evidence, reexamine it—"

"And make Huber look good. Somehow, it will be him and the governor who look good. You're kidding yourself if you think otherwise."

"It will make *me* look good. And you're going to make sure of that—"

She abruptly stops talking as the office door opens and coincidentally, maybe too coincidentally, her law clerk walks in without knocking. Huber's son. It briefly crosses her mind that he's been eavesdropping. But the door is shut. It isn't possible.

"Toby?" she warns. "Am I psychotic or did you just walk in without knocking again?"

"Sorry about that. Man, I got too much on my mind."

He sniffs, shakes his shaved head, looks half stoned. "I just wanted to remind you I'm taking off."

For good, she wishes. "I'm completely aware," she says.

"Be back next Monday. Hanging out at the Vineyard, chilling, my dad knows where to find me if you need me."

"You've taken care of all pending matters?"

He sniffs again. Lamont's pretty sure he's fond of cocaine. "Uh, like what?"

"Uh, like everything I've put on your desk," she says, tapping a gold pen on a legal pad.

"Oh, yeah, sure. And I was a good boy, cleaned up everything, straightened up so you won't have to pick up after me." He smirks, his resentful feelings toward her peeking through his fog, leaves, shuts the door.

"One of my bigger mistakes," she says. "Never do a favor for a colleague."

"It's obvious you've made your decision and it's as final as death," Roy picks up where he left off. "And I reiterate my belief that you're making a very big mistake. Maybe a fatal one."

"Cut the death analogies, Roy. They really annoy me. I could use a coffee."

GOVERNOR MILES CRAWLEY sits in the backseat of his black limousine, the partition up, his executive protection out of sight, unable to hear him on the phone.

"Don't be so damn sure you get careless," he says, staring down at his long, pinstripe-clad legs stretched out, staring blankly at his shiny black shoes. "What if someone talks? And we shouldn't be talking about this . . ."

"The *someone* involved isn't going to talk. That's guaranteed. And I'm never careless."

"No guarantees except death and taxes," the governor says, cryptically.

"In this instance, you've got a guarantee, no way to lose. Who didn't know where it was? Who lost it? Who hid it? No matter what, who looks bad?"

The governor gazes out the window at the darkness, the rain, the lights of Cambridge shining through, not so sure he should have gone along with this, decides, "Well, there's no turning back since it's out to the press. You'd damn well better hope you're right, because the person I'll blame is you. It was your damn idea."

"Trust me, it will all be good news for you."

The governor could use a little good news. His wife is a real pain in the ass these days, his bowels are acting up, and he's off to another dinner. This one is at the Fogg Art Museum, where he'll walk around looking at Degas paintings, then say a few words to make sure all the art-loving philanthropists and Harvard elitists are reminded of what a cultured man he is.

"I don't want to talk about this any further," the governor says.

"Miles . . ."

He hates being called by his first name, no matter how long he has known the person. It's *Governor Crawley*. Someday *Senator Crawley*.

". . . you'll be thanking me, I promise . . ."

"Don't make me repeat myself," Governor Crawley warns. "This is the last time we have this conversation." He ends the call, tucks his cell phone back in his jacket pocket.

The limousine pulls up to the front of the Fogg. Crawley waits for his private protection to let him out, lead him on to his next political performance, alone. Damn his wife and her damn sinus headaches. He was briefed on Degas not even an hour ago, at least knows how to pronounce his name and that he was French.

LAMONT GETS UP, slowly paces, looking out the window at a depressingly dark, wet dusk, sipping coffee that tastes burned.

"The media's already started calling," Roy says as a warning.

"I believe that was the plan," she says.

"And we need a damage-control plan . . ."

"Roy. I can't hear much more of this!"

He's such a coward, the gutless wonder, she thinks, her back to him.

"Monique, I just don't see how you can possibly believe

that any scheme of the governor's is going to benefit you in the end."

"If we're going to get fifty million dollars to build a new crime lab," she repeats herself slowly, as if he is stupid, "we have to get attention, show the public, the legislators, we're completely justified in upgrading technology, hiring more scientists, buying more lab equipment, building the biggest DNA database in the country, maybe even in the world. We solve some old case that people in the good ol' South have left in a cardboard box for twenty years, and we're heroes. The taxpayers support us. Nothing succeeds like success."

"More of Huber's brainwashing. What crime lab director wouldn't want to talk you into that, despite the risk to you?"

"Why can't you see what a good idea this is?" she says in frustration, looking out at the rain, the relentless, dreary rain.

"Because Governor Crawley hates you," Roy replies flatly. "Ask yourself why he would hand this off to you."

"Because I'm the most visible DA in the common-wealth. I'm a woman. So he doesn't look like the small-minded, sexist, right-wing bigot he really is."

"And running against him—any failure will be on your head, not his. You'll be Robert E. Lee surrendering your sword, not him . . ."

"So now he's Ulysses S. Grant. Win will get this done."

"More likely do you in."

She slowly turns around, faces Roy, watches him flip through a notebook.

"Just how much do you know about him?" he says.

"He's the best investigator in the unit. Politically, a perfect choice."

"Vain, obsessed with clothes." He reads his notes. "Designer suits, a Hummer, a Harley, raising questions about his finances. A Rolex."

"A Breitling. Titanium. Probably *gently used,* from one of his many secondhand shops," she says.

Roy looks up, baffled. "How do you know where he gets his stuff?"

"Because I recognize the finer things in life. One morning I asked him how he afforded the Hermès tie he happened to be wearing that day."

"Consistently late when called to crime scenes," Roy goes on.

"According to whom?"

He flips several more pages, runs down one of them with his finger. She waits for his lips to move as he silently reads. *There, they just moved. Dear God. The world is full of imbeciles.*

"Doesn't appear he's gay," Roy continues. "That's good news."

"Actually, it would be rather huge-minded of us if our poster-boy detective was gay. What does he drink?"

"Well, he's not gay, that's for sure," Roy says. "A womanizer."

"According to whom? What does he like to drink?"

Roy pauses, confounded, says, "Drink? No, he doesn't have that problem at least . . ."

"Vodka, gin, beer?" She's about to lose her patience entirely.

"I got no friggin' idea."

"Then you call his pal Huber and find out. And I mean before I get to the faculty club."

"Sometimes I just don't understand you, Monique." He returns to his notes. "Narcissistic."

"Who wouldn't be if he looked like him," she says.

"Conceited, a pretty-boy empty suit. You should hear what the other cops have to say about him."

"I believe I just did."

Win Garano enters her mind. His dark, wavy hair, flawless face. A body that looks sculpted of creamy tan stone. And his eyes, something about his eyes. When he looks at her, she gets the uncanny sensation that he is read- ing her, knows her, maybe even knows something she doesn't.

He'll be perfect on TV, perfect in photo shoots.

". . . probably the only two good things I can say about him is he shows well," poor inadequate Roy is saying, "and has somewhat of a minority status. Albeit high-yellow, nei- ther nor."

"What did you just say?" Lamont stares at him. "I'm going to pretend you didn't."

"Then what do we call it?"

"We don't call it anything."

"African-Italian? Well, I guess so," he answers his own questions as he skips through the notebook. "Father was black, mother Italian. Apparently decided to give him his mother's name, Garano, for obvious reasons. Both parents dead. Faulty heater. Some dump they lived in when he was a kid."

Lamont fetches her coat from the back of the door.

"His upbringing's a mystery. Got no idea who raised him, lists no closest next of kin, the person to contact in an emergency someone named Farouk, apparently his land-lord."

She digs her car keys out of her bag.

"Less about him, more about me," she says. "His history isn't important. Mine is. My accomplishments. My record. My stand on the issues that matter. Crime. Not just today's crime. Not just yesterday's crime." She walks out the door. "Any crime, any time."

"Yup," Roy follows her. "Some campaign slogan you got there."

2

LAMONT SNAPS SHUT her umbrella and unbuttons her long, black raincoat as she notices Win on an antique sofa that's about as comfortable as a wooden plank.

"Hope you haven't been waiting long," she apologizes.

If she cared about inconveniencing him, she wouldn't have ordered him to fly all the way here for dinner, interrupted his training at the National Forensic Academy, interrupted his life, as usual. She's carrying a plastic bag that has the name of a liquor store on it.

"Meetings, and the traffic was awful," she says, forty-five minutes late.

"Actually, I just got here." Win gets up, his suit covered

with water spots that couldn't possibly have dried if he'd only just come in out of the rain.

She slips off her coat and it's hard not to notice what's beneath it. Lamont wears a suit better than any woman he knows. It's a shame Mother Nature wasted such good looks on her. Her name is French and she looks French, dark and exotic, sexy and seductive in a dangerous way. Had life turned out differently and Win had gone to Harvard and she wasn't so driven and selfish, they would probably get along fine and end up in bed.

She eyes his gym bag, frowns a little, says, "Now that's obsessive. You somehow fit in a workout between the airport and here?"

"Had to bring some stuff." He self-consciously shifts the bag to his other hand, careful not to clank the glass items inside it, items a tough cop like him shouldn't carry, especially not around a tough DA like Lamont.

"You can leave it in the cloakroom. Over there by the men's room. You don't have a gun in it, do you?"

"Just an Uzi. The only thing they'll let you carry on planes anymore."

"You can hang this up while you're at it." She hands him her coat. "And this is for you."

She hands him the bag, he peeks inside, sees a bottle of Booker's bourbon in its wooden crate, expensive stuff, his favorite.

"How did you know?"

"I know a lot about my staff, make that my mission."

It rankles him to be referred to as *staff.* "Thanks," he mutters.

Inside the cloakroom, he carefully tucks the bag out of sight on top of a shelf, then follows Lamont into a dining room with candles and white cloths and waiters in white jackets. He tries not to think about his spotted suit and soaked shoes as he and Lamont sit across from each other at a corner table. It is dark out, lamps along Quincy Street blurry through the rain and fog, and people heading into the club for dinner. They don't have spots on their clothes, belong here, probably went to school here, maybe teach here, are the sort of people Monique Lamont dates or has as friends.

"At Risk," she starts in. "Our governor's new crime initiative, which he has handed off to me." She shakes open a linen napkin and drapes it over her lap as the waiter appears. "A glass of sauvignon blanc. The one from South Africa I had last time. And sparkling water."

"Iced tea," Win says. "What crime initiative?"

"Indulge yourself," she says with a smile. "We're honest tonight."

"Booker's. On the rocks," he tells the waiter.

"DNA is as old as time," she starts in. "And ancestral DNA can take the John Doe out of John Doe cases. You familiar with the new technology they're doing in some of these private labs?"

"Sure. DNAPrint Genomics in Sarasota. I've heard about a number of serial murder cases they've helped solve . . ."

She goes on without him: "Biological samples left in cases where we have no idea who the perpetrator is and come up with nothing in database searches. We retest using this cutting-edge technology. We find out, for example, the suspect turns out to be male, 82 percent European, eighteen percent Native American, so we know he looks white and quite possibly we even know his hair and eye color."

"The *At Risk* part? Besides the fact the governor has to call some new initiative something, I suppose."

"It's obvious, Win. Every time we get another offender out of circulation, society is less *at risk*. The name is my idea, it's my responsibility, my project, and I intend to give it my full attention."

"With all due respect, Monique, couldn't you have just e-mailed me all this? I had to fly up here in a rainstorm all the way from Tennessee so you could tell me about the governor's latest publicity stunt?"

"I'll be brutally candid," she interrupts him, nothing new.

"You're good at brutal." He smiles at her, the waiter suddenly back with their drinks, treating Lamont like royalty.

"Let's be frank," she says. "You're reasonably intelligent. And a media dream."

It's not the first time he's thought about quitting the Massachusetts State Police. He picks up his bourbon, wishes he had ordered a double.

"There was a case in Knoxville twenty years ago . . ." she continues.

"Knoxville?"

The waiter hovers to take their order. Win hasn't even looked at the menu.

"The bisque to start with." Lamont orders. "Salmon. Another sauvignon blanc. Give him that nice Oregon pinot."

"Whatever your steak is, rare," Win says. "A salad with balsamic vinegar. No potato. Let me see. It's just chance I happen to be sent down South to Knoxville, and suddenly you've decided to solve some cold case from down there."

"An elderly woman beaten to death," Lamont continues. "Apparently a burglary gone bad. Possible attempt at sexual assault, nude, her panties down around her knees."

"Seminal fluid?" He can't help himself. Politics or not, cases pull him in like black holes.

"I don't know the details." She reaches into her bag, pulls out a manila envelope, hands it to him.

"Why Knoxville?" He won't let it go, his paranoia clutching him harder.

"Needed was a murder and someone special to work on it. You're in Knoxville, why not see what unsolved cases they might have, and there we are. This one apparently sensational at the time, now as cold and forgotten as the victim."

"There are plenty of unsolved cases in Massachusetts." He looks at her, studies her, not sure what's really going on.

"This one should be easy."

"I wouldn't count on that."

"It works out well for a number of reasons. A failure down there won't be as obvious as one up here," she says. "The way we play it, while you were attending the Academy, you heard about the case and suggested Massachusetts could assist, try this new DNA analysis, help them out . . ."

"So you want me to lie," he says.

"I want you to be diplomatic, smart," she says.

Win opens the envelope and slides out copies of newspaper articles, the autopsy and lab reports, none of them very good quality, probably from microfilm.

"Science," she says with confidence. "If it's true there's a God gene, then maybe there's also a Devil gene," she adds. Lamont loves her cryptic quasi-brilliant pronouncements.

She is almost quotable.

"I'm looking for the devil that got away, looking for his ancestral DNA."

"I'm not sure why you're not using the lab in Florida that's known for all this." Win looks over the blurry copy of the autopsy report and adds, "Vivian Finlay. Sequoyah Hills.

Knoxville old money on the river, can't touch a house for under a million. Someone really beat the hell out of her."

Although there are no photographs included in the records Lamont has given him, the autopsy protocol makes several things clear. Vivian Finlay survived long enough to have substantial tissue response, her face lacerated and bruised, her eyes swollen shut. When her scalp was reflected back, it revealed huge contusions, a cranium with punched-out areas caused by the repeated violent blows of a weapon that had at least one round surface.

"If we're testing for DNA, then there must be evidence. Who's had it all this time?" he asks.

"All I know is the FBI did the lab work back then."

"FBI? What interest did the Feds have?"

"I meant the state authorities," she says.

"TBI. Tennessee Bureau of Investigation."

"I don't think they were doing DNA back then."

"Nope. The dark ages when they still did good ol' fashioned serology, ABO typing. Exactly what was analyzed and who's had it all this time?" he tries again.

"Bloody clothing. As I understand it, it was still in the evidence room at the Knoxville PD, was sent to the lab in California . . ."

"California?"

"This has all been carefully researched by Huber."

Win indicates the photocopies she gave him, then asks, "This is everything?"

"Apparently the Knoxville morgue's moved since then, their old records in storage somewhere. What you've got is what Toby tracked down."

"Meaning what he had the ME's office print out from microfilm. What a sleuth," he says sarcastically. "I don't know why in the world you have an idiot like that . . ."

"You know why."

"Don't know how Huber could have an idiot son like that. You should be careful doing favors for the director of the crime labs no matter how great a guy he is, Monique. Could be construed as a conflict of interest . . ."

"How about leaving that to me," she says coldly.

"All I can say is Huber owes you big-time if he's dumped Toby on you."

"Okay. We said we're honest tonight?" She looks him in the eye, holds his gaze. "It was a bad call on my part. You're right. Toby's useless, a disaster."

"What I need is the police file. Maybe Toby the disaster got a photocopy of that, too, in the course of his arduous and thorough research?"

"I suppose you can take care of that yourself when you return to Knoxville. Toby just left for vacation."

"Poor guy. Probably exhausted from working so hard."

Lamont watches the waiter return with his silver tray and two glasses of wine, says, "You'll like the pinot. A Drouhin, the daughter, actually."

He slowly swirls it, smells it, tastes it. "Have you

forgotten? You sent me to the Academy because it's the, and I quote you, *Harvard of Forensic Science.* I've got one month left."

"I'm sure they'll accommodate you, Win. Nobody said anything about your dropping out. In fact, this is going to make the NFA look good, too."

"So I'll work it in my sleep. So let's see." He sips his wine. "You're using the NFA, using the Knoxville Police Department, using me, using everyone for political gain. Tell me something, Monique." He pushes his luck, his eyes intense on hers. "Do you really give a damn about this dead old lady?"

"Headline: BIG-SHOT MASSACHUSETTS DETECTIVE HELPS OUT SMALL-TOWN POLICE DEPARTMENT, SOLVES TWENTY-YEAR-OLD CASE, VINDICATES OLD WOMAN MURDERED FOR SPARE CHANGE."

"Spare change?"

"It's in one of the newspaper articles I gave you," she says. "Mrs. Finlay collected silver coins. Had a box of them on her dresser. The only thing missing, as far as anybody knows."

IT IS STILL RAINING when they leave the Harvard Faculty Club and follow old brick pavers to Quincy Street.

"Where now?" Lamont asks, half hidden by a big, black umbrella.

Win notices her tapered fingers tightly curled around

23

the umbrella's wooden handle. Her nails are neatly squared, no polish, and she wears a large white-gold watch with a black crocodile band, a Breguet, and a Harvard signet ring. Doesn't matter what she earns as a DA and for the occasional class she teaches at the law school, Lamont comes from family money—a lot of it, from what he hears—and has a historic home near Harvard Square and the British racing-green Range Rover parked across the dark, wet street.

"I'm all set," he says as if she offered him a ride. "I'll walk to the Square and grab a taxi. Or maybe stroll over to the Charles, see if they've got any good jazz going on at the Regattabar. You like Coco Montoya?"

"Not tonight."

"I didn't say he was playing tonight."

He wasn't inviting her, either.

She is digging into her coat pockets, getting impatient, looking for something, says, "Keep me informed, Win. Every detail."

"I'll go where the evidence goes. And a fine point that shouldn't get lost in all the excitement, I can't go where the evidence doesn't go."

She digs in her expensive handbag, exasperated.

"And I hate to emphasize the obvious," he says as rain falls on his bare head, trickles down his collar. "I don't see what good your At Risk initiative is going to do if we can't solve the case."

"At the very least, we'll get an ancestral DNA profile, say

the case was reopened as a result. That in itself is newsworthy and compassionate, and we'll never admit to failure, just continue to keep the case open. A work in progress. You graduate from the NFA, return to your usual assignments. Eventually everybody will forget about the case all over again . . ."

"And by then maybe you'll be governor," he says.

"Don't be so cynical. I'm not the cold-blooded person you seem determined to paint me to be. Where the hell are my keys?"

"In your hand."

"My house keys."

"Want me to go with you, make sure you get in all right?"

"I've got a spare in a key box," she says, and abruptly leaves him in the rain.

3

Win looks up and down the street, watching people moving with purpose along sidewalks, watching cars drive by, water spitting out from the tires, watching Lamont drive off.

He walks toward the Square, where the cafés and coffee shops are crowded despite the weather, and he ducks into Peet's and squeezes between people, mostly students, the privileged and self-consumed. When he orders a latte, the girl behind the counter gawks so openly at him, her face turns red. He's used to it, usually is somewhat flattered, amused, but not tonight. He can't stop thinking about Lamont and the way she makes him feel about himself.

He carries his latte through Harvard Square, where the Red Line train comes in and most people traveling on it aren't enrolled at Harvard, maybe don't even know that Harvard isn't just the local college. He loiters on the sidewalk along John F. Kennedy Street, squinting at oncoming headlights, and the rain slashing the bright lights reminds him of pencil marks, of childish drawings of falling rain, like the ones he used to draw when he was a boy, when he drew something besides crime scenes and ugly conclusions about people.

"Tremont and Broadway," he says as he climbs into a cab, carefully setting the gym bag on the vinyl bench seat.

The driver is the shape of a head talking without turning around, a Middle Eastern accent.

"Tray-mond? Where?"

"Tre-mont and Broad-way, you can drop me off on the corn-er. You don't know the way, you can stop and I'm getting out."

"Tray-mont. Is close to where?"

"In-man Square," he says loudly. "Head that way. You can't find it, I'll walk and you don't get paid."

The driver stomps on the brake. He turns around, his dark face and dark eyes glowering at him.

"You don't pay, you get out!"

"You see this?" Win snatches out his wallet, shoves his Massachusetts State Police shield closer to the driver's face. "You want tickets the rest of your life? Your inspection sticker's expired. You realize that? One of your taillights is burned out. You aware of that? Just take me to Broadway. Think you can find the damn City Hall Annex? I'll direct you from there."

They ride in silence. Win sits in back, his hands clenched in his lap because he just had dinner with Monique Lamont, who's running for governor and oddly expects him to make Governor Crawley, who's running for reelection, look good so she'll look good, the two of them looking good when they run against each other. *Politics. Christ.* As if either one of them really cares about some murdered old lady down in the boonies of Tennessee. He gets more resentful by the moment as he sits in the dark and the taxi driver drives, having no idea where he's going unless Win tells him.

"That's Tremont there, take a right," Win finally says, pointing. "Just up there on the left. Okay, you can let me out here."

The house pains him every time he sees it, two-story, paint-peeled wood siding that is overgrown with ivy. Like the woman who lives inside, Win's family home has seen nothing but bad times for the last fifty years. He climbs out of the cab and hears the chiming of wind chimes in the dark backyard. He sets his latte on the taxi's roof, digs in a pocket, and throws a crumpled ten-dollar bill through the driver's window.

"Hey! It's twelve dollars!"

"Hey! Get a GPS," he says as the wind chimes play their magical, airy music, as the taxi speeds off and the latte slides off the roof and pops open on the road, and milky coffee streams over the black pavement, and the chimes sweetly chime as if excited to see him.

The thick, moist air stirs and sweet, light chimes sound from the shadows and the trees, from doors and windows he can't see, chimes sound from everywhere because his grandmother believes chimes should chime all the time to ward off bad spirits, and he's never said, *Well, if it really works, then how do you explain our lives?* He digs a key out of his pocket and unlocks the front door, pushes it open.

"Nana? It's me," he calls out.

Inside the foyer are the same family photographs and paintings of Jesus and crucifixes crowded over the horsehair plaster, all dusty. He shuts the door, locks it, sets his keys on an old oak table that he's looked at most of his life.

"Nana?"

The TV is on in the living room, turned up high, sirens screaming, Nana and her cop shows. The volume seems higher since he was here last, maybe because he's gotten used to quiet. Anxiety touches him as he follows the sound to the living room where nothing has changed since he was a boy except that Nana continues to accumulate crystals and stones and statues of cats and dragons and Saint Michael the Archangel and magical wreaths and bundles of herbs and incense, hundreds of all of it everywhere.

"Oh!" she exclaims when the sound of him finally jettisons her out of some *Hill Street Blues* rerun.

"Didn't mean to startle you." He smiles, goes to the couch, and kisses her cheek.

"My darling," she says, clasping his hands.

He picks up the remote control from a table covered with more crystals and magical trinkets and stones and her deck of tarot cards. He turns off the TV and makes his usual assessment. Nana looks all right, her dark eyes alert and bright in her sharp-featured face, a face very smooth for her age, beautiful once, her long, white hair piled on top of her head. She's wearing her usual silver jewelry, bracelets practically up to her elbows, and rings and necklaces, and the blaze-orange UT football sweatshirt he sent her a few weeks ago. She never fails to put on something he gave her when she knows she'll see him. She always seems to know. He doesn't have to tell her.

"You didn't have your alarm on," he says, opening his gym bag, setting jars of sourwood honey, barbecue sauce, and bread-and-butter pickles on the coffee table.

"I have my wind chimes, darling."

It occurs to him that he left the bottle of bourbon in the faculty club cloakroom. He didn't remember, and Lamont didn't notice that he didn't have it when they left. *That figures.*

"What did you bring me?" Nana is asking.

"I don't pay the alarm company all that money for wind

chimes. Some local stuff, made right there in Tennessee. If you'd rather have moonshine, I'll bring that next time," he teases, settling in a worn-out chair she keeps covered in a purple afghan one of her clients crocheted for her a few years back.

She picks up her cards and says, "What's this about money?"

"Money?" He frowns. "Now don't go doing your juju on me, Nana."

"Something about money. You were just doing something that had to do with money."

He thinks of "Money" Monique Lamont.

"That boss lady of yours, I suppose." She slowly shuffles through her cards, her way of having a conversation, and she places a moon card next to her on the couch. "You watch out for that one. Illusions and madness or poetry and visions. You get to choose."

"How are you feeling? You eating something besides whatever people bring you?"

People give her food for readings, give her all sorts of things, whatever they can afford.

She places another card faceup on the sofa, this one a robed man carrying a lantern, and the rain has picked up again, sounds like a drumroll, tree branches scraping against window glass, wind chimes a distant, frantic clanging.

"What did she want with you?" his grandmother says. "That's who you were with tonight."

"Nothing for you to worry about. The good thing is, I get to see you."

"She keeps things hidden behind a curtain, very troublesome things, this high priestess in your life." She turns another card faceup, this one the colorful image of a man hanging by one foot from a tree, coins falling out of his pockets.

"Nana." He sighs. "She's the DA, a politician. She's not a high priestess and I don't consider her *in my life.*"

"Oh, she's in it, all right," his grandmother says, looking keenly at him. "There's someone else. I'm seeing a man in scarlet. Ha! That one goes in the freezer right away!"

His grandmother's way of taking care of destructive people is to write their names or descriptions on scraps of paper and tuck them in the freezer. Clients pay good money to have her consign their enemies to her old Frigidaire, and the last time he checked, her freezer looked like the inside of a paper-shredder basket. Win's phone vibrates and he removes it from his jacket pocket, looks at the display, the number blocked.

"Excuse me," he says, getting up, moving closer to a window, rain flailing the glass.

"Is this Winston Garano?" a man asks in a voice that is obviously disguised, a really bad fake accent that almost sounds British.

"Who wants to know?"

"I think you might want to have a coffee with me, Davis

Square, the Diesel Café, where all the freaks and fags hang out. It's open late."

"Let's start with you telling me who you are."

He watches his grandmother shuffle through more tarot cards, placing them faceup on the table, thoughtful and at ease with them as if they are old friends.

"Not over the phone," the man says.

The murdered old woman suddenly enters Win's mind. He imagines her purplish-blue swollen face, the huge, dark clots on the underside of her scalp, and the holes punched into her skull, bits of bone driven into her brain. He imagines her pitiful, brutalized body on a cold steel autopsy table, doesn't know why he's suddenly thinking about her, tries to push her away.

"I don't meet strangers for coffee when they don't tell me who they are or what they want," he says into the phone.

"Vivian Finlay ring a bell? I'm pretty sure you want to talk to me."

"I'm not seeing any reason at all why I should talk to you," Win says as his grandmother sits calmly on the sofa, going through cards, placing another one faceup, this one red and white with a pentacle and a sword.

"Midnight. Be there." The man ends the call.

"Nana, I've got to go out for a while," Win says, pocketing his phone, hesitating by the rain-splattered window, getting one of his feelings, the wind chimes a discordant banging.

"Watch out for that one," she says, picking another card. "Your car running?"

Sometimes she forgets to put gas in it, and not even divine intervention keeps the engine from quitting.

"Was last time I drove it. Who's the man in scarlet? You find that out, you tell me. You pay attention to the numbers."

"What numbers?"

"The ones coming up. Pay attention."

"Keep your doors locked, Nana," he says. "I'm setting the alarm."

Her 1989 Buick with its peeling vinyl top and rainbow bumper stickers and beaded dream catcher hanging from the rearview mirror is parked behind the house beneath the basketball hoop that's been rusting on its pole since he was a boy. The engine resists, finally gives itself up, and he backs all the way out to the street because there is no room to turn around. His headlights flash in the eyes of a dog wandering along the roadside.

"Oh, for God's sake," Win says loudly as he stops the car and gets out.

"Miss Dog, what'cha doing out here, girl?" he says to the poor, wet dog. "Come here. It's me, come on, come on, that's a good girl."

Miss Dog, part beagle, part shepherd, part deaf, part blind, a name as stupid as her owner, creeps forward, sniffs Win's hand, remembers him, wags her tail. He strokes her wet, dirty fur, picks her up, and puts her in the front seat, massaging her neck as he drives her to a run-down house two blocks away. He carries her to the front door, bangs on it for a long time.

Finally, the woman inside yells, "Who is it?"

"I've got Miss Dog again!" Win yells back to her.

The door opens, the ugly, fat woman on the other side wearing a shapeless pink robe, has no bottom teeth, stinks like cigarettes. She turns on the porch light, blinks in the glare, looks past him to Nana's Buick parked on the street, never seems to remember the car or him. Win gently puts down Miss Dog and she darts inside the house, gets away from the ungrateful sloth as fast as she can.

"I told you, she's going to get hit by a car," Win warns. "What's the matter with you? This is how many times I've had to bring her home because she's wandering the damn street?"

"What am I supposed to do. I let her out to potty, she doesn't come back. Then he came over tonight, left the door open, not that he's supposed to be here. You can blame him. Kicks at her, mean as a snake, leaves the door open on purpose so she'll get out because that stupid dog gets killed it will break Suzy's heart."

"Who's he?"

"My damn son-in-law the police keep arresting."

Win thinks he might know who she's talking about, has seen him in the area, drives a white pickup.

"And you let him on the property?" Win says severely to her.

"Just try to stop him. He ain't afraid of no one, nohow. It's not me who's got the restraining order."

"You call the cops when he showed up earlier?"

"No point in it."

Through the open door, Win can see Miss Dog flat on the floor, cowering under a chair.

"How about I buy her from you," Win says.

"There's no amount of money," she retorts. "I love that dog."

"I'll give you fifty dollars."

"Can't put a price on love," she wavers.

"Sixty," he says, and that's all the cash he's got, his checkbook in Knoxville.

"No sir"—she's thinking hard about it—"my love for her's worth a whole lot more than that."

4

TWO TUFTS KIDS with green hair and tattoos clack pool
balls not far from Win's table. He watches them disdain-
fully.

Maybe he isn't from money, didn't get sixteen hundred
on his SATs or compose a symphony or build a robot, but at
least when he applied to the schools of his dreams, he was
respectful enough to buy a khaki suit (on sale) and new
shoes (also on sale) and get a haircut (he had a five-dollar
coupon) in the event he was invited by the dean of admis-
sions to tour the campus and talk about what he wanted in
life, which was to become a scholar and poet like his father,
or maybe a lawyer. Win was never called for a campus tour

or an interview. All he got were boilerplate letters that regretted to inform him . . .

He watches everything and everybody inside the Diesel Café, looking for a man he is supposed to meet about a murder that happened twenty years ago in Tennessee. It is almost midnight, still raining, and Win sits at his small table, sipping cappuccino, watching scruffy students with their horrible hair and grungy clothes and coffees and laptops, watching the front door, his temper heating up by the moment. At quarter past midnight, he angrily gets up from the table as some pimple-faced, thinks-he's-an-Einstein punk clumsily racks pool balls, talking loud and fast to his girlfriend, both of them oblivious, self-consumed, hyped up on something, maybe ephedrine.

"No there isn't," the girl is saying. "There's no such word as *sodomitical.*"

"*The Portrait of Dorian Gray* was called a sodomitical book." Clack. "In some of the reviews back then." A striped ball wobbles into a pocket.

"It's *Picture* of Dorian Gray, not *Portrait,* genius," Win says to the pedantic, body-pierced punk now twirling the pool cue like a baton. "And it was called a sodomitical book during Oscar Wilde's trial, not in book reviews."

"Whatever."

Win starts to walk off, catches *mulatto fag.*

He walks back, grabs the pool cue out of the punk's hands, says, "My turn to break." He snaps the pool cue in half over his knee. "Now then. You said something to me?"

"I didn't say anything!" the punk exclaims, glassy eyes huge.

Win tosses the broken halves of the pool cue on top of the table, strides off, ignores the girl behind the counter, who has been staring at him ever since he got here. She's blasting steam into a big coffee cup and says *excuse me* as he reaches for the door. *Sir?* she calls out above the noise of the espresso machine.

He walks over to the counter and says, "Don't worry. I'll pay for it." He pulls a few bills out of his wallet.

She doesn't seem interested in his pool-hall vandalism, says, "Are you Detective Geronimo?"

"Where'd you get a name like that?"

"I take that as a yes," she replies, reaching below the counter, retrieving an envelope, handing it to him. "This guy came in earlier, asked me to give this to you when you were about to leave."

"How much earlier?" He slips the envelope into a pocket, mindful of who might be watching.

"Maybe a couple hours."

So the man with the fake accent called Win *after* the letter was dropped off here, never intended on a meeting.

"What did he look like?" Win asks.

"Nothing special, kind of old. Had on tinted glasses, a big trench coat. And a scarf."

"A scarf this time of year?"

"Shiny, silky. Sort of a deep red."

"Of course." A man in scarlet, just like Nana said.

Win walks out into the rain, and the dampness of the night makes him feel sticky and wilted. His grandmother's car is a dark-finned hulk on Summer Street, in front of the Rosebud Diner, and he walks along the wet pavement, looking around, wondering if the man in scarlet is nearby, watching. He unlocks the car, opens the glove box, finds a flashlight and a stack of napkins from Dunkin' Donuts, wraps several of them around his hands, and slits open the envelope with one of the keys dangling from the steering column. He slips out a folded piece of lined paper, reads what's neatly printed on it in black ink.

You're the one AT RISK, half-breed.

He dials Lamont's home number and she doesn't answer. He tries her cell phone. She doesn't answer. He doesn't leave a message, changes his mind and tries again, and she answers this time.

"Hello?" Her voice doesn't have its usual energy.

"You want to tell me what the hell's going on!" He cranks the engine.

"No need to be upset with me," she weirdly says, sounds strained, something off about her.

"Some wacko with a wacko fake accent just called me about the Finlay case. What a coincidence. Somehow the guy has my cell-phone number, another amazing coincidence, and coincidentally said he'd meet me and didn't show up, left me a threatening note. Who the hell have you been talking to? You send out a press release or something . . . ?"

"This morning," she replies, and a muffled male voice in the background says something Win can't make out.

"This morning? Before I even got to town! And you couldn't bother to tell me?" he exclaims.

"That's fine," her non sequitur follows.

"It's not fine!"

The person Lamont is with—some man at almost one o'clock in the morning—says something and she abruptly ends the call, and Win sits in the dark inside his grand-mother's old Buick staring at the lined piece of paper in his napkin-wrapped hands. His heart pounds so hard he can feel it in his neck. Lamont alerted the media about a case that's now supposed to be his and didn't ask his permission or even bother telling him. She can take her At Risk shit and shove it.

I quit.

See what she does when he tells her that.

I quit!

He has no idea where to look for her. She didn't answer her home phone, only her cell phone. So she probably isn't home. Well, it's hard to say. He decides to cruise past her Cambridge house anyway. In case she's there. The hell with who else might be there, and he wonders who Lamont sleeps with, if she's one of these alpha-dog women who doesn't like sex or maybe the opposite. Maybe she's a pira-nha, eats her lovers to the bone.

He roars away from the curb, fishtails—damn rear-wheel drive—skids on the slick pavement, and the windshield wipers drag loudly across the glass, driving him crazy because he's already feeling crazy, as if he's in the middle of something crazy that he was crazy to get in the middle of, dammit. He should have refused to fly back up here, should have stayed in Tennessee. It's late to call Sykes. It's rude. He's always doing this to her and she always lets him. She won't mind, and he enters her number, remem-bering it's Tuesday night, and usually on Tuesday nights at this late hour, the two of them are dressed like preppies, lis-tening to jazz at Forty-Six-Twenty, drinking fruit-infused martinis and talking.

"HEY GORGEOUS," Win says. "Don't kill me."

"Figures the one time I was actually sleeping," says Sykes, an agent with the Tennessee Bureau of Investigation, and an insomniac, her hormones hateful these days.

She sits up in bed, doesn't bother with the lamp. For the past six weeks she has spent a lot of time talking to Win on the phone, in bed in the dark, alone, wondering what it would be like to talk to him in bed, in the dark, in person. She listens for her roommate through the wall, doesn't want to wake her up. The funny thing is, when Sykes drove Win to the Knoxville airport, she said to him, *Well, for once our roommates will get a full night's sleep.* Since she and Win began their training at the National Forensic Academy, they've talked the nights away, and since the student apartments don't have thick walls, their roommates get the raw end of that deal.

"I think you miss me," Sykes says, joking but hoping it's true.

"Need you to do something," Win says.

"Are you all right?" She switches on the lamp.

"I'm fine."

"You don't sound fine. What's going on?" She gets out of bed, stares at herself in the mirror over the dresser.

"Listen. An old lady was murdered in Knoxville twenty years ago, Vivian Finlay. Sequoyah Hills."

"Let's start with why the sudden interest."

"Something damn weird's going on. You were in Tennessee back then. Maybe you remember the case."

Sykes was in Tennessee, all right, yet another reminder of her age, and she looks at herself in the mirror, her silvery blond hair sticking up everywhere, *like Amadeus* is the way Win once described it. *If you saw the movie,* he said. She hadn't.

"I vaguely recall the case," she is saying. "Rich widow, someone broke in. An unbelievable thing to happen in Sequoyah Hills in the middle of the day."

The mirror is especially unkind at this hour. Her eyes are

puffy. Too much beer. She doesn't know why Win likes her so much, why he doesn't seem to see her the same way she does, maybe sees her the way she used to be, twenty years ago when she had creamy skin and big blue eyes, a tight, round butt, and perky boobs, a body that flipped the finger at gravity until she turned forty and gravity flipped the finger back.

"I need the original police file," he is saying over the phone.

"By chance you got the case number?" Sykes asks.

"Only the autopsy case number. Just microfilm printouts from that, no scene photos, no nothing. Got to have that file too if we can ever find it in the Bermuda Triangle of storage. You know, when the old morgue moved. Or at least Lamont said it did. I'm assuming she's right."

Her again. "Yeah, it moved. Okay, one thing at a time," she says, getting stressed, irritable. "First, you want the police file."

"Got to have it, Sykes."

"So I'll try to track it down first thing in the morning."

"Can't wait. Whatever you can get your hands on now. E-mail it to me."

"And who do you think's going to help me out at this hour?" She is already opening her closet door, yanking a pair of blue cargo pants off a hanger.

"The Academy," Win says. "Call Tom, get him out of bed."

*

HE DRIVES FAST toward Mount Auburn Hospital, turns off Brattle Street, headed to Monique Lamont's house so he can ruin the rest of her night.

I quit.

Maybe he'll sign on with the TBI, the FBI, the FYI— *for your information, Monique, nobody jerks me around like this.*

I quit.

Then why are you sending Sykes on a mission in the middle of the night? another part of his brain asks him. A minor technicality. Just because he quits Lamont doesn't mean he'll quit the Vivian Finlay case. It's personal now. Some man in scarlet screws with him, insults him, and it gets personal. Win drives through an intersection, barely slows at the stop sign, turns left near the fire station, onto the narrow street where Lamont lives on a sliver of an acre in a nineteenth-century pale plum house, a Queen Anne Painted Lady, showy and intricate and formidable, like its owner. Her property is dense with crepe myrtles, oaks and birch trees, and the dark shapes of them rock in the wind and water drips from branches and leaves.

He parks in front, turns off his headlights, cuts the engine. The front porch light isn't on, no lights along the property are on, and only one window is lit up, the one on the second floor to the left of the front door, and he has one of his feelings. Her Range Rover is in the cobbled driveway, and his feeling intensifies. If she's not home, somebody picked her up. Well, big deal. She could have anybody she wants, so her date du jour picked her up, maybe took her to his place, big deal, but the feeling persists. If her date du jour is inside the house with her, where's his car? Win tries her home phone and gets voicemail. He tries her cell phone and she doesn't answer. He tries it a second time. She doesn't answer.

Some man in a red scarf sending him on a wild-goose chase, making a fool of him, threatening him, taunting him. *Who?* Win worries about what's going to appear in the news. Maybe Lamont's idiotic press release is screaming through cyberspace, landing all over the Internet. Maybe that's how the man in the red scarf found out about At Risk, about Win, but it doesn't make sense. As far as he knows, Vivian Finlay wasn't from New England, so why is some man in New England interested enough in her case to go to all the trouble to call Win, set up a phony meeting, and taunt him?

He continues staring at Lamont's house, at her densely wooded property, looking up and down the street—for what, he doesn't know. For anything. He grabs the flashlight and gets out of his grandmother's prehistoric-looking car, keeping up his scan, listening. Something doesn't feel right, feels worse than not right. Maybe he's just rattled, expecting something not to feel right, getting spooked the way he did as a boy when he started imagining monsters, bad people, bad things, death, having premonitions because *it's in his blood,* as his grandmother so often declared. He has no gun. He follows the brick walk to the front porch, climbs the steps, looking, listening, deciding that what he's really uneasy about is Lamont.

She won't be nice about this. If she's with someone, she'll have Win's head. He starts to ring the bell, looks up at the same time a shadow moves past the curtained, lighted window directly overhead. He stares up, waiting. He shines the flashlight at the brass mailbox to the left of the front door, lifts the lid. She didn't pick up her mail when she came in, and he remembers what she said about a key box. He doesn't see anything like that.

Water drips in big, cool drops from leaves and smacks the top of his head as he goes around to the back of the house, where it is thickly wooded and very dark, where he finds the key box open, the key still in the lock, the door ajar. He hesitates, looks around, listening to water dripping, shining the flashlight in the trees, the shrubbery, directing the beam back to something dark red between two box-woods, a gas can with rags on top of it, wet from the rain but clean. His pulse picks up, begins to race as he silently steps into the kitchen, hears Lamont's voice, then a male voice, an angry male voice, on the second floor, the room with the lighted window above the front door.

He moves fast up wooden stairs that creak, three stairs at a time, cuts across a hallway that creaks. Through an open doorway he sees her on the bed, nude, tied to the bedposts, a man in jeans, a T-shirt, sitting on the edge of the bed, stroking her with a pistol.

"Say it, *I'm a whore.*"

"I'm a whore," she repeats in a shaky voice. "Please don't do this."

Left of the bed is the window, the drapes drawn. Her clothes are strewn on the floor, the same suit she had on hours earlier at dinner.

"*I'm nothing but a filthy whore.* Say it!"

Overhead is a large art-glass chandelier with painted flowers—blue, red, green—and Win hurls the flashlight and it crashes into the chandelier and it shatters and sways and the man jumps up from the bed, whips around, and then Win has him by the wrist, struggling to get the pistol away from him, the man's breath in his face, reeking of garlic, and the gun fires into the ceiling, just missing Win's head.

"Drop it! Drop it!"

His voice sounds muffled and distant in his ringing ears as he struggles, and the pistol fires again and again and the man's grip suddenly goes limp. Win grabs hold of the gun, shoves him hard and he collapses to the floor, blood flowing out of his head, pooling on the hardwood, quiet on the floor next to the bed, bleeding, not moving, a young, Hispanic-looking man, maybe in his teens.

Win yanks a comforter over Lamont, frees her from the electrical cords lashing her to the bedposts as he repeatedly says, "It's all right. You're safe now. It's all right." He calls

911 on his cell phone and she sits up, pulling the comforter around her, gasping for breath, shaking violently, eyes wild.

"Oh, God," she says. "Oh God!" she screams.

"It's okay, it's okay, you're safe now," he says, standing over her, looking around, watching the man on the floor, blood and bloody shards of colorful art glass everywhere.

"Is he the only one?" Win yells at Lamont as his heart pounds and his eyes dart around, his ears ringing, the pistol ready. "Is there anybody else?" he shouts.

She shakes her head, her breathing rapid and shallow, her face blanched, her eyes glazed, about to pass out.

"Deep, slow breaths, Monique." Win takes off his suit jacket, places it in her hands, helps her hold it up to her face. "It's all right. Breathe into it like it's a paper bag. That's good. Good. Deep, slow breaths. No one's going to hurt you now."

5

MONIQUE LAMONT wears a hospital gown inside an examination room at Mount Auburn Hospital, but a few blocks from where she lives.

It is a nondescript room, white, with an examination table, the kind with stirrups, and a counter, a sink, a cabinet filled with medical supplies, swabs and specula, a surgical lamp. Moments earlier, a forensic nurse was alone in the room with Lamont, examining the powerful district attorney's orifices and other very private areas of her body, swabbing for saliva and seminal fluid, plucking hairs, getting fingernail scrapings, looking for injuries, taking photographs, gathering whatever might be potential evidence. Lamont is holding up amazingly well, maybe bizarrely well, playing the role of herself, working her own case.

She sits in a white plastic chair next to the white paper-covered table, Win on a stool across from her, another investigator with the Massachusetts State Police, Sammy, standing near the shut door. She had the option of being interviewed in more civilized surroundings, her home, for example, but refused, made the rather chillingly clinical observation that it was best to compartmentalize, keep related conversations and activities to the confined spaces where they belong. Translated: Win seriously doubts she'll ever sleep in her bedroom again. He won't be surprised if she sells her house.

"What do we know about him?" she asks again, the prosecutor who seems to have no feelings about what just happened.

Her attacker is in critical condition. Win is careful what he tells her. It is, to say the least, a highly unusual situation. She is accustomed to asking the state police anything she wants and having nothing withheld from her. She is the district attorney, is in charge, is programmed to demand details and get them.

"Ms. Lamont," Sammy says respectfully, "as you know, he had a gun and Win here did what he had to do. Things happen."

But that's not what she's asking. She looks at Win, holds

his gaze remarkably well considering that just hours ago he saw her nude, lashed to her bed.

"What do you know about him." She poses it not as a question but a command.

"This much," Win says. "Your office prosecuted him in juvenile court about two months ago."

"For what?"

"Possession of marijuana, crack. Judge Let-'em-Loose Lane gave him a reprimand."

"The prosecutor certainly wasn't me. I've never seen him before. What else?"

"Tell you what," Win says. "How about letting us get our job done first, then I'll tell you anything I can."

"No," she says. "It won't be what you can. It will be what I ask."

"But for now . . ." Win starts to say.

"Information," she demands.

"I got a question." It is Sammy who says this from his remote position near the wall. "About your getting home last night."

His ruddy face is grim, something in his eyes. Maybe it's embarrassment. Maybe talking to the district attorney after she's been through something like this somehow makes him a voyeur. Lamont ignores him, ignores his question.

"I had dinner with you," she says to Win. "I got in my car and drove back to the office to finish up a few things, then drove straight home. Because I didn't have my keys, I went around to the back of the house, put my code into the key box, got out the spare key, and was unlocking the back door when suddenly a hand clamped over my mouth and someone I couldn't see said *one sound, you're dead.* He pushed me into the house."

Lamont does a fine job reciting the facts. Her assailant, now identified as Roger Baptista of East Cambridge, an address not far from the court building where Lamont works, forced her up to her bedroom, began yanking electrical cords from lamps, from the clock radio. Then her home phone rang. She didn't answer it. Then her cell phone rang. She didn't answer it.

Win calling her.

Her cell phone rang again and she thought fast, said it was her boyfriend, he was getting worried, might show up, so Baptista told her to answer the phone and if she tried anything he'd blow her head off and then kill her boyfriend, kill everybody, and she answered. She had the brief, peculiar conversation with Win. She says she ended the call and Baptista forced her to undress and tied her to the bedposts. He raped her. Then put his pants back on.

"Why didn't you resist?" Sammy asks her as delicately as possible.

"He had a gun." She looks at Win. "I had no doubt he would use it if I resisted, probably would use it, regardless. When he finished with me. I did what I could to control the situation."

"Meaning?" Win asks.

She hesitates, her eyes cutting away from him, says, "Meaning, I told him to do what he wanted, acted as if I wasn't frightened. Or repulsed. Did what he wanted. Said what he told me to say." She hesitates. "As calm and non-combative as I could muster under the circumstances. I, uh, I said it wasn't necessary to tie me up, I, well, I worked with cases like this all the time, understood them, knew he had his reasons. I, well, I . . ."

The small room echoes with the ensuing silence and it is the first time Win has ever seen Lamont's face turn red. He suspects he knows exactly what she did to stall Baptista, to calm him, to connect with him in the remote hope he would let her live.

"Maybe you acted like you wanted a little," Sammy suggests. "Hey, women do it all the time, make the rapist think it's okay, they're good in bed, fake an orgasm and even ask the guy to come back another time like it's a date or . . ."

"Out!" Lamont fires at him, pointing her finger. "Get out!"

"I'm just—"

"Didn't you hear me?"

He leaves the room, leaves Win alone with her, not his first choice. Considering he critically injured her assailant, it would be preferable and prudent to interview her with at least one witness present.

"Who is this piece of shit?" Lamont asks. "Who? And

do you think it's a goddamn coincidence he decided to show up at the house the same night my keys mysteriously disappeared? Who is he?"

"Roger Baptista . . ."

"That's not what I'm asking."

"When's the last time you saw your keys?" Win says. "You lock up with them when you left for work this morning? Actually, yesterday morning."

"No."

"No?"

She is silent for a moment, then, "I didn't come home that night."

"Where were you?"

"I stayed with a friend. Left there for work in the morning. After work I had dinner with you, checked by my office. That's the chronology."

"You mind telling me who you stayed with?"

"I do."

"I'm just trying . . ."

"I'm not the one who committed a crime." She stares coldly at him.

"Monique, I assume your alarm was set when you unlocked the door with your spare key," Win pointedly says. "Baptista clamps his hand over your mouth as you're unlocking the door. So what about the alarm after that?"

"He told me if I didn't disarm it he'd kill me."

"No panic code that silently alerts the police?"

"Oh, for God's sake. And you would think of that if it were you? See what security precautions you revert to when someone's got a gun to the back of your head."

"You know anything about a can of gasoline and some rags found by your back door, in the bushes?"

"You and I need to have a very important conversation," she says to him.

SYKES DRIVES her personal car, a '79 blue VW Rabbit, through the Old City, as Knoxville's historic downtown is called.

She passes Barley's Taproom & Pizzeria, the Tonic Grill, deserted and dark, then a construction site that was shut down the other day when a backhoe dug up bones that turned out to be cow, the site having been a slaughterhouse and stockyard in a long-ago life. Her uneasiness—the jitters, as she calls them—gets worse the closer she gets to where she's going. She sure hopes Win's insistence that she track down the Vivian Finlay case records *immediately* is really urgent enough to merit her waking up the Academy director, then the chief of the Knoxville Police Department, next several other people with the Criminal Investigative Division and Records, who couldn't find the case, only its accession number, KPD893-85.

Last and most unpleasant of all, Sykes woke up former detective Jimmy Barber's widow, who sounded drunk, and asked what her late husband might have done with his old files, paperwork, memorabilia, et cetera, when he retired and packed up his office at headquarters.

All that crap's in the basement. What you people think he's hiding down there, Jimmy Hoffla? The damn Da Vin-shay code?

I sure am sorry to bother you, ma'am. But we're trying to locate some old records, careful what she said, mindful that Win made it clear something unusual is going on.

I don't know what's got such a bug up y'all's butt, Mrs. Barber complained over the phone, swearing, slurring, nasty. *It's three damn o'clock in the morning!*

In what the locals call Shortwest Knoxville, the city begins to fray around the edges, disintegrating into housing projects before it improves a little, not much, about two miles west of downtown. Sykes parks in front of a small rancher, vinyl siding, the yard a mess, the only house with empty supercans haphazardly parked near the street because Mrs. Barber is too lazy to roll them back to the house, it seems. The neighborhood has very few streetlights and a lot of souped-up gaudy old cars—Cadillacs, a Lincoln painted purple, a Corvette with those stupid spinning hubcaps. The crapmobiles of dirtbags, drug dealers, no-account kids. Sykes is mindful of the Glock .40-caliber pistol in the shoulder holster under her jacket. She follows the sidewalk and rings the bell.

Momentarily, the porch light blinks on.

"Who is it?" a voice slurs from the other side of the door.

"Agent Sykes, Tennessee Bureau of Investigation."

A burglar chain rattles. A dead-bolt lock snaps free. The door opens and a cheap-looking woman with dyed blond hair and makeup smudges under her eyes steps aside to let Sykes in.

"Mrs. Barber," Sykes politely says. "I sure appreciate . . ."

"I don't get what all the fuss is about, but go on." Her housecoat is buttoned crooked, eyes bloodshot, smells like booze. "The basement's thataway," she indicates with a nod, fumbles to relock the door, has a very loud voice with a very strong twang. "Rummage through his junk all you want. You can load it in a truck and haul it the hell away for all I care."

"I won't be needing to load it in a truck," Sykes says. "I just need to look through some police files he may have had in his office once."

"I'm going back to bed," Mrs. Barber says.

LAMONT SEEMS TO HAVE forgotten where she is.

It crosses Win's mind that she's delusional, believes she's in her big office surrounded by her big glass collection, maybe in one of her big-ticket designer suits, sitting at her big glass desk instead of in a hospital gown, in a plastic chair, inside a hospital examination room. She acts as if she and Win are doing their usual thing, working a high-profile case, a bad one destined for a lot of complications and press.

"I'm not sure you're hearing me," she says to Win as a knock sounds on the shut door.

"Just a minute." He gets up to answer it.

It's Sammy, pokes his head in, quietly says, "Sorry."

Win steps out into the corridor, pulls the door shut. Sammy hands him this morning's *Boston Globe,* the local section. The headline across the top of the front page is big and bold.

ANY CRIME, ANY TIME
DA ENLISTS SPACE-AGE SCIENCE TO SOLVE OLD MURDER

"Four things you should know," Sammy says. "First, your name's all over this thing, a damn road map for how you're supposedly going to solve the governor's whodunit. More accurate, *her* whodunit"—he looks at the shut door—"since he's delegated it to her. Good luck if the killer's still out there and reads all this shit. Second, well, the second thing's sure as hell not good."

"What?"

"Baptista just died. To state the obvious, now we don't get to talk to him. Third, I went through his clothes, found a thousand bucks in hundred-dollar bills in his back pocket."

"Loose, folded up, what?"

"Plain white envelope, no writing on it. Bills new-looking, you know, crisp. Not folded or nothing. I called Huber at home. The labs are going to process them right away, look for prints."

"What's the fourth thing?"

"The media's found out about . . ." He again nods toward the shut door. "There's like three TV trucks and a crowd of reporters out there in the parking lot and it isn't even daylight yet."

Win steps back inside the examination room, shuts the door.

Lamont is sitting in the same plastic chair. It occurs to him she's got nothing to wear unless she can handle the warm-up suit she put on before he drove her to the hospital. After the assault, she couldn't shower, he didn't have to give her instructions, she knows the routine. She still hasn't showered, and it's not a subject he is entirely comfortable bringing up.

"The press has found out," he says, sitting back down on the stool. "I need to get you out of here without them ambushing you. I'm sure you know you can't go back to your house right now."

"He was going to burn it down," she states.

The gas can was full. It certainly wasn't left there by her yardman.

"He was going to kill me and burn down my house." A

steady, firm voice, the DA working the case as if she's talking about some other victim. "Why? To make my death look like an accident. To make it look like I burned up in my house. He's no beginner."

"Depends on whether it was his idea," Win says. "Or if someone gave him instructions. In any event, disguising a homicide with fire isn't very reliable. Most likely, the autopsy would have revealed soft-tissue injury, the bullet, and possible damage to cartilage, bone. Bodies don't completely burn up in house fires. You know that."

He thinks about the money in Baptista's pocket, something telling him it's not a good idea to give that detail to Lamont just yet.

"I need you to stay here," she says, tightly gripping the blanket she holds around herself. "Forget the lady in Tennessee, what's-her-name. We need to find out who's behind this. Not just some little nobody piece of . . . maybe someone else who put him up to it."

"Huber's already getting the labs mobilized . . ."

"How does he know about it?" she blurts out. "I haven't told—" She stops short, her eyes wide. "He's not going to get away with this," and she's talking about Baptista again. "This is one case that isn't going to be . . . I want you in charge of it. We're going to bury him."

He resists the obvious pun, says, "Monique, he's dead."

She doesn't flinch.

"Justified or not, struggle or not, I killed him. It was a

good shooting. But you know what happens. Your office can't investigate it alone, will either have to transfer the case to another DA's office or bring in the Boston Homicide Unit. Not to mention Internal Affairs doing its thing. Not to mention the autopsy and every other test known to man. I'll be put on administrative duties for a while."

"I want you on this right now."

"Not even a mental-health day? That's nice."

"Go drink a few beers with the stress unit. I don't want to hear about your so-called mental health." Her face is livid now, her eyes dark holes of hate, as if he is the one who attacked her. "If I don't get a mental-health day, I'll be damned if you do."

Her change in demeanor is startling, unnerving.

"Maybe you don't grasp the magnitude of what just happened," he says. "I see it all the time with other victims."

"I'm not a victim. I was victimized." Just as suddenly, she is the DA again, the strategist, the politician. "This has to be handled precisely right or you know what I'll be known for? The gubernatorial candidate who was raped."

He doesn't reply

Any crime, any time, including mine," she says.

6

MONIQUE STANDS in the middle of the examination room, the white blanket wrapped around her.

"Get us out of here," she says to Win.

"It's not *us*," he says. "I can't be involved . . ."

"I want you in charge of this. Now come with me," she says, her face calm, masklike. "Get us out of here. Stay with me until know I'm safe. We don't know who's behind this. I must be safe."

"You'll be safe, but I can't be your protection."

She stares at him.

"I've got to let them investigate this, Monique. I can't be involved in a deadly-force case and go about my business as if nothing happened."

"You can and you will."

"You're not really expecting me to be your bodyguard . . . ?"

"That would be your fantasy, wouldn't it," she says, and she stares at him, something in her eyes he's never seen before, not from her. "Get me out of here. There must be a basement, a fire exit, something, get me out of here. Doesn't this goddamn hospital have a rooftop helipad?"

Win calls Sammy on the cell phone, says, "Get one of the choppers in and fly her out of here."

"To where?" Sammy asks.

Win looks at Lamont, says, "You got some safe place to stay?"

She hesitates, then, "Boston."

"Where in Boston? I need to know."

"An apartment."

"You have an apartment in Boston?" That's news to him. Why would she have an apartment less than ten miles from her house?

She doesn't reply, doesn't owe him any further explanations about her life.

He tells Sammy, "Get an officer to meet her when she lands, escort her to her apartment."

He gets off the phone, looks at her, has one of his bad feelings, says, "Words aren't enough, Monique, but I can't tell you how sorry . . ."

"You're right, words aren't enough." She gives him the same disconcerting stare.

"I'm out of commission for a few days, starting now," he says. "It's the best thing to do."

Her eyes bore into him as she stands in the small, white room, the white blanket wrapped around her.

"What do you mean, *the best thing*? I should think I'm the one who decides what the best thing is for me."

"Maybe this isn't only about you," he says.

Her scary eyes don't leave his.

"Monique, I need a few days to take care of things."

"Right now, your job is to take care of me," she says. "We have to do damage control, turn this into something positive. *You* need *me*."

She stands perfectly still, her eyes staring. Behind them is a darkness seething with hatred and rage.

"I'm the only witness," she states in a flat tone.

"Are you threatening to lie about what happened if I don't do what you say?"

"I don't lie. That's one thing people know about me," she replies.

"You're threatening me?" He says it again, and now he's a cop, now he isn't the man who saved her life. "Because there are more important witnesses than you. The silent witnesses of forensic science. His body fluids, for example. Unless you're going to say it was consensual. Then I guess his saliva, his seminal fluid are irrelevant. Then I guess I inadvertently interrupted a tryst, some creative sex scenario. Maybe he thought he was protecting you from me, thought

I was the intruder, instead of the other way around. That what you're going to say, Monique?"

"How dare you."

"I'm pretty good with scripts. You want a few more?"

"How dare you!"

"No. How dare you. I just saved your goddamn life."

"You sexist pig. Typical man. Think all of us want it."

"Stop it."

"Think all of us have some secret fantasy about being . . ."

"Stop it!" Then he lowers his voice. "I'll help you all I can. I didn't do this to you. You know what happened. He's dead. He got what he deserved. The best revenge, if you want to look at it that way. You won, made him pay the ultimate price, if you want to look at it that way. Now let's repair what we can, get things on the right track as best we can. Damage control, as you put it."

Her eyes clear. Thoughts move in them.

"I need a few days," Win says. "I need you to refrain from taking this out on me. If you can't do that, I'll have no choice but to . . ."

"Facts," she interrupts him. "Fingerprints on the gas can. DNA. The pistol—is it stolen? My missing keys, probably a coincidence unless they were on his person, in his residence. If so, why wasn't he waiting inside my house?"

"Your alarm."

"Right." She paces, wrapped in her white blanket like an Indian chief. "How did he get to my house. Does he have a car. Did someone else drive him. His family. Who did he know."

Past tense. Her attacker is dead and she thinks of him as dead already. It hasn't even been an hour. Win looks at his watch. He calls Sammy. The chopper's nine minutes out.

THE BELL 430 lifts off from Mount Auburn Hospital's rooftop helipad, hovers and noses around, flies off toward the Boston skyline. It's a seven-million-dollar bird. Lamont had a lot to do with making sure the Massachusetts State Police has three of them.

At the moment she doesn't take much pride in that, doesn't take much pride in anything, isn't sure how she feels except heavy, stony. From where she sits in back, she can see frantic journalists on the ground, their cameras pointed in her loud, dramatic direction, and she shuts her eyes and tries to ignore her desperate need for a shower and clean clothing, tries to ignore areas of her body that were invaded and violated, tries to ignore nagging fears about sexually transmitted diseases, pregnancy. She tries to concentrate on who and what she is and not on what happened hours earlier.

She takes a deep breath, looks out the window, looks at

the rooftops passing below her as the helicopter beats its way toward Massachusetts General Hospital, where the pilots plan to land so some state policeperson can pick her up and transport her to an apartment no one is supposed to know about. She'll probably pay for that mistake, doesn't know what else she could have done.

"You all right back there?" A pilot's voice sounds through her headset.

"Fine."

"We'll be landing in four minutes."

She is sinking. She stares without blinking at the partition that separates the pilots from her, and she feels herself getting heavier, sinking lower. Once when she was an undergraduate at Harvard she got drunk, really drunk, and although she never said a word about it to anyone, she knew that at least one of the men she was partying with had sex with her while she was unconscious. When she came to, the sun was up and the birds were making noise, and she was alone on a couch and it was obvious what had happened, but she didn't accuse the suspect she had in mind, certainly didn't consider an examination by a forensic nurse. She remembers how she felt that day—poisoned, dazed. No, not just dazed, maybe dead. That was it, she recalls as she flies into the downtown skyline. She felt dead.

Death can be liberating. There are things you don't have to care about anymore if you're dead. People can't injure or maim parts of you that are dead.

"Ms. Lamont?" A pilot's voice sounds in her headset again. "When we land, it will take us a minute to shut down and I want you to sit tight. Someone will open the door for you and get you out."

She imagines Governor Crawley. She imagines his ugly, smirking face when he hears the news. He probably already knows. Of course he does. He'll be sympathetic, heartbroken, and degrade and destroy her in the election.

"Then what?" she says, pushing the mic close to her lip.

"The state police officer on the ground will tell you . . ." one of the pilots answers.

"You're the state police," she says. "I'm asking you what the plan is. Is the media there?"

"You'll be briefed, I'm sure, ma'am."

They are hovering over the hospital's rooftop helipad now, a blaze-orange windsock whipping around in the rotor wash, some state policewoman in a blue uniform bending her head against the wind. The helicopter sets down, goes into flight idle, and Lamont sits, staring out at the unfamiliar, plain-looking woman officer, someone low on the food chain who's supposed to get the traumatized and besieged DA to safe asylum. A damn escort, a damn bodyguard, a damn woman to remind Lamont that she's a woman who has just been violated by a man and therefore most likely doesn't want to be escorted by a man. She's damaged. A victim. She imagines Crawley, imagines what he'll say, what he's already saying and thinking.

The engines go silent, the blades whining quietly, winding down, then braking to a stop. She takes off her headset and shoulder harness and imagines Crawley's smarmy, pious face looking into the camera and offering compassion from the people of Massachusetts to Monique Lamont. Victim Lamont.

Victim Lamont for governor. Any crime, any time, including mine.

Lamont opens the helicopter door herself before the officer can, climbs out herself before anybody can help her.

Any crime, any time, including mine Lamont.

"I want you to find Win Garano for me. Right now," Lamont says to the officer. "Tell him to drop everything he's doing and call me right now," she orders.

"Yes, ma'am. I'm Sergeant Small." The woman in blue offers a handshake, does everything but salute.

"An unfortunate name," Lamont says, walking off toward a door that leads inside the hospital.

"You mean the investigator, right? The one they call Geronimo." Sergeant Small catches up with her. "If I was fat it would be a really unfortunate name, ma'am. I get made fun of enough." She removes her radio from her big black belt, opening the door. "I've got my car downstairs, hid out of view. You mind some stairs? Then where can I take you?"

"The *Globe*," she says.

*

JIMMY BARBER'S BASEMENT is dusty and mildewy with nothing but one low-wattage bare bulb to illuminate what must be a hundred cardboard cartons stacked to the rafters, some labeled, most not.

Sykes has spent the past four hours pushing aside boxes of miscellaneous crap—ancient tape recorders, scores of tapes, several empty flowerpots, fishing tackle, baseball caps, an old-style bulletproof vest, softball trophies, what must be thousands of photographs and letters and magazines, files, notepads, the handwriting horrible. Crap and more crap. The man was too lazy to organize his memorabilia so he just threw it into boxes, packed up everything short of fast-food wrappers and what was in his wastepaper basket.

So far, she's been through plenty of cases, ones he probably thought were worth saving: a fugitive who hid in a chimney and got stuck, a deadly assault with a bowling pin, a man struck by lightning while sleeping in an iron bed, an intoxicated woman who stopped in the middle of a road to pee, forgot to put her car in gear, ran over herself. Cases and more cases that Barber shouldn't have decided were his to carry home when he retired. But she has yet to find KPD893-85, not even in a box that contained a lot of papers, correspondence, and cases for 1985. She calls Win's cell phone for the third time, leaves another message, knows he's busy but takes it personally.

She can't help thinking that if she were someone really important, maybe like that Harvard-educated woman DA he complains about so much, he'd call back promptly. Sykes went to a tiny Christian college in Bristol, Tennessee, flunked out her second year, hated school, didn't see a practical reason in the world why she should learn French or calculus or go to chapel twice a week. She's not the same caliber as Win and that DA and all those other people way up north who are part of his life. She's practically old enough to be his mother.

Sykes sits on top of an overturned five-gallon plastic pickle bucket, staring at stacks of cardboard boxes, her throat scratchy, her eyes itchy, her lower back aching. For a moment she is overwhelmed, not merely by the task before her but by everything, sort of the way she felt when she began the Academy and on day two, the class was taken on a tour of that notorious University of Tennessee research facility known as The Body Farm, two wooded acres littered with stinking dead bodies in every condition imaginable, donated human remains rotting on the ground or under concrete slabs or in car trunks or in bodybags or out of bodybags, clothed or naked, anthropologists and entomologists wandering around day after day, taking notes.

Who could do this? I mean, what kind of person does something this disgusting for a living or graduate school or whatever? she asked Win as they crouched down, looking at maggots teeming over a partially skeletonized man whose hair had slid off his skull, looked like roadkill, about three feet away.

Better get used to it, he said as if the stench, the insects didn't bother him at all, said it as if she didn't know squat. *Dead people aren't nice to work with and they never say thanks. Maggots are good. Just little babies. See?* He picked one up, put it on his fingertip, where it perched like a grain of rice, a wiggly one. *Snitches. Our little friends. Tell us time of death, all kinds of things.*

I can hate maggots all I want, Sykes said. *And I don't need you treating me like I just fell off the turnip truck.*

She gets up from her pickle bucket, surveys layers of boxes, wondering which ones contain more old cases that walked out of the office with Detective Barber. Selfish, pinheaded idiot. She lifts a box four layers up, grunting under the weight of it, hoping she doesn't pull something. Most of the boxes are open, probably because the old goat couldn't bother retaping them shut after going in and out of them over the years, and she starts rummaging through charge-card statements and phone and utility bills going back to the mid-eighties. It's not what she's looking for, but the funny thing about bills and receipts is that they often reveal more about a person than confessions and eyewitness accounts, and she entertains an idle curiosity as she imagines August 8 twenty years ago, the day Vivian Finlay was murdered.

She imagines Detective Barber going to work that day, probably as if it were any other day, and then getting called to Mrs. Finlay's expensive riverfront home in Sequoyah

Hills. Sykes tries to remember where she was twenty years ago in August. Getting divorced, that's where. Twenty years ago she was a police dispatcher in Nashville and her husband worked for a recording company, exposing himself to new female talent in a way that turned out to be a little different from what Sykes thought was acceptable.

She pulls out files sloppily labeled by month and sits back down on the pickle bucket with credit-card receipts and utility and telephone bills. The address on the envelopes is the one for the house that belongs to this hellhole of a basement, and as she looks over MasterCard charges, she begins to suspect that Barber lived alone back then, most of his charges made at places like Home Depot, Wal-Mart, a liquor store, a sports bar. She notes that throughout the first half of 1985, he made very few long-distance calls, in some months no more than two or three. Then in August, that abruptly changed.

She shines the flashlight on a phone bill and recalls that twenty years ago cell phones were these big, cumbersome contraptions that looked like a Geiger counter. Nobody used them. Cops didn't. When they were away from their desks and needed to make calls they asked the dispatcher to do it and relay the information over the radio. If the information the detective needed was confidential or involved, he returned to headquarters, and if he was on the road, he charged the calls to the department and then had to fill out forms for reimbursement.

What cops didn't do was make case-related calls from their homes or charge them to their home numbers, but beginning the evening of August 8, when Mrs. Finlay was already dead and in the morgue refrigerator, Barber started making calls from his home phone, seven of them between five p.m. and midnight.

7

WIN'S CONDO is on the third floor of a brick-and-sandstone building that in the mid-eighteen-hundreds was a school. For someone who had so much trouble getting into schools, it's strange that he ended up living in one.

It wasn't premeditated. When he was hired by the Massachusetts State Police, he was twenty-two, had nothing to his name but a ten-year-old Jeep, secondhand clothes, and the five hundred dollars that Nana had scraped together for a college graduation present. Finding an affordable place in Cambridge was out of the question until he happened upon the old schoolhouse on Orchard Street, abandoned for decades, then being converted into condominiums. The building wasn't habitable yet, and Win made a deal with Farouk, the owner: If the rent was sufficiently cheap and Farouk promised not to raise it more than 3 percent per year, Win would live there during the extensive renovation and provide security and supervision.

Now his police presence is enough. He doesn't have to supervise anything and Farouk lets him park his Hummer H2 (seized from a drug dealer and sold at auction for a song), his Harley-Davidson Road King (repossessed, gently used), and his unmarked police car in a small paved area in back. None of the other tenants have parking, fight it out along the narrow street, get dinged and crunched and scraped.

Win unlocks the back door and walks up three flights of stairs to a hallway lined with units that once were class-rooms. He lives at the end of the hall, number 31. He unlocks the heavy oak door and steps inside a private enclave of old brick walls that still have the original chalk-boards built into them, and fir floors and wainscoting and vaulted ceilings. His furniture isn't of the period, a brown leather Ralph Lauren couch (secondhand), a chair and Oriental rug (eBay), a Thomas Moser coffee table (floor sample, slightly damaged). He looks, listens, engages all of his senses. The air seems stagnant, the living room lonely, and he retrieves a flashlight from a drawer, shines it obliquely over the floor, the furniture, the windows, looking for footprints or fingermarks in dust or on shiny surfaces.

He doesn't have an alarm system, can afford just the one in Nana's house. Doesn't matter, he has his own way of dealing with intruders.

Inside the coat closet near the front door, he opens a safe built into the wall, gets out his Smith & Wesson .357, model 340, internal hammer, or "hammerless," so it doesn't get snagged on clothing, and constructed of a titanium and aluminum alloy, so lightweight it feels like a toy. He tucks the revolver into a pocket and walks into the kitchen, fixes a pot of coffee, looks through mail Farouk has stacked on the counter, most of it magazines, thumbs through *Forbes* while coffee drips, skims an article on the fastest cars, Porsche's new 911, the new Mercedes SLK55, Maserati Spyder.

He heads into his bedroom with its brick walls, another chalkboard (for keeping score, he tells some of the women he dates, winks at them, just kidding), sits on the bed, sips coffee, thinking, his eyes heavy.

SYKES WISHES she had thought of bringing a bottle of water with her and something to eat. Her mouth is dry, tastes like dust. Her blood sugar's dropping.

Several times she has thought about venturing upstairs again and asking Detective Jimmy Barber's widow for a little hospitality, but the one time she went up to inquire if she could use the bathroom, Mrs. Barber, who was supposed to be asleep, was sitting at the kitchen table, drinking straight vodka and as unfriendly and unpleasant as a skunk.

"Go on." Drunk as hell, jerks her head toward the bathroom down the hall. "Then get on with your business and leave me the hell alone. I'm sick and tired of all this, done my bit."

Alone and exhausted in the basement, Sykes continues studying Barber's baffling phone bills, trying to make sense of his charging so many of them to his home phone. Five of them have the area code 919, the same number each time, and Sykes tries it, gets an answering service for the North Carolina State Medical Examiner's Office, someone asking if she wants to report a case.

"No. Oh, I'm sorry," she says. "I must have the wrong number," and she hangs up.

She notes that at least a dozen other calls Barber charged to his home phone over the days after Vivian Finlay's murder have the area code 704. She tries the number and gets a recording—the area code has been changed to 828. She redials.

"Hello?" a groggy male voice answers.

Sykes checks her watch. It's almost seven a.m., says, "Really sorry to bother you so early, sir. But do you mind telling me how long you've had this phone number?"

He hangs up on her. Maybe it wasn't the best approach. She tries again and says right off, "I promise this isn't a crank call, sir. I'm an agent with the Tennessee Bureau of

Investigation and I've come across this phone number in a case I'm looking at."

"Good Lord," he says. "You're kidding."

"No, sir. Serious as a heart attack. A case that happened twenty years ago."

"Good Lord," he says. "You must mean my aunt."

"And that would be . . . ?" Sykes asks.

"Vivian Finlay. This number was hers. I mean, we've never changed it."

"So I'm assuming she had another home besides the one in Knoxville."

"That's right. Here in Flat Rock. I'm her nephew."

Sykes calmly asks, "Do you remember Jimmy Barber, the detective who worked your aunt's case?"

She hears a female voice in the background: "George? Who is it?"

"It's all right, honey," he says, then to Sykes, "My wife, Kim." Then back to his wife, "I'll just be a minute, honey." Then to Sykes, "I know he tried hard, probably too hard. Was downright territorial about it, and I kind of blame him for it not going anywhere. You know, the case of his career, him not sharing information, working in secret. I bet you're familiar with things like that."

"'Fraid so."

"As best I recall, he seemed to have this notion he was onto something, hot on the trail, wouldn't say just what that trail was, guess nobody else knew what it was, either. That's probably one reason it never got solved. That's always been my belief."

Sykes thinks of the calls made from Barber's home phone. Maybe that's the explanation. He was secretive, didn't want any dispatchers or his fellow investigators to catch the scent of what he was following. Maybe Barber wanted to solve the case himself, didn't want to share the glory. Yes, she's all too familiar with that MO.

"Honey," George is talking to his wife again, clearly trying to soothe her. "Why don't you go make us some coffee? It's all right." Back to Sykes. "Kim took it the hardest, was as close to my aunt as a daughter. Oh, Lord, I hate all this has to come up." He keeps sighing.

Sykes questions him a little further. George was in his early forties when his aunt was murdered, is the son of her only sibling, Edmund Finlay, and when Sykes tries to make sense of how George and his aunt could have the same last name, he explains that she was quite strong-willed, proud of her distinguished family name, and refused to give it up when she married. George is an only child. He and his wife, Kim, have two grown children who live out west, the couple spend all of their time in Flat Rock, left Tennessee for good not long after the murder, just couldn't be there anymore, couldn't handle the memories, especially Kim couldn't, practically had a nervous breakdown afterward.

Sykes promises to get back with him or, more likely, an

investigator named Winston Garano will. George doesn't sound very happy when he hears that part.

"It's just awfully painful to open up all this," he explains. "You mind my asking why it's necessary after all these years?"

"We're just looking into a few things, sir. I appreciate your cooperation."

"Of course. Whatever I can do to help."

He'd rather eat dirt than help, Sykes thinks. When the anger goes away and the ugliness fades, a lot of people don't care about justice anymore. They just want to forget.

"Too bad," she mutters to Barber's dark, wretched basement. *It's not like I'm having fun, either.*

She ponders and contemplates, perched on the pickle bucket like that statue *The Thinker,* resumes going through more bills, finds a MasterCard bill for September, pulls out what is in the envelope, finds something that gives her a disk error, as she calls it.

"What the hell?" she mutters, staring at a document with a cover sheet stamped with an autopsy case number, then another case number, this one a police file number sloppily scribbled in pencil: KPD893-85.

The page underneath it is a medical examiner's inventory of Vivian Finlay's personal effects, and stapled to it is a Polaroid photograph of mutilated male body parts, grimy and gory: feet, arms and legs, pieces and parts, guts, a decapitated head, arranged on top of a steel autopsy table covered with a green sheet. The case number written on a six-inch ruler used as a reference scale indicates that the death occurred in North Carolina in 1983.

WIN WAKES UP with a start, for an instant not sure where he is. He realizes he's been asleep for more than two hours, still in his clothes, his neck stiff, the coffee on his bedside table cold.

He checks his phone messages, skipping over the earlier ones left by Sykes when he was too busy with Lamont to deal with the Finlay case. Sykes has left him another message: She's sent him files over the Internet and he needs to look at them right away and call her. His computer is neatly centered on a Stickley desk (yard sale), and he sits down, enters Sykes's number, gets her on her cell phone.

"Good God!" She hurts his ear. "I just heard!"

"Whoa," he says. "You near a landline?"

She gives him a number he recognizes as the Academy. He calls her back.

"Good God!" she starts in again. "It's all over the news. Good God, Win! What happened?"

"I'll tell you about it later, Sykes."

"You get in a shootout and you're going to tell me later? At least you killed him. Goddamn, and her. How's that gonna work? The DA? That's all anybody's talking about down here."

"Can we move on, Sykes?"

"The part I don't get is how you ended up at her house, walked right into it. She invite you there for a nightcap or something?"

It doesn't take a detective to pick up on her jealousy. The beautiful, powerful Lamont, all the more formidable because Sykes has never met her, and now she imagines him heroically saving her life, probably thinks Lamont is devoted to him forever, wants to quit her job for him, get married, have his children, throw herself on a funeral pyre when he dies.

"Tell me what you've got," he says. "You find the file?"

"After spending half the night in Barber's damn basement, everything but."

He sips his cold coffee, goes into his e-mail, sees files from her, converts them to documents as she talks fast, hardly takes a breath, tells him about MasterCard and phone bills, about Barber's probable territoriality and glory-hunting and secrecy, what Mrs. Finlay's nephew had to say. Then gets to the part about some man who had a bad encounter with a train in Charlotte two years before Mrs. Finlay's murder.

"Whoa, slow down," Win interrupts her, scanning a document on his screen. "What's a train death got to do with anything?"

"You tell me. You looking at the picture?"

"Looking at it now." He studies the photograph on his screen, not very good quality, a Polaroid of raggedly severed limbs and intestines and chunks of flesh piled next to a mutilated torso and severed head, what looks like black grease and dirt everywhere. White guy. Black hair. Pretty young, as best Win can tell. "You checked it out with the ME's office?"

"You know, I didn't realize this was my case."

His cell phone rings. He doesn't answer, impatiently silences it.

"Hey," Win says to Sykes. "You sound pissed at me."

"I'm not pissed at you," Sykes says angrily.

"Good. Because I've got plenty of people pissed at me and don't need you added to the list."

"Like who?"

"Her, for starters."

"You mean after what you did . . . ?"

"Exactly. I've tried to tell you. She's borderline, a sociopath, Bonnie without Clyde, doesn't need a Clyde, thinks all of us are Clydes. Hates Clydes, actually."

"You saying Lamont doesn't like men?"

"Not sure she likes anybody."

"Well, it'd be nice if you'd say thanks." Sykes tries to sound gruff. "I've been up all night running down crap for you, and I'm supposed to be in class in five minutes and where am I? In the damn media room sending files to you, trying to call people, mostly getting cussed at. I'm going to look at the case later today, on a flight to Raleigh, the ME's office in Chapel Hill."

"Who *cussed* at you?" He smiles a little. When she gets riled, she sounds like a little kid, one as Southern as pecan pie.

"Some damn Charlotte cop. And who's going to reimburse me for my plane ticket, by the way?"

"Don't worry. I'll take care of everything," he says, scrolling through another file, information that came from Detective Barber's basement, puzzled by a medical examiner's inventory of personal effects removed from a dead body in the morgue. "What did the *damn Charlotte cop* who worked the train fatality have to say?"

One pair of ruffled blue tennis panties with ball pocket, he reads the inventory.

One Izod white tennis skirt and matching shirt, bloody . . .

His cell phone rings again. He ignores it.

"The big jerk." Sykes continues to vent all over the map. "He's the police chief now, you know what they say about what floats to the top."

He zooms in on a number written in pencil on the upper-right corner of the personal effects report.

KPD893-85.

"Sykes?"

". . . Said I'd have to submit my request in writing if I want copies of the reports, which by now would probably be on microfilm," she is saying. "But he said he didn't understand the interest, there was nothing to it . . ."

"Sykes? KPD893-85. Vivian Finlay? She was wearing tennis clothes when she was murdered?"

"Try telling that to him, the guy smashed to smithereens by the damn freight train. *Nothing to it . . .*"

"Sykes! This inventory is Vivian Finlay's personal effects when she came into the morgue?"

"That's the next bizarre part, the only thing I could find from her case file. Where the hell's the rest of it?"

"These bloody tennis clothes are what's been in the Knoxville PD's evidence room for twenty years, what's being tested for DNA in California?"

The autopsy report Lamont gave him depicts a tiny seventy-three-year-old lady.

"You sure this personal-effects form is from her case?" Win asks.

"That's her case number for sure. I looked at every damn thing in every damn box while that Roller Derby drunk wife of his rattled around in the kitchen upstairs, stomped around, made sure I knew how unwelcome I was. There's nothing else."

He looks at the personal-effects inventory again, realizes something he should have noticed immediately.

"Her nephew says he'll be glad to talk to us," Sykes says. "Well, not *glad.* But he will."

"Size ten," Win says as someone knocks on the door. "The tennis clothes are size ten. A five-foot, ninety-one-pound woman doesn't wear size ten. Now what!" as the knocking becomes more insistent.

"Got to go," he tells Sykes, gets up from his desk,

walks into his living room as the urgent knocking continues.

He looks through the peephole, sees Sammy's flushed, unhappy face, opens the door.

"I've been trying to get you for a damn hour," Sammy blurts out.

"How'd you know I was here?" Win asks, confused, his mind going everywhere.

"I'm a detective. Your home phone's busy. She just screeched at me like an air-raid siren."

"Who?"

"Who do you think. You got to come with me right now. She's waiting for you at the *Globe*."

"Forget it," Win says.

8

STUART HAMILTON, the managing editor, maintains his appropriate demeanor as he sits inside his office with Lamont and a senior reporter and a photographer. The office is glass. Everyone in the newsroom is witness to what no doubt will be an unprecedented interview, maybe the biggest news in the city since the Red Sox won the World Series.

Everyone, and there must be a hundred people beyond the glass, can see the well-known, formidable DA Monique Lamont, in a dark warm-up suit, exhausted, no makeup, sitting on a sofa, their commander in chief, Hamilton, listening, nodding, his face somber. Journalists, secretaries, editors are guarded in their glances from the other side of the glass, but Lamont knows she is being watched, talked about, that looks are being exchanged, that e-mails are firing from desk to desk. It is what she wants. The interview will run on A1, above the fold. It will race through cyberspace and land in papers and on Internet news sites all around the world. It will be talked about on television, the radio.

Crawley can go to hell.

"Because I have no choice," she is saying from the sofa, her shoes off, her legs curled under her as if she is having coffee with old friends. "I owe it to women everywhere." She catches herself. "To men, women, children, all victimized people everywhere."

Careful. Don't suggest that sexual violence is a problem restricted to women. Don't refer to yourself as a victim.

"If we are going to destigmatize sexual violence. Pedophilia. Rape—and not only women are raped—" she continues, "then we must be open about it and speak of it in the context of violence and not simply in the context of sex."

"So you're basically desexualizing it at the same time you're demythologizing it," the reporter says, Pascal Plasser-something, she never can get his name right.

Last time he interviewed her, he was reasonably fair, reasonably truthful, and not particularly bright, which is why she requested him when she showed up unannounced at the newspaper, rang Hamilton, told him that if he assured her the coverage she deserves for an exclusive of this magnitude, she would talk openly about what just happened.

"No, Pascal," she says. "That's not what I'm doing at all."

She wonders where Win is and her anger spikes, fear sits in her stomach like lead.

She says, "I can't possibly desexualize what happened to me. It was a sexual crime. Sexual violence that could have exacted the ultimate price. My life."

"It's incredibly courageous for you to do this, Monique," Hamilton says with an air of solemnity, of sorrow, like he's a damn funeral-home director. "But I must point out that some of your detractors will view this as a political ploy. Governor Crawley, for example . . ."

"A *ploy*?" She leans forward on the sofa, holds Hamilton's gaze. "Someone puts a gun to my head, ties me up, rapes me with the intention of murdering me and burning down my house, and that's a *ploy*?"

"Your talking about it might be construed as . . ."

"Stuart," she says, and her mettle, her self-control are remarkable. "I welcome anybody to suggest such a thing. I challenge them. I dare them."

She's not quite sure how she can be so poised, and a part of her is terrified that it isn't normal for her to be this pulled together, that maybe it's the dead calm before a horrific storm, the sane moment before the straitjacket or suicide.

"Why do you say you'd welcome it?" Pascal What's-his-name asks, scribbling notes, flipping a page.

"Anybody," she says ominously. "*Anybody* who says or suggests such a thing will only succeed in revealing his true character. Good. Let him try."

"Him?"

"Let anybody try."

She looks through the glass, surveys the expanse of bleak partitioned space, journalists in their cubicles, rodents who feed on the garbage and tragedies of others. She looks for Win, waits for his formidable, striking presence to suddenly dominate the newsroom, striding her way. But there is no sign of him, and her hope begins to fade. Anger flares.

He has defied her directive. He has degraded her, belittled her, shown his misogynistic contempt.

"Your new crime initiative—in fact published in this very paper this morning—*any crime, any time,*" Hamilton says. "What might you say now?

"And will this new cold-case initiative, At Risk, the murder in Tennessee, somehow take a backseat to . . . ?"

Win isn't coming. She'll punish him for this.

"I couldn't be more motivated and determined to bring about justice in any violent crime, no matter how long ago it was committed," Lamont says. "In fact, I've assigned Investigator Garano to At Risk full-time while he's on leave from my Middlesex County headquarters."

"Leave? So there's a question about whether the shooting

of Roger Baptista was merited?" Pascal is suddenly alert, more alert than he has been throughout her brave, painful interview.

"Any time deadly force is used, no matter the apparent circumstances," Lamont says, placing emphasis on the word *apparent*, "we must investigate the incident to the fullest."

"Are you implying that the force might have been excessive?"

"I can make no further comment at this time," she says.

WIN FEELS a little guilty walking into the state police crime laboratory with his sealed envelope, knowing it really isn't fair to bypass backlogs and protocols when he wants evidence analyzed right away.

He doesn't feel the least bit guilty for not showing up at the *Globe* to further Lamont's relentless political aspirations, to participate in behavior that is inappropriate, outrageous, and, in his opinion, self-destructive. Sammy says her *exclusive tell-all* is already being talked about in cyberspace, on TV and the radio, getting everybody primed to read her prurient and pitiful interview. He has decided she's reckless and irrational, and that's not a good thing if the person is your boss.

The modern brick building with its heavy steel front doors is a haven for Win, a place to go when he wants to unload on Captain Jessie Huber, discuss cases, complain, confide, ask for advice, maybe a favor or two. Win walks through the green and blue glass-block lobby, heads down a long hallway, and helps himself to the familiar open door where he finds his friend and mentor, typically dapper in a conservative dark suit and a gray silk cravat, typically on the phone. Huber is tall and thin, bald as a full moon, and women find him sexy, maybe because he is formidable and a good listener. Three years ago he was the senior investigator in Win's unit, then was appointed to take over the labs.

He hangs up when he sees Win, bolts up from his desk, blurts out, "Dammit, boy!" and hugs him the way men hug, more backslapping than anything else. "Sit, sit! I can't believe it. Tell me what the hell's going on." He shuts the door, pulls a chair close. "I send you to Tennessee, best damn forensic training facility on the planet, right up your alley. Then what? What the hell you doing back up here and what the hell have you gotten yourself into?"

"You sent me?" Win sits, puzzled. "Thought it was Lamont. Thought it was her brilliant brainstorm to send me to the Academy, maybe so she could have me handy to work a *small-town case*, as she views it, that would make all us *big-city folks* up here look good."

Huber pauses, as if considering what he's going to say next, then, "You just killed somebody, Win. Let's don't talk politics."

"I killed somebody because of politics. Politics are why I was ordered back up here to have dinner with her, Jessie."

"I understand."

"I'm glad somebody does."

"You're very angry."

"I'm being used. Given nothing to work with. Can't even find the damn case file."

"Looks like you and me share the same opinion of this At Risk mess she's gotten us into," Huber says.

"I thought it was the governor's initiative, that she's just the quarterback. That's how it was explained . . ."

"Yes and no," Huber interrupts, leaning forward in his chair, lowering his voice. "This is all about her. She cooked it up, suggested it to Crawley, convinced him it would make the Commonwealth, make him look good. She might get most valuable player, but he's the team owner, right? Not hard to talk a governor, especially Crawley, into something like this—you know how out of touch governors can be when it comes to minutiae. What do you mean you can't find the case file?"

"Just what I said. The Finlay police case file—gone. Lost in space."

Huber gets a disgusted look on his face, almost rolls his eyes, mutters, "Jesus, wouldn't you suppose she would have had it sent to her office?" He picks up the phone, dials, glances up at him, adds, "Before she dragged you into this?"

"She says . . ." Win starts to reply.

"Hey," Huber says to the person who answers the phone. "I got Win Garano here with me. The Finlay case file. You ever see it?" A pause, then Huber stares at Win, says, "No big surprise. Thanks," and hangs up.

"What?" Win asks, a bad feeling fluttering in his stomach.

"Toby says he got it weeks ago, put it on Lamont's desk."

"She told me she's never seen it. Knoxville PD's never seen it, either. How 'bout giving me Toby's phone number."

Did Lamont lie? Did she lose the file? Did somebody take it before she ever saw it?

"Politics, my boy." Huber is saying. "Maybe dirty politics," he emphasizes with an ominous look in his eyes, writes down a phone number, hands it to him. "When she first told me about At Risk, I was emphatic she should never have talked Crawley into it and should try to talk him out of it. *Any crime, any time.* Jesus. What? We start doing DNA testing on every unsolved violent crime since the Great Flood? Meanwhile, we've got a backlog of some five hundred cases. Real cases with real people out there raping, killing."

"I'm not sure I understand why you would send me to Knoxville." Win can't get past that, feels shaky, a little dazed.

"Thought I was doing you a service. Great place and great on your résumé."

"I know you've always looked out for me . . . but it just seems coincidental I'm down there and then . . ."

"Look. It's coincidental to a point," Huber says.

"Lamont was determined to work an old case that wasn't local. You happened to be in Tennessee, Win, and happened to be the investigator she wanted involved."

"What if I hadn't been in Tennessee?"

"She would have found some other old case in some other distant town and probably loaned you out one way or another. You know, us enlightened New Englanders to the rescue," he adds sarcastically. "Send in the Yankee troops from the land of MIT and Harvard. Easy to bury, too, right? If things don't go so well down there in some quaint little Southern town, eventually—maybe even by election time—everyone up here forgets about it. Lot harder to bury some cold-case homicide that might have happened in Massachusetts, right?"

"Probably."

Huber leans back in his chair, adds, "I hear you're the star down there at the Academy."

Win doesn't reply, his thoughts stuck in multiple places. He's sweating under his suit, a cold sweat.

"Your future, Win. I don't think you want to work for her the rest of your life or run around all hours of the day and night working misdemeanor murders, one scumbag killing another. Not to mention the money. I sure as hell got tired of it. Training. The best. Grooming. You're so damn talented. I'm thinking you'll be replacing me as lab director when I retire, and I'm counting the days. All depending on the powers to be, who the governor is." He gets a knowing look on his face. "You following me?"

Win isn't following much. Stays silent, has a feeling about Huber. One he's never felt before.

"You trust me?"

"Always have," Win replies.

"You trust me now?" Huber says, his face very serious.

Win won't go there, says, "Trust you enough to spend my mental-health day with you, Jessie. That's the way we do things here in the land of Oz when we kill somebody on the job. How 'bout it?"

"I'm not in the stress unit anymore, my good friend. You know that."

"Doesn't matter. And you know that. I'm declaring this an official counseling session with the experienced counselor of my choice. Anybody inquires, I just had my mental-health day. Go on, ask me how I feel."

"Tell me."

"Regretful that deadly force was necessary," Win mechanically recites. "All broken up about it, can't sleep. Did everything I could to stop him, but he left me no choice. It's tragic. Just a kid, maybe he could have been rehabilitated, added something positive to society."

Huber stares at him for a long moment, then, "I'm gonna throw up."

"All right then. Grateful he didn't kill Lamont. Or me. Angry the worthless piece of shit did this to her, to me. Glad he's dead so he doesn't sue me. You mind if I borrow Rake for a little while?" Win holds up the envelope, the back of it sealed with yellow evidence tape initialed by him. "Maybe try out her ESDA magic box or that fancy image-enhancement software you just got or both on a letter? Reminds me, any prints on the money, the thousand dollars in Baptista's pocket?"

"Already ran them in IAFIS. Nothing." Huber gets up, goes back behind his desk, sits in his swivel chair.

"You got any thoughts about it?" Win then says. "Robbery gone bad or something else?"

Huber hesitates, says, "Enemies? The list is long, Win. I think by now you're seeing the scary truth for yourself, and I'd be very careful what you tell her, what you ask her, very, very careful. A shame. A damn shame, because you know what? She wasn't like that when she got started, was a real ballbuster, took down a lot of dirtbags, had my respect. Let's just put it this way, the word *ethics* probably isn't in her fancy vocabulary anymore."

"I thought the two of you were buddies. Here she's doing this little favor for your son."

"Right, buddies." He smiles ruefully. "In this business, never let people know what you really think of them. She certainly has no clue what Toby really thinks of her."

"Or you?"

"Incompetent and blames everything on everybody else, including Toby. Two guys talking? Between you and me, Geronimo? She's going down," Huber says. "It's really sad."

9

THE FORENSIC PATHOLOGIST who conducted the autopsy on the train fatality died one week later during a Sunday afternoon of skydiving when his parachute didn't open.

If Sykes didn't have the original case file in front of her, she might not believe it. *Bad karma,* she thinks uncomfortably. As a kid, she loved archaeology. It was one of the few subjects that interested her, maybe because it wasn't taught in school. She lost interest when she read about King Tut's tomb, about curses and people mysteriously dying.

"Twenty years ago, Mrs. Finlay's death," she is saying to Win over the phone. "Two years before that a train death, then the ME's death. I'm getting a little freaked out."

"Possibly coincidence," he says.

"Then why was the picture stapled to Mrs. Finlay's personal-effects inventory?"

"Maybe we shouldn't talk about this right now," says Win, who doesn't like cell phones and certainly doesn't assume that any conversation on them is secure.

Sykes is alone in the small morgue office on the eleventh floor of a tall, beige building behind the UNC–Chapel Hill medical school's hospitals. She is bewildered, seems the more she looks into Vivian Finlay's violent death, the more mysterious it gets. First, her case file has disappeared except for an inventory of clothing she supposedly had on when she was murdered, tennis clothes that would appear to be the wrong size. Second, a train fatality may somehow be connected to her case, and now the ME and his skydiving accident.

"Just a few things," Win adds. "Keep the details to a minimum. How?"

"Chute didn't open."

"There should have been an autopsy on the chute."

"How about I e-mail all this to you," Sykes says. "How about you read it yourself. When you getting back this way?"

She's feeling very isolated, abandoned. He's up there with that DA, the two of them headline news. As far as Sykes is concerned, he was involved in a shooting, should get out of town and be down here to help her out. It's his case. Well, that's not how it's feeling anymore. But the fact is, it's his case. Typically, now that something sensational has happened, an old lady murdered twenty years ago is a throwaway. Who cares.

"As soon as I can," is all Win has to say about it.

"I know you got some real problems up there," she replies as reasonably as possible. "But this is your case, Win. And if I don't get back to the Academy, the TBI will be all over me like white on rice."

"Whatever happens, I'll fix it," he says.

He always promises that and so far he hasn't fixed a damn thing. She spends all her time talking to him, doesn't study or hang out with the other students discussing what they just learned that day in class, then gets behind and doesn't fully comprehend the newest forensic technology and investigative techniques or have friends. She complains and he says, *Don't worry. You got me and I'm a great tutor.* She says maybe she shouldn't devote so much of herself to a man almost young enough to be her son, and he says he doesn't care about age, then pays attention to some younger woman or obsesses about that DA, Lamont, who's smart and beautiful, well, maybe damaged goods now. Not nice to think it, but a lot of men don't want a woman after she's been raped.

Sykes goes through the medical examiner's case. His name was Dr. Hurt. That figures, might be funny if it wasn't so sad. Fell from an estimated five thousand feet, she reads, suffered massive trauma to his head, part of his brain avulsed, femurs driven up into his hips, crushed and fractured this, ruptured that. The only mention of the parachute is a brief description by a police officer who responded to the scene. He stated it appeared the chute was improperly packed. Witnesses claimed Dr. Hurt packed it himself. The possibility was raised that he might have committed suicide.

Colleagues and family acknowledged he was deeply in debt and getting divorced but claimed he wasn't depressed or acting oddly at all—in fact, seemed to be in good spirits. Sykes has heard that tall tale before, people didn't notice a thing. Well, guess why. If they admit there was even the slightest reason for concern, they might feel guilty about being so caught up in their own lives that they couldn't take a moment to worry about somebody else. She looks up as a knock sounds and the door opens. The chief medical examiner walks in, a mousy kind of pinched-looking woman somewhere in her fifties, granny glasses, a loose lab coat, a stethoscope around her neck.

"Now that's something," Sykes says, looking pointedly at the stethoscope. "You making sure everybody's dead before you start cutting and sawing?"

The chief smiles, says, "My secretary asked me to check her lungs. She's getting bronchitis. Just making sure you don't need anything."

It's more than that.

"I don't guess you were around here when Dr. Hurt died," Sykes says.

"I succeeded him. What's this about, exactly? Why all the interest?" She glances at the two case files on the table.

Sykes isn't going to tell her, says, "Several seemingly unrelated deaths may have something in common. You know how it is, you have to look at everything."

"I think it was pretty clear he was a suicide. Why's the TBI involved?"

"It's not, exactly."

"Then you're not working the case?" she interrupts.

"I'm helping. It's not my case." As if Sykes needs to be reminded of that one more time. "Like I said, I'm just checking out a few things."

"Well, I see. I guess it's all right. I'll be in the morgue if you need me," the chief says, and she shuts the door behind her.

Guess it's all right. As if Sykes is a Girl Scout.

Then she thinks about Dr. Hurt, wonders about his state of mind, his level of professional competence, the effort he put forth if he was anxious and depressed and no longer valued his life. She imagines herself in a similar situation and is fairly certain she would miss important details, might not try very hard, maybe wouldn't care. She keeps that in mind as she reviews the train fatality, a terribly mutilating death that occurred at a rail crossing on a two-lane rural highway, the freight train's engineer stating that when he rounded a sharp curve at approximately eight fifteen that morning, he saw the decedent lying facedown across the tracks and couldn't stop the train in time to avoid running over him. The victim's name was Mark Holland, a thirty-nine-year-old detective with the Asheville Police Department.

His widow, Kimberly, was quoted in the newspaper as saying that her husband left their Asheville home early the previous evening en route to Charlotte, where he was to meet with someone, she didn't know who, but "it was related to work." He was not depressed and she could think of no reason whatsoever to account for his alleged suicide, that she was extremely upset and adamant that he would not have done such a thing, especially since "he just got promoted and we were excited about starting a family."

The autopsy revealed a laceration to Mark Holland's head and an underlying fracture (*Well, no friggin' wonder*) that was *consistent with a fall.*

Dr. Hurt wasn't just depressed, Sykes thinks, he was lights on, nobody home, bought into the Charlotte cop's suggestion that Holland was crossing the railroad tracks on foot, perhaps on his way to have a secret meeting with a witness, tripped, fell, knocked himself unconscious. Dr. Hurt signed out the case as an accident.

FORENSIC SCIENTIST RACHAEL—or "Rake," as Win calls her—places the letter on top of a porous metal platen called a vacuum bed. She hits a switch and begins vacuuming down the box.

He has watched her work the electrostatic imaging system before, and sometimes they've been lucky, most recently in a kidnapping case, the ransom note written on a sheet of paper that obviously had been under one the kidnapper had used earlier to jot down a phone number that led the police to a Papa John's Pizza where he had placed a take-out order and paid for it with a credit card. Rake wears white cotton examination gloves, was happy when Win told her he hadn't touched the letter with his bare hands. After they've finished looking for indented writing, the letter the man in the red scarf left for Win at the Diesel Café will go to the fingerprints lab to be processed with ninhydrin or some other reagent.

"How's Knoxville?" asks Rake, a nice-looking brunette who started out with the FBI lab in Quantico but decided after 9-11 and the Patriot Act that she didn't want to work for the Feds. "You gonna start talking with a dueling-banjo twang?"

"That's North Georgia, *Deliverance* country. No dueling banjos in Knoxville, just blaze-orange everywhere."

"Hunting?"

"UT football."

Rake covers the letter and the platen with a clear plastic imaging film that reminds Win of Saran Wrap.

"Win?" she says without looking up. "Sounds trite, but I'm sorry about what happened."

"Thanks, Rake."

She passes what she calls a corona discharge unit over the surface. Win always smells ozone when she does it, as if it might rain.

"I don't care what anybody says. You did the right thing," she adds. "I don't see how anybody can even question it."

"I didn't realize anybody was," he says, getting one of his uneasy feelings.

She tilts the tray and cascades toner-coated beads over the image-film-covered document, says, "Heard it on the radio during a coffee break."

The electrostatic charge causes the toner to migrate to indentations that aren't visible to the unaided eye, areas of the paper with microscopic damage caused by handwriting.

"Go on. Tell me," Win says, already knows.

He's being screwed.

"Just that Lamont said you're being investigated, like maybe it wasn't a good shooting. A big story's being run tomorrow and they're already promoting it with teases." She looks at him, adds, "How's that for grateful?"

"Maybe what I expected," he says as latent images appear in faint black, partial words, confusing.

Rake isn't impressed, points out something on the threatening letter the man in the red scarf left for Win, decides, "Think we'd better try three-D enhancement."

*

TOBY HUBER IS COLD, shivering as he sits on his balcony of the Winnetu Inn in South Beach, Edgartown, smoking a joint, looking at the ocean, at people in long pants and jackets walking along the beach.

"I'm sure it's gone, just not where, exactly," he says over his cell phone, annoyed but with a nice buzz going. "Sorry, man. But at this point, it doesn't matter."

"That's not for you to judge. Try to think for once."

"Look. I told you, okay? It must be when I threw out everything in trash bags, whatever. And I mean everything, including any food in the fridge, any beer, anything. Even hauled the trash about five miles away to a Dumpster behind . . . some restaurant, can't remember which one. Damn it's freezing here. I've checked and rechecked and it's not here. Man, you need to chill before you have a stroke . . ."

A knock from inside the one-bedroom suite, and then the door opens, the housekeeper is startled as Toby steps inside and glares at her.

"What is it you don't understand about *Do Not Disturb*!" he screams at her.

"Sorry, sir. The card's not on the door." She quickly vanishes.

Toby returns to the balcony, takes a toke, almost yells into the phone, "I'm out of here. You got that? Where it's warm. Boring as goddamn hell here. You've put me through enough and it'd better be worth it."

"Not quite yet. It will look suspicious if you're suddenly flying off to L.A. You need to stay put a few more days. We've got to make sure it's not someplace where it might be found and cause us a lot of trouble. Think, Toby!"

"If it's anywhere, it's still inside the damn apartment. I don't know . . ." Something glimmers. He's not sure he checked under the bed, mentions that, adding, "You know, when I was reading it, could have stuck it there. Why don't you go check your goddamn self?"

"I already have."

"Then you're so spazzed out about it, go check again!"

"Think! Where did you have it last? You sure you didn't leave it at the office . . ."

"I told you. I took it with me, know that for fact because I was reading it."

"I didn't tell you to take it so you could read it!"

"Yeah, so you've said about a hundred times by now, so you can just shut up about it, okay?"

"You put it in your car, drove it there? What? Reading it in bed? So you could look at the damn pictures? Are you insane! Where did you have it last!"

"I told you to shut up, don't act like such a hysterical old woman. It's not like I can exactly go look. So you help yourself, look 'til the cows come home. Maybe I missed it, okay? I had it all kinds of places when I was there. In a drawer, maybe in a pile by the bed, under the pillow. At one point I had it in a basket of dirty clothes. Or maybe it was in the dryer . . ."

"Toby, are you sure you didn't take it with you to the Vineyard?"

"How many times you going to ask me! What difference does it make. So what if it's gone? Nothing worked the way it was supposed to, anyway."

"Well, we don't *know* it's gone, now do we? And that's a problem, a very serious problem. You were supposed to leave it where it would be found. The last thing you did before you left. But you didn't. You completely ignored my orders."

"So it probably ended up in the trash, okay? That's probably what happened when I cleaned things out." He takes another toke. "You know, it's not like I didn't have a lot on my mind, right? And he kept wanting to know about the money, said I'd better give it to him in advance, and I said half of it up front, and then you took forever getting it for me . . ."

"How the hell did I end up with someone like you?"

Holding in smoke. Exhaling. "Because you're lucky. So far. But that can change, you know."

RAKE IS LOST in a software world of pixels and Z ranges and histograms, panning, zooming, rotating, manipulating light angles, surface reflection, contour enhancement while Win stares at the big flat screen, looking at shadowy shapes in magnified 3-D.

He starts seeing a word, maybe numbers.

"An *e*, an *r*, a *w*, lowercase?" he suggests. "And three and ninety-six?"

There's more. She keeps working, the words and numbers materializing. Odd-looking, almost overlaid.

"More than one note that's left indented writing?" Win considers.

"That's what I'm thinking," Rake says. "Could very well be indentations from different writings on different sheets from the same pad of paper. You know, you write a note, then another page down, write another one, and the pressure of the pen or pencil pressed against the paper is sufficiently strong to create an indented image multiple sheets down."

She works some more and they make out what they can: *three-year market exclusivity,* and *okay,* and partly overlaying that, suggesting it was a separate writing on a separate sheet of paper, is *$8.96* and what appears to be *up from an earlier forecast of $6.11.*

10

MONIQUE LAMONT SITS in a marble and cherry kitchen on Mount Vernon Street in Beacon Hill, one of the most expensive and coveted addresses in Boston. She is drinking her first martini of the day, straight up, Grey Goose, one pimiento-stuffed green olive, and a glass that she took out of the freezer.

She wears jeans and a loose-fitting denim shirt. The warm-up suit she had on earlier is in the Dumpster behind the nineteenth-century brick complex where the apartment was safely and secretly tucked away until this morning when Sammy disclosed the location to the troops, insisting that the police patrol the area, insisting that she can't stay in her

Cambridge house, not now, not that she would. She will always see the back door, the key box, the gas can. She will always see him in her bedroom, the gun pointed at her head as he did what he wanted, as he re-created her into his own image—a small, filthy creature, a nothing, a nobody.

"I only wish I'd killed him myself," she says.

Huber sits across the table from her, drinking his second beer. He is having a hard time looking at her, his gaze interrupted as if his eye muscles are suddenly palsied.

"You've got to get beyond this, Monique," he says. "I know that's easy for me to say. But you're not thinking right, couldn't possibly be under the circumstances."

"Shut up, Jessie. If it ever happens to you, you'll find yourself howling at the damn moon. Then you'll understand empathy."

"So it helps if you ruin everything else in your life? You shouldn't have told them about this place."

"And what? Refuse police protection when I don't know who's behind what happened, who put him up to it?"

"We don't know for a fact that anybody did."

"Go to a hotel? Walk into the lobby, find the media in packs, waiting to tear into me?"

"You're the one who went to the media," he says somberly, his eyes moving around, doing their cold, calculating thing. "Now we have to take your crap and make caviar out of it."

He has the worst metaphors and analogies of anyone

Lamont has ever met. She says, "Why did you let him? You could have told him the documents lab was tied up, that Rachael wasn't there, was busy, something. That was stupid, Jessie."

"Win's always had a special membership to Club Crime Lab. He's too smart. If I'd started making excuses, he would have known right away something was going on. He trusts me like a father."

"Then he's not as smart as you think." She sips her martini, drains the glass, eats the olive.

"And you're a Harvard snob." Huber gets up, opens the freezer, gets out the Grey Goose, a frozen glass, makes her another, forgets the olive.

She stares at the martini he sets on the table, stares at it long enough for him to remember the olive.

"You know what that guy's IQ is?" Huber says from inside the refrigerator. "Higher than yours and mine put together."

She replays that unforgiving footage, Win seeing her, handing her his jacket, telling her to take deep breaths. She sees him seeing her naked and powerless and degraded.

"He just can't take tests, the damndest thing," Huber continues, opens another beer. "Graduated from high school with a four-point-oh, valedictorian, most likely to succeed, best-looking, best everything except for one minor thing. Tanked his SATs. Then, after college, tanked his GREs, his LSATs. He can't take tests. Something happens to him."

Win didn't show up at the *Globe.* He defied her. He has no respect for her after seeing her . . .

"I hear there are people like that." Huber sits back down. "Brilliant but can't take tests."

"I'm not interested in his learning disabilities," Lamont says. "What exactly did he find out at the lab?" The vodka has made her tongue bigger, less nimble, her thoughts stuttering. "Or what does he think he found out?"

"He probably doesn't know what it means. Can't prove anything, anyway."

"That's not what I asked!"

"Notes from a phone conversation with my broker."

"Oh, God."

"Don't worry. They won't find fingerprints, nothing to link that letter to me. One thing I do know is forensic science." He smiles. "Win probably thinks it's you. For that matter, probably thinks you're behind it. Probably thinks Roy did it, called him a *half-breed.*" Huber laughs. "Now that for sure pissed him off."

"Another one of your impulsive, high-risk decisions."

He didn't ask her, just did it. Then he told her after the fact because the more she knows, the more implicated she is, that's been his strategy all along.

"It did exactly what I said it would." Huber drinks his beer. "You threaten him, insult him, try to scare him off a case, and he locks his jaws on it like a pit bull."

She is silent, sips her martini, trapped.

She says, "It wasn't necessary. He's a pit bull anyway."

"Your fault for insisting on talking to him in person instead of over the phone. You should have left him down there in Knoxville." He pauses, his face twitching. "Maybe you got a thing about him. That's what it looks like."

"Go to hell, Jessie."

"Of course, it's a blessing he was here. Providence, your guardian angel, living right, whatever," he indelicately, indifferently goes on. "Win got pissed and came to see you. As it turns out, my little ploy actually did us all quite a favor. You're still alive, Monique."

"Don't sound so disappointed."

"Monique . . ."

"I'm not joking." She holds his gaze, doesn't flinch, realizes she has come to hate him, to wish him harm, misery, poverty, death. Then, "I don't want Toby coming back. He's worthless. I'm done with that favor. I'm done with any favors."

"He can't stand working for you anyway."

"I've had enough of you, Jessie. I have for a long time." The vodka is making her uninhibited. He can go to hell. "I told you I'm not playing along with it anymore. I goddamn meant it. It's not worth it."

"Of course it is. You've gotten what you want, Monique. What you deserve," he says, and there is no mistaking what he means.

She stares at him, shocked. "What I deserve?"

He stares back at her.

"I deserve *that*? You're saying I deserve *that*! You bastard!"

"I meant you work hard, should get something for it." His eyes don't jump around this time. They look at her, flat, nothing in them.

She starts to cry.

IT IS DARK NOW, the moon new.

Win opens the driver's door of Nana's old Buick, stopped in the middle of the road again, watching Miss Dog wandering aimlessly again, headlights flashing in her old, blind eyes.

"That's it. The end," Win says, furious. "Come here, girl," he coaxes, whistling. "Come on, Miss Dog. What'cha doing on the street again, huh? She forget to shut the door? Let you out, her fat ass too lazy to make sure you got back in? Her son-in-law lowlife kick you again?"

Miss Dog's tail droops, her head hangs. She drops to her belly as if she's done something wrong. Win gently picks her up, keeps talking, wonders if she can hear him at all, places her inside the car, drives off, tells her where she's going and what will happen next. Maybe she hears him, maybe she doesn't. She licks his hand. He parks behind Nana's house, and the wind chimes are chiming softly, the night clear, the cool air barely stirring, the chimes quietly chiming as if telling secrets, and he unlocks the back door, Miss Dog draped over his shoulder like a furry sack of potatoes.

"Nana?"

He follows the sound of the TV.

"Nana? We have a new addition to the family."

SYKES HAS BEEN on the phone for more than an hour, getting bounced from one old-timer to the next. Twenty-three years ago is forever. So far, no one at the Asheville Police Department remembers Detective Mark Holland.

She dials another number as she drives west toward Knoxville, approaching headlights confusing her, reminding her what a rip-off it is to get old. She can't see worth crap anymore, can't read a menu without glasses, her night vision awful. *Damn airlines. Damn delays and cancellations.* The only rental car left, one with four cylinders, got the pep of a sea cow.

"I'm trying to reach Detective Jones," she tells the man who answers the phone.

"Been quite awhile since I was called that," the voice pleasantly says. "And who's this?"

She introduces herself, says, "As I understand it, sir, you were a detective with the Asheville PD back in the eighties, and I'm wondering if you might remember another detective named Mark Holland."

"Not well because he'd only been a detective a couple of months when he got killed."

"What do you remember about that?"

"Only he'd gone to Charlotte supposedly to interview some witness in a robbery case. You want to know my opinion, he wasn't no accident. I think he just didn't want to take his own life in a place where one of us would have had to work his case."

"You have any idea why he might have wanted to take his own life?"

"The way I heard it, his wife was cheating on him," he says.

NANA IS ASLEEP on the couch, in her long, black robe, her long, white hair loose and splayed over the cushion, Clint Eastwood on the TV, making somebody's day with his big, bad gun.

Win sets down Miss Dog and she instantly puts her head in Nana's lap. Animals always react to her like that. She opens her eyes, looks at Win, holds out her hands to him.

"My darling." She kisses his face.

"You didn't have your alarm on again. So I have no choice but to give you a guard dog. This is Miss Dog."

"Welcome my friend Miss Dog." She pets her, gently pulls on her ears. "Don't you worry, Miss Dog. She won't find you here. That nasty woman, I can see her plain as day, could use a few teeth, couldn't she." Petting Miss Dog. "Don't you worry, my little one," Nana says indignantly. "I have ways of taking care of people like her."

If you want to incur Nana's wrath, treat an animal badly, incite her to go out on one of her mysterious missions late at night, flinging 999 pennies into a bad person's yard, a payment to the old crone goddess Hecate, who knows how to take care of cruel people.

Miss Dog is fast asleep in Nana's lap.

"Her hips are hurting," she says. "Arthritis. Gum problems, pain. Depressed. She yells at her a lot, that big, unhappy woman, not a nice person, treats her the same way she treats herself. Terrible. Poor baby." Petting her as she snores. "I know all about it," she then says to Win. "It's all over TV, but you're all right." She takes his hand. "You remember that time your father beat up that man who lived three streets over?" She points. "He had no choice."

Win isn't sure he knows what she's talking about, nothing new. Her world isn't always obvious or logical.

"You were four and this man's son—he was eight—shoved you to the ground and started kicking you, calling you awful names, calling your father awful names, racist names, and oh, when your father found out, he went to their house and that was that."

"Did Dad start it?"

"Not your father. But he ended it. It happens. And

you're all right. If you go back and look around, you'll find a knife."

"No, Nana. It was a gun."

"There's a knife. You know, the kind with a handle that's got a thing." She draws it in the air. Maybe she means a knife with a guard, like a dagger. "You look. The one you killed, and you mustn't blame yourself for that. He was very bad, but there's another one. He's worse. Evil. I tried the honey on a muffin this morning. Tennessee is a pure place with lots of good people, not necessarily good politics, but good people. The bees don't care about politics so they like it there, are joyful making their honey."

Win laughs, gets up. "I think I'm going to head down to North Carolina, Nana."

"Not yet. You have unfinished business here."

"Will you please set the burglar alarm?"

"I have my wind chimes. And Miss Dog," she says. "Tonight the moon is aligned with Venus, has entered Scorpio. Misconceptions abound, my darling. Your perceptions are veiled, but that's all about to change. Go back to her house and you'll find what I'm talking about and something else." She stares off, says, "Why am I seeing a small room with rafters overhead? And a narrow staircase, maybe plywood?"

"Probably because I still haven't gotten around to cleaning out your attic," he says.

11

THE NEXT MORNING Sykes and the director of NFA, Tom, are squatting, moving through the grass like crabs, picking up brass.

On the Knoxville Police Department firing range, no one is above picking up after himself, and everyone is expected to live up to the privilege of attending the Academy. Showing up for class goes without saying. Sykes is sleep-deprived and depressed as she glances around at her classmates, fifteen men and women in blue cargo pants, polo shirts, and caps, returning firearms and ammo to the golf cart, finishing up an eight o'clock session of analyzing trajectories, cartridge case ejections, marking evidence with tiny orange flags and taking photographs like they do at crime scenes.

Sykes is humiliated, dejected, certain the other students are shunning her, have no respect for her. The way it must look to them, she's a fair-weather crime scene investigator, turns up when there's something fun going on like firing the AK-47, the Glock, the 12-gauge riot gun, blasting away at what she calls the *ugly bastard targets,* her favorite because it is far more gratifying to rip into a paper thug pointing a pistol at her than to go for a bull's-eye. She clinks several brass cartridge cases into the plastic bucket she and Tom share, the air humid and heavy, the distant Smoky Mountains hazy, living up to their name.

"So far it's not making the Knoxville PD look good." She is trying to explain, sweat running into her eyes.

"Yesterday was blunt-force and pattern injuries," Tom says, clinking in another cartridge case.

"Kind of funny," she says, parting grass, plucking out more brass. "That's what killed her. Blunt force." Clink. "And she had pattern injuries." Clink. "Win says she had holes punched in her skull, like maybe somebody went after her with a hammer." Clink. "So I'm learning about it anyway, even if I missed class."

"You've missed drug-abuse deaths. SIDS. Child abuse," Tom goes on, moving through the grass, clinking more brass into the bucket.

"You know I'll make it up." She's not sure she can and Win isn't here to help her.

"You've got to." Tom gets to his feet, stretches his back, his young face serious, maybe more serious than he really feels.

He's not the hardhead he pretends to be. Sykes knows. She's seen him with his kids.

"What about the PD, exactly," he then says.

She explains about Jimmy Barber's basement, about a case file that should never have been taken home and now is missing, tells him about what is seeming like an incredibly careless and inept investigation of an incredibly vicious murder. She's a bit dramatic, emphatic, hoping he'll understand the importance of what she's doing instead of focusing on what she's not doing.

"I don't want to make anybody look bad," she says. "And if I just drop all this and walk away . . . ? If Win and I do?"

"Don't make excuses for him. He can answer for himself. If we ever see him again. And it's his case, Sykes. His department put him on it."

It may be his case, but that's not how it's feeling. Seems to her she's doing all the work.

"And the KPD isn't going to look bad. That was a long time ago, Sykes. Law enforcement has changed dramatically in the past twenty years. Back then all they had was ID techs, nothing like this." He looks around at his students.

"Well, I don't think I can turn my back on it and walk away," she says.

"Our Academy students don't turn their backs and walk away from anything," Tom says, almost kindly. "Tell you what. Tomorrow's gunshot wounds, we'll be working with a couple ballistic gelatin dummies."

"Well, hell." She likes shooting up jelly men, as she calls them, even more than the ugly bastard targets.

"Not as crucial as some other things, I can let it slide, find some time later to get you back out on the range. But all next week is bloodstain-pattern analysis. That you can't miss."

She takes off her dark blue cap, wipes the sweat off her brow, watches the other students walking off toward the field house, toward the trucks, toward their futures.

"I'll give you until Monday," he says.

"NOTHING," WIN ANNOUNCES as he creaks down the creaking wooden stairs, remembering how loud they sounded only a few early mornings ago, when his entire life changed.

"I told you. We really did play detective and look around after the fact," Sammy says from a wing chair near a fire-place covered with a stained-glass screen. "No other areas of the house were involved. It fits with what she said. He came in behind her, forced her up to the bedroom, and that was it, thanks to you."

"That wasn't it, unfortunately." Win looks around.

Lamont's glass fetish doesn't end in her office. Win has never seen anything quite like it. Every light fixture is the same kind he shattered in her bedroom, an exotic half moon suspended from a hammered iron chain, hand-painted in vivid colors, signed Ulla Darni, expensive as hell. Her dining-room table is glass, and there are crystal bowls and figurines, art-glass mirrors and vases everywhere.

"You know what I'm saying." Sammy gets up slowly, sighs, as if he's too tired to move. "Man oh, man. I need a new back. You satisfied? Can we go now?"

"She's got a garage," Win reminds him.

"Already been in there. Nothing."

"I haven't been in there."

"Whatever you want," Sammy says, shrugging, and out the door they go.

In the late eighteen-hundreds, it was a carriage house, brick, a slate roof, now a bit tired and half hidden by the low branches of an old oak tree. Sammy finds the key to the side door, realizes the lock is broken, has been pried open.

"It wasn't like this when I was here . . ." Sammy slides out his gun. Win's already got his out.

Sammy shoves the door open and it bangs against the inside wall, and he lowers his pistol, returns it to its holster. Win lowers his .357, stands just inside the door, looking around, noticing oil stains on concrete, noticing dirty tire tracks, what he would expect inside a garage. Hanging from Peg-Boards are the usual yard and garden tools, and in a corner is a lawn mower, a wheelbarrow, and a plastic gallon gas can, half full.

"Doesn't look like the gas can came from in here," Sammy remarks.

"Never thought it did," Win replies. "You plan on torching a place, usually you bring your own accelerants."

"Unless it's an inside job, like a domestic situation. Seen my share of those."

"That's not what this is. Roger Baptista sure as hell wasn't a domestic situation," Win says, looking at a rope hanging from the exposed beam ceiling, a pull-down ladder.

"You already check?" Win asks.

Sammy looks up where Win is looking and says, "No."

THE WINDOWS of the imposing Tudor home glint in the sun, the Tennessee River bright blue and gracefully bending in either direction as far as Sykes can see. She climbs out of her old VW Rabbit, figures she looks like a harmless, middle-aged realtor in a denim pants suit.

The businessman who owns the house where Vivian Finlay was murdered isn't in, Sykes checked, wonders if anyone has bothered to tell him that twenty years ago a seventy-three-year-old woman was beaten to death inside his ritzy house. If he was told, he must not care. That's something. Sykes wouldn't live in a place where someone was murdered, not even if it was given to her. She starts walking around, wondering how Mrs. Finlay's killer got in.

There's the front door, and on both sides of the house plenty of windows, but they're small, and it's hard for her to imagine someone climbing through a window in the middle of this neighborhood in the middle of the day. Another door closer to the back of the house appears to lead into the basement, then facing the river is one more door, and through windows on either side of it is a handsome modern kitchen with stainless-steel appliances and lots of tiles and granite.

Sykes stands in the backyard, taking in the flowers and lush trees, the low wall built of river rock, then the dock and the water. She watches a motorboat roaring past, pulling a hotdog skier, calls a number she stored in her cell phone as she was driving over here after an Academy class that might be the last one she ever attends.

"Sequoyah Hills Country Club," a polite voice answers.

"The business office, please," Sykes says, and the call is transferred, then, "Missy? Hi. Special Agent Delma Sykes again."

"Well, I can tell you this much," Missy says. "Vivian Finlay was a member from April 1972 until October 1985 . . ."

"October? She died in August," Sykes interrupts.

"October was probably when her family got around to

canceling her membership. These things can take awhile, you know, people don't even think about it."

Sykes feels stupid. What does she know about country clubs or memberships of any type?

"Had a full membership," Missy is explaining, "meaning it included tennis and golf."

"What else you got in that file?" Sykes asks, sitting on the wall, wishing she could look at water without trespassing or going on vacation. Must be something to have so much money you can help yourself to a river.

"I'm sorry?"

"I mean, old itemized bills that might give some details as to what she bought and did, maybe? For instance, if she ever bought tennis clothes in the pro shop?"

"We don't throw away business files, but they wouldn't be here in the office. We have a storage facility . . ."

"I need her old bills, all of them for 'eighty-five."

"My word, twenty years' worth to dig through. That could take . . ." Dismay, an audible sigh.

"I'll help you look," Sykes says.

THE UPPER STORY of Lamont's garage has been converted into a guest room that doesn't appear to have been used except for the indentations and a little dirt left by feet walking around the dark brown carpet. Fairly big feet, Win notes. Two different tread patterns.

The walls are painted beige and hung with several signed prints—sailboats, seascapes. There is a single bed covered with a brown spread, a bedside table, a small dresser, a swivel chair, and a desk that has nothing on it except an ink blotter, a green glass lamp, and a brass letter opener that looks like a dagger. The furniture is inexpensive maple. A small bathroom with a stacked washer-dryer, very neat and clean, looks unlived-in, except, of course, for the footwear indentations all over the carpet.

"What you got up there?" Sammy yells from the bottom of the pull-down plywood stairs. "Want me to come up?"

"No need and there's no room," Win says, looking down through the opening at the top of Sammy's graying head. "Doesn't look like anybody's been staying here, working here. Or if they were, they moved out and cleaned up pretty well. For sure, someone or maybe more than one person has been walking around."

Win pulls a pair of latex gloves out of a pocket, puts them on, starts opening drawers, all of them. He gets down on his hands and knees, looks under the dresser, looks under the bed, something telling him to look everywhere, not sure what for or why except that if someone has been in and out of the apartment, obviously since it was cleaned and vacuumed last, then why? And who pried open the locked door downstairs? Did someone come here after Lamont was almost murdered, and if so, what was the person looking for? He opens a closet, opens cabinets under the sinks in the kitchenette and the bathroom, stands in the middle of the living room, looks around some more, his attention wandering to the oven. He walks to it and opens the door.

On the bottom rack is a thick manila envelope with the handwritten address of the DA's office and a Knoxville return address, lots of stamps pasted on crooked, hastily, more postage than needed.

"Jesus Christ," he says.

The envelope has been slit open, and he looks at the letter opener on the desk, the one that reminds him of a dagger. He pulls out a thick case file bound with rubber bands.

"You're shittin' me!" he exclaims.

Sammy's feet sound on the pull-down stairs.

"The case. She's had it here all along." Then he's not so sure. "Or someone has."

"Huh?" Sammy's baffled face appears in the opening.

"The Finlay case file."

Sammy holds on to a rope railing, doesn't climb up any farther, says, "Huh?" again.

Win holds up the file, says, "She's had it for three damn months. Since before I started the Academy, before she'd even told me I was going. Christ."

"That doesn't make sense. If Knoxville PD sent it to her, wouldn't they have mentioned that when you started looking for it?"

"No name." Win is reading the label again. "Just the

address, which I don't recognize. Postmark June tenth. Zip code's 37921, the Western Avenue–Middlebrook Pike area. Hold on."

He calls Sykes, gets his answer, goes calm the way he does when everything is unraveling. The return address is Jimmy Barber's.

"Looks like his Roller Derby wife dug in the basement long before you did," Win says to Sykes. "Sent the Finlay file up here where it's been hiding in an oven."

"A what? The bitch lied to me!"

"That depends. Did you ever tell her exactly what you were looking for?" Win asks.

Silence.

"Sykes? You there? Did you tell her?"

"Well, not exactly," she says.

AT HALF PAST TWO, he parks Nana's old Buick behind her house, can see her wind chimes in daylight, their long, hollow tubes moving in the trees and from the eaves and not quite as magical as they are at night.

Another car is parked near the basketball hoop, almost in the bushes, an old red Miata. He needs a landline and right now his apartment seems like a bad idea. He has a feeling about it and has decided to heed it, wouldn't be far-fetched to suppose cops or someone who pries open locks might be patrolling his neighborhood. He knocks, then

139

walks in through the back door, into the kitchen, where Nana sits across from a distraught young woman who is cutting the deck of tarot cards into three stacks. Nana has made hot tea, a house specialty, with sticks of cinnamon and fresh slivers of lemon peel. He notices a jar of Tennessee honey on the counter, a spoon nearby.

"Guess what we tried, my darling," Nana says to him, reaching for a card. "Your special honey made by joyful bees. This is Suzy. We're taking care of that husband of hers who thinks he doesn't have to abide by the restraining order."

"He been arrested?" Win asks Suzy, in her twenties, delicate-looking, face puffy from crying.

"My boy's a detective," Nana proudly says, sipping her tea as nails click and Miss Dog wanders in.

Win sits on the floor, starts petting her, and she wants her tummy scratched, and Suzy is saying, "Twice. Don't do any good. Matt just bails himself out, shows up like last night at my mama's house, waiting behind the hedge, and gets in my face as I'm getting out of the car. He'll kill me. I know it. People don't understand."

"We'll see about that," Nana warns.

Win asks her where her mama lives, notices Miss Dog is looking remarkably improved. Her sightless eyes seem full of light. She seems to be smiling.

"Just down the road," Suzy tells him with a question in her voice. "You should know." She looks at Miss Dog.

He gets it. Suzy's mother is Miss Dog's owner. That

figures. "Miss Dog's not going anywhere," he says, and that's that.

"I don't care, won't say a word. Mama's awful to her. Matt's worse. I've been telling her the same thing you have. She's gonna get run over by a car."

"Miss Dog's doing just fine," Nana says. "She slept in my bed last night with both the cats."

"So Mama doesn't protect you from Matt." Win gets off the floor.

"Nothing she can do. He cruises past her house all he wants. Walks right in if he wants. She doesn't do anything."

Win heads into the living room to use the phone. He sits among his grandmother's crystals and mystical clutter and asks to speak to Dr. Reid, a geneticist who works for the DNA lab in California that is analyzing the bloody clothing in the Finlay case. He's told Dr. Reid is on a conference call, can get back with Win in half an hour, and he walks out of the house, starts walking toward Miss Dog's house, her former house. He's seen Matt before, pretty sure of it, small, fat, lots of tattoos, the type to be an abusive bully.

His cell phone rings. Sykes.

"Don't bother me. I'm about to get into a fight," he says.

"I'll make this quick, then."

"No sense of humor today?"

"Well, I didn't want to tell you. But if you and me aren't back in class by Monday, we're getting kicked out of the Academy."

It will disappoint her more than it will disappoint him. The Massachusetts State Police has its own crime scene investigators, doesn't need Win out there gathering evidence himself, and he doesn't give a damn about being director of the crime labs or anything else at the moment. It enters his mind that maybe he's lost his enthusiasm because he suspects the only reason he was sent down South to school was to set him up to work the Finlay case, to position him for selfish, political, and, at this point, unknown purposes. And he's no longer sure who is behind what.

"Win?" Sykes is asking.

The house is in sight, about a block up ahead on the left, a white Chevy truck in the drive.

"Don't worry," Win says. "I'll take care of it."

"You can't take care of it! I'm going to be in so much trouble with the TBI, probably get fired. I wish you wouldn't keep saying you'll fix something you can't, Win!"

"I told you I'm going to take care of it," he says, walking faster as Matt emerges from the back of the house, heading to the pickup truck, that brazen, stupid loser.

"I should tell you the other thing," Sykes says dejectedly. "I checked with Ms. Trailer-Park Barber. Soused again, by the way. And you were right."

"And?" Win begins to trot.

"She sent the case to the DA's office about two months ago, said some guy, sounded young, kind of rude, called her, gave her instructions. She didn't mention it to me because I didn't ask, says a lot of people call about stuff. I'm sorry."

"Gotta go," Win says, running fast.

He grabs the truck's door as it is shutting, and the fat little bully looks at him, shocked, then furious.

"Get your damn hands off my truck!"

He's mean, stupid, stinks like beer and cigarettes, his breath so bad Win can smell it as he opens the door wide, stands between it and the front seat. He looks into the small, cruel eyes of Suzy's worthless husband, who's probably been hanging around here, waiting for her to show up or, if nothing else, waiting for her to drive past and see him and speed off in terror.

"Who are you and what do you want!" Matt yells.

Win just stares at him, a trick he learned a long time ago on the school playground, after he got bigger, got tired of being picked on. The longer you stare at somebody and don't say anything, the more freaked out the person gets, and Matt's eyes seem to be retreating like little clams digging into the sand, hiding. He's not so tough now. Win stands there, blocking the door, staring at him.

"Man, you're crazy," Matt says, beginning to panic.

Silence.

"Now just go on, I'm not doing nothing to nobody."

He's spitting as he talks, so scared he just might soil himself.

Silence.

Then Win says, "I hear you're into kicking dogs and abusing your wife."

"That's a lie!"

Silence.

"Whoever said that's lying!"

Silence.

Then, "I just want you to remember my face," Win says very quietly, staring, not a trace of emotion. "You bother Suzy one more time, ever hurt an animal one more time, and this face is going to be the last one you ever see."

12

WIN GETS THE FRUSTRATING news that the DNA analysis isn't completed yet. He explains that the situation is urgent, asks how quickly the analysis can be finished. Maybe in another day or so. He asks exactly what the results might mean.

"A genealogical history," Dr. Reid explains over the phone. "Based on four major biogeographical ancestry groups, sub-Saharan African, Indo-European, East Asian, or Native American, or an admixture."

Win sits in Nana's favorite rocking chair by the open window, and wind chimes quietly chime, light, sweetly.

". . . Technology based on SNPs," Dr. Reid is

explaining. "Single Nucleotide Polymorphisms. Different from normal DNA screening that requires the analysis of millions of base pairs of genes when looking for patterns, many of them irrelevant. Basically, what we're interested in are the some two thousand ancestry information-markers . . ."

Win listens to a typical scientist typically overexplaining, going on and on about some beta version of some machine that is 99.99 percent accurate, about some test that can predict human eye color from DNA with 95 percent accuracy, about Harvard Medical School and a license the lab has with it to develop some anemia drug . . .

"Whoa." Win stops rocking. "What do drugs have to do with this?"

"Pharmacogenetics. When we started doing ancestral profiling, it wasn't to work criminal cases. The original objective was to assist pharmaceutical companies with determining how genetics can be applied to developing drugs."

"You've got something going on with Harvard Medical School?" Win gets a feeling, a strong one.

"Maybe you've heard of PROHEMOGEN? For the treatment of anemia associated with renal failure, cancer chemotherapy, Zidovudine-treated HIV. Can help reduce the need for blood transfusion."

A breeze stirs the trees beyond Nana's window and the chimes seem to chime louder.

"Dr. Reid," Win says, "you mind telling me how long ago the sample was submitted in the Finlay case."

"I believe about two months or so ago."

"It takes that long?"

"Theoretically, five days, a week, but it's a question of priorities. We're currently analyzing DNA in a hundred or so other active criminal cases, several of them serial rapists, serial murderers. I was told there was no rush."

"I understand. Twenty years ago. The guy we're talking about probably isn't killing people anymore."

"It's not a guy. The first thing we always do is run a standard STR panel, which happens to give us gender from one of those markers. Both DNA sources are from females."

"Both? What?"

"Samples from areas of clothing around the neck, under the arms, the crotch, where you might find cells from sweat, skin shedding, gave us a profile of a female who has a different DNA profile from the bloodstains, which have always been assumed to be the victim's and are," he says. "That much they got right back then."

THE STORAGE FACILITY where the country club keeps decades of records is a massive complex of cinder-block units connected like train cars over a two-acre lot.

Although the units are temperature-controlled, they have no lighting, and Sykes runs the narrow beam of her small flashlight over white cartons while Missy checks her inventory list so she can tell what's inside.

"E-three," Sykes reads.

"November 1985," Missy says. "Getting close."

They move on. It is stuffy in here, dusty, and Sykes is getting tired of digging through old boxes in dark, claustrophobic spaces while Win runs around New England doing who knows what.

"E-eight," she reads.

"June 1985. Looks like they're a bit out of order."

"You know what?" Sykes decides, lifting another heavy box off metal shelving. "Let's just get them for the whole year."

THE DOORMAN of the historic brick building in Beacon Hill isn't inclined to let Win do what he wants, which is to appear at Lamont's door unannounced.

"I'm sorry, sir," says the older man in his gray uniform, a bored doorman who spends most of his time behind a desk, obviously reading newspapers. There's a stack of them under his chair. "I have to ring her first. What's your name?"

Numb-nut. You just told me she's home.

"All right. I guess you leave me no choice." Win sighs, reaching inside his jacket pocket, slipping out his wallet, flipping it open, showing his creds. "But I really need you to keep quiet about this. I'm in the middle of an extremely sensitive investigation."

The doorman takes a long time looking at Win's shield, his ID card, then looks closely at his face, something odd and uncertain in his own, maybe a glint of excitement, then, "You're that . . . ? The one I've been reading about. I recognize you now."

"I can't talk about it," Win says.

"You want my opinion, you did what you had to do. Damn right. Kids these days, worthless hoodlums."

"I can't talk about it," Win says as a woman in her fifties enters the lobby, yellow designer suit, a Chanelian, as Win calls rich women who have to flaunt those huge Chanel double C's.

"Good afternoon." The doorman politely nods at her, almost bows.

She dismisses Win's existence, then does a sharp double take, stares openly at him, smiles at him, a little flirtation going. He smiles back, watches her head to the elevator.

"I'll just ride up with her," Win says to the doorman, doesn't give him a chance to protest.

He strides across the lobby as polished brass elevator doors part and steps aboard a mahogany vessel that is about to carry him on a mission Monique Lamont isn't likely to appreciate or forget.

"They really need to replace this. How many times do I

need to tell them? As if the building can't afford a new elevator," the Chanelian says, tapping the button for the eighth floor, looking him over as if he's a trunk show and she might just buy everything in it.

The elevator creaks like the *Titanic* sinking. Lamont is staying in this building but no one seems to know which apartment. There isn't one in her name.

"You live in the building? Don't believe I've seen you before," the Chanelian says.

"Just visiting." He looks confused, staring at the elevator buttons. "She said the penthouse, but there seem to be two of them. PH and PH two. Or maybe it was . . . ?" He starts digging in his pockets, as if looking for notes.

The elevator stops. The doors take their time opening. The Chanelian doesn't move, gets thoughtful, replies, "If you tell me who you're here to see, perhaps I can help you."

He clears his throat, lowers his voice, leans closer, her perfume piercing his sinuses like an ice pick. "Monique Lamont, but please keep that confidential."

Her eyes light up, she nods. "Tenth floor, south corner. But she doesn't live here. Just visits. Often. Probably to have a little privacy. Everyone is entitled to a life." Her eyes on his. "If you know what I mean."

"You know her?" he asks.

"Know of. She's rather hard to miss. And people talk. And you? You look familiar."

Win sticks out his arm, keeps the doors from closing,

replies, "A lot of people say that. Have a nice rest of the day."

The Chanelian doesn't like being dismissed, walks off, doesn't look back. Win gets out his cell phone, calls Sammy.

"Do me a favor. Lamont's apartment." He gives Sammy the address. "Find out who owns it, who leases it, whatever."

He gets off on the tenth floor, where there are two doors on either side of a small marble foyer, and he rings the bell for 10 SC. He rings it three times before Lamont's wary voice sounds on the other side.

"Who is it?"

"It's me, Win," he says. "Open the door, Monique."

Locks unlock, the heavy wooden door opens, Lamont on the other side, looking like hell, looking like she just got out of the shower.

"What do you want? You had no right coming here," she says furiously, pushing damp hair out of her face. "How did you get in?"

He moves past her, stands beneath a Baccarat chandelier, looks around at ornate molding and wainscoting and rich, old wood.

"Nice place you've got here. Worth what? A couple mil? Four or five, maybe six?" he says.

SYKES SITS INSIDE an office at a club she could never afford and wonders if Vivian Finlay thought she was better than everybody else and would have dismissed Sykes as a klutzy country girl who probably doesn't know which fork to use for salad. The truth about crime victims is a lot of them are unlikable.

She sorts through paperwork, has gotten as far as May. What she has learned so far is that Mrs. Finlay was very active, played tennis at the country club as often as three times a week, always had lunch afterward, and based on how much the bill was each time, she never ate alone and had a habit of picking up the check. It appears she ate dinner there once or twice a week and liked Sunday brunch. Again, she didn't dine alone, based on the substantial size of the bills.

Mrs. Finlay was conspicuously generous, and Sykes suspects the reason for the rich old woman's largesse wasn't so she could spread around her good fortune, since it is unlikely that her guests were on tight budgets, not at this club. More likely, she was one of those people who nod for the check every time because she likes to be the big shot, likes to be in charge, controlling people, proud people, the sort who have always made Sykes feel simple and small. She's dated plenty of men like that, thinks about how different Win is from any man she's ever known.

Like the other night at the Tennessee Grill, the two of them watching the sun set over the river, a special evening of big cheeseburgers and beer, her aching with the hope that maybe he was as attracted to her as she was to him. Well, *is.*

She can't deny it, keeps thinking it will go away. That night it was her turn to treat, and she did because unlike most men, Win doesn't mind—not that he's cheap, because he sure isn't. He's generous and kind but believes things ought to be equal so both people feel *empowered and experience the pleasure of giving,* is the way he explains it. Win takes turns. On the firing range, driving places, paying tabs, or just talking, he is as fair as he can be.

Sykes begins looking through the statement for the month of July, starts getting excited when she notices that in addition to Mrs. Finlay's court times and lunches, a *guest* played tennis and golf at the club. Whoever this *guest* was, or perhaps it was a different guest on different occasions, Sykes considers, within a two-week period, almost two thousand dollars was spent on "clothing" in the pro shops and charged to Mrs. Finlay's account. Sykes starts on the month of August.

On the eighth, the day Mrs. Finlay was murdered, a *guest* played tennis, apparently alone because there is a rental fee for the ball machine, something it doesn't seem the sociable Mrs. Finlay ever used. That same day, a *guest* spent almost a thousand dollars in the tennis pro shop and charged it to Mrs. Finlay's account.

THERE IS NOTHING between Lamont and Win except an antique table and her red silk robe.

It is almost seven p.m., the sun fiery orange, a band of pink spreading across the horizon, the window open and warm air drifting in.

"Why don't you get dressed," he says to her for the third time. "Please. We're two professionals, two colleagues talking. Let's keep it like that."

"You're not here because we're colleagues. And it's my apartment and I'll wear what I want."

"Actually, it's not your apartment," he says. "Sammy had a little chat with the supervisor. It seems your crime lab director is doing quite well."

She is silent.

"Monique? Where does Huber get his money?"

"Why don't you ask him."

"Why are you staying in his apartment? The two of you got something going?"

"I'm rather homeless at the moment. Get this over with, won't you?"

"All right. We'll get back to that." Win leans forward, rests his elbows on the table. "I can go first or give you a chance to tell me the truth."

"Yes, colleagues, as you put it." Her eyes are on his. "Will you Mirandize me next for some crime you seem to think I've committed?"

"Truth." He says it again. "You're in trouble. I can't help you if you don't tell me the truth."

"I have no idea what you're talking about."

"The office over your garage," he goes on. "Who uses it?"

"Did you get a search warrant before you went charging in there?"

"Your property is a crime scene. All of it, every inch of it. I don't need to explain that to you."

She picks up a pack of cigarettes, slides one out, her hands trembling. It's the first time he's ever seen her smoke.

"When's the last time you were in the apartment over your garage?" he asks.

She lights the cigarette, takes a deep drag, is considerate enough to blow smoke out sideways instead of in his face.

"What is it you intend to accuse me of?"

"Come on, Monique. I'm not after you."

"Feels like it." She slides an ashtray close.

"Here, let me walk you through it." Win tries a different approach. "I enter your garage through the side door—which, by the way, had been broken into, the lock pried open."

She blows out smoke, taps an ash, a glint of fear that turns to anger.

"And I see some evidence of a car having been in there, tire tracks, dirty, possibly made when it rained last. Which would have been the night you were attacked."

She listens, smokes.

"I see the pull-down stairs and climb up and find a guest

apartment that appears unlived-in except for footprints on the carpet."

"And of course, you ransacked the place," she says, leaning back in her chair as if inviting him to look at her in a way he shouldn't.

"If I did, what did I find? Why don't you tell me?"

"I have no idea," she says.

13

LAMONT TAPS AN ASH, blowing out smoke, her eyes not leaving his, her robe nothing but a red sheen over her naked flesh, tied tightly around her waist, cleavage showing.

"All these high-tech labs you deal with in California?" Win is saying. "There's a lot of money in biotechnology, pharmaceuticals. A lot of potential for fraud, scams. Funny how stuff like that metastasizes from person to person. Sometimes to people who weren't bad, then got exposed."

She is listening, smoking, looking at him, the same unsettling glint in her eyes.

He exclaims, "Are you hearing me?"

"You going to play bad cop now, Win? Won't work. I know the routine better than you do."

"You think you can do this to me?" he says. "Agree to have me sent off to Tennessee, then jerk me back up here to work this publicity-stunt case of yours. A threatening letter. Accusations that the shooting wasn't a good one, how could you do that to me, what kind of person would do something like that . . . ?"

"A suggestion that the shooting had to be investigated. A suggestion made by a DA who plays by the rules." Her eyes stare at him. "I played it by the books."

"Oh, yeah. You and your rules. You and your ego and machinations. A missing police file, a homicide case file no one's been able to find. Well, guess what. I found it. And guess where. In your damn apartment over the garage. Are you crazy?"

"What?" She looks confused, startled.

"You heard me."

"The Finlay case file was in my garage apartment? I didn't even know it was missing or that my office ever had it . . . Where in my apartment?"

"You tell me." He is getting very angry.

"I would if I knew!"

"How about the oven."

"Is this supposed to be funny?"

"The Vivian Finlay case file was in your oven."

The look returns to her eyes, suspicion, contempt.

"Somebody stoned and damn stupid," she mutters. "Someone with the memory of a gnat. To make me look bad."

"You hide it in there?"

"I'm not stupid," she says, crushing out her cigarette as if she's killing it slowly. "Thank you, Win. You've just given me extremely important information."

She leans forward, rests her arms on the table, affording him a view he shouldn't have, her eyes filled with an invitation she has never offered in the past.

"Stop it, Monique," he says.

She doesn't move, waits, watching him look, and his eyes have a will of their own, and it enters his mind more than it ever has before what it would be like with her . . .

"Don't do this." He looks away. "I know what you must feel. I've worked with victims of sexual violence . . ."

"You don't know anything! I'm not a victim!"

Her outburst seems to shake the kitchen.

"And I'm not going to be one," he says quietly, coldly. "You're not going to use me to validate that you're still desirable. Save it for your therapist."

"*You* validate *me*?" she says, snatching her robe together. "I believe it's the other way around. I believe I would be the one doing the validating." She sits up straight in the chair, looking down, blinking back tears.

A long silence follows as she struggles to control herself.

Then, "I'm sorry." She wipes her eyes. "Unfair and I'm sorry. I didn't mean that."

"Talk to me," Win says.

"If you'd bothered to look into all this a little more thoroughly"—she regains her composure and sharp edge—"you might have found out I don't use the garage. Haven't parked my car in there for months. Someone else does. Or did. I haven't stepped foot inside the place."

"Who?"

"Toby."

"Toby?" he says furiously, feeling something else. "You've been letting that brain-dead idiot live on your property? Jesus."

"You sound jealous." She smiles, smoking.

"And you sound like you think you owe Huber . . ." His thoughts are tangled. He almost sputters.

"It doesn't matter."

"It does matter!"

"He asked if Toby could live there while clerking for me. Get him out of the house."

Win thinks of the hundred-dollar bills in Baptista's pocket, the gasoline can, the rags. He thinks of the missing keys that forced Lamont to go around to the back of her house, where it was dark and wooded, so she could get the spare key out of the box. He thinks of Toby's penchant for drugs, thinks of Baptista's drug charges and recent visit to juvenile court.

"Let me ask you something," Win says. "You know any reason why Huber might want you dead?"

*

LAMONT LIGHTS ANOTHER CIGARETTE, her voice getting hoarse from smoke. She's laying off the martinis, is pouring herself a glass of white wine.

She watches him, appraises him, watches him watching her, waiting for his eyes to find her. My God, he is the most beautiful male specimen she has ever seen. Dark, pleated trousers; open-neck white cotton shirt; smooth, tan skin; hair as black as a raven's; and eyes that change like the weather. She reminds herself that she's a little drunk, wonders what it would be like . . . then stops herself from going there.

Win doesn't say a word. She can't tell what he is thinking.

"I know you have no respect for me," she then says, smoking.

"I feel sorry for you," he says.

"Of course." She feels hate rising, squeezing her heart. "You and your kind take it from us and then cast us aside. Turn us into garbage, then treat us like garbage. Save your pity for one of your loser bimbo girlfriends."

"I feel sorry for you because you're empty."

She laughs and her laugh sounds hollow.

Empty. She feels like crying again, doesn't understand what is wrong with her, in control one minute, falling apart the next.

"Looking for something to fill up your vast emptiness, Monique. The best of everything. Power. Fame. More power. Beauty. Any man you want. All of it so fragile, like all of your glass. The slightest trauma or disappointment and everything breaks."

SHE TURNS AWAY from him, won't give him her eyes.

"I'm going to ask you again, did you have anything to do with the Finlay case file ending up in your apartment, where Toby was staying?"

"Why!" She blurts out in a trembling voice, looking at him again. "To keep it from you? No. I told you. I've never even seen that file. I assumed it was in Tennessee."

"Then you didn't see it when it arrived at your office? Toby claims he put it on your desk."

"He's a goddamn liar. I didn't even know it was being sent to my office. Obviously he intercepted it."

"So I'm to assume he took it to your garage apartment and hid it. Or misplaced it. Or whatever the hell he did."

"I don't go in there, not since he's been there. It's just a guest room, rarely used."

"Doesn't appear he used it much, either. You never saw him coming or going?"

"I didn't pay any attention."

"Never saw his car?"

"Sometimes heard it, usually very late at night. I stayed out of his business. Frankly, didn't care. Assumed he was out all the time, partying with his druggie friends."

"Maybe a druggie friend named Roger Baptista. By the looks of it, Toby was never planning on coming back to your office or your apartment after his vacation in the Vineyard."

She is thinking, her face tight, angry. Scared.

"Why would Toby remove that file from your office?" Win presses her.

"Forgetful, brain rotted by drugs, no memory left . . ."

"Monique?"

"Because someone asked him to, what do you think! To make me look incompetent, corrupt. You don't have what you need to work the case. Without the file, it's rather impossible, isn't it? If that file was found there, it's terrible for me."

Win just listens.

"Someone told Toby to take it and the brain-rotted fool did." She is silent for a minute, then, "Stupid, incompetent. Dead or alive. Either way, Crawley gets reelected."

"You think he had something to do with this?"

"How convenient Toby was out of town that night. When you showed up, when it happened, Toby wasn't there. Had just left for the Vineyard. No witnesses. The purpose of that ridiculous letter left at the Diesel Café was probably to make sure you didn't decide to show up at my house and prevent the very thing you did."

"So you know about that, too," Win says. "Let me guess. Huber and his silk cravats. A scarlet one that night."

"I found out after the fact. Now maybe I see a different reason why he did it. A taunting letter to keep you occupied. In case you might have decided to drop by, come see me . . ."

"Why would he think that?"

"Pathological jealousy. He thinks everybody wants me. He thinks everybody wants you. Toby probably hand-picked him, you're probably right." She's back to something else, back to Baptista. "Probably one of his drug sources. Probably met him hanging around the courthouse. Do you think he paid him?"

"Who's *he*?"

She looks at him, looks at him a long time, then, "You know damn well."

"Huber," Win says, and it's not going to be easy interrogating him when that time comes.

"Jessie's probably the one who broke into my apartment . . ."

"Why? To find the file?"

"Yes." Then, "I don't know. I don't know. All I know is he wanted me to look bad. Destroy my reputation. After death. Or now. In life . . ."

Her voice is shaking, her eyes filled with enraged tears. Win watches her, waits.

"So tell me." She can barely talk. "He pay him to rape me, too?" She raises her voice, tears falling.

Win doesn't know. He doesn't know what to say.

"Or paid him just to kill me and burn up the house and the worthless nothing piece of shit threw in the rape free. Oh, yes. The proverbial crime of opportunity."

"Why?" Win quietly asks. "Why the—"

"Why the *overkill*?" Lamont interrupts with a harsh laugh. "Why? Come on, Win. You see it every day. Hate. Envy. Being scorned, dissed, threatened. Payback. Kill somebody as many times and in as many different horrific ways as you can, right? Degrade them, cause them as much pain and suffering as possible."

Images of that night, of her. Win tries to push them back.

"Well, he tried," she says. Then, "How much?"

He knows what she's asking. He doesn't answer her.

"How much!"

He hesitates, says, "A thousand dollars."

"So that's all I'm worth."

"It has nothing to do with that and you know—"

"Don't bother," she says.

14

REX'S GUNS & AMMO is on Upward Road in East Flat Rock, a good spot for a private meeting because the shop is closed on Sundays. Nice to know that the folks in North Carolina who believe in firearms and camouflage observe the Sabbath.

Sykes and Win sit in folding chairs somewhere between racks of rifles and fishing tackle, a seven-pound bass mounted on the wall giving Sykes the fisheye. Leaning against a glass showcase of pistols is the Henderson County Sheriff, Rutherford, a friend of Rex's, which is how he came upon the key to let Win and Sykes in so they could have a little discussion about the Finlay case. Rutherford sort of

PATRICIA CORNWELL

looks like his name, an odd thing about that, a phenomenon
Sykes has been aware of all her life.

He's big and rumbling like a freight train, intimidating
and hell-bent in one direction—his. He has reminded them
more than once in one way or another that Flat Rock is his
jurisdiction, made it clear that if anybody picks up George
and Kimberly, "Kim," Finlay, it will be him, says he needs to
understand why they should be picked up in the first place.
So Sykes and Win are doing their best to patiently explain
the facts of the case, details that became apparent when
they stayed up all last night driving here from Knoxville,
then holing up in a Best Western motel, picking apart and
piecing together information from a case file that they
should have had access to from the start, pages and pages of
reports, witness statements, and about a dozen gruesome
photographs that make many things disturbingly obvious.

It was Kim who discovered Mrs. Finlay's brutalized
body and called 911 at 2:14 p.m., August 8. She claims she
was driving George's white Mercedes sedan, was out running errands and decided to drop by for a visit. Yet several
hours earlier, between ten thirty and eleven a.m., a retired
man who lived only a few blocks from Mrs. Finlay's
Sequoyah Hills home saw Kim in the area driving her red
Mercedes convertible. When Detective Barber questioned
her about it she offered the simple explanation that while
she was out and about she stopped in the Sequoyah Hills
neighborhood to walk her Maltese, Zsa Zsa, on Cherokee

Boulevard, or *the Boulevard*, as she called it. Nothing particularly suspicious about that, since Cherokee Boulevard was and is a popular place for people, including nonresidents, to walk their dogs. Kim, who didn't live in Sequoyah Hills, was known to walk Zsa Zsa there daily, depending on the weather, and August 8 happened to be a beautiful day.

In her statement to Barber, she continued to spin her reasonably credible story, claiming she took Zsa Zsa home around noon, checked on George, who was *sick in bed with a cold*, then went back out in his Mercedes because her Mercedes convertible *needed gas and was making a funny noise*. On her way to the dry cleaner's, she decided to *drop in* on Mrs. Finlay, and when she didn't answer the door Kim let herself in and had *the most awful shock* of her life. She went on to tell Barber, very tearfully, that she had been very worried about Mrs. Finlay's safety. *She has all this money and is ostentatious and lives alone, and is naïve, much too trusting,* she said, adding that earlier in the week when *George and I came by to have dinner with her, we both saw a suspicious-looking black man near her house, staring at it. When we turned into the driveway, he walked away very quickly.*

George, of course, verified his wife's story. George, of course, had a few good stories of his own, including that he was *fairly sure* his aunt had noticed this same black man several days earlier, just walking up and down the street near her house—*loitering,* in her words. George was also *fairly sure* he *probably* left a hammer on a windowsill in his aunt's master bedroom, having used it to help her hang a painting, he wasn't exactly sure when, but not long before *it happened.* A plausible theory evolved: Mrs. Finlay returned home from tennis or shopping or something and interrupted her assailant, who had gotten only so far as stealing a box of silver coins that supposedly was *in plain view on a dresser in the master bedroom.*

In one of Barber's notes, he wrote that when the police arrived, there was water in the tub, a damp towel draped over the side of it, and another, larger damp towel on the bedroom floor not far from where the body was found. He speculated that when the killer heard Mrs. Finlay drive up, he *may have hid himself* and watched her undress to take a bath, which *may have sexually excited him.* At the point when she may have had nothing on but her *ruffled blue tennis panties,* he confronted her, and when she started screaming, he noticed the hammer on the windowsill and used it.

What Barber didn't entertain, at least not in writing, was the possibility that Mrs. Finlay was in the tub when her assailant appeared, that in fact her assailant might have been someone she knew so well as to allow this person to come into the bedroom, perhaps even talk to her while she was still in the tub or drying off, maybe a close female friend or relative, maybe someone who didn't always get along with her. It never seemed to occur to Barber that Mrs. Finlay might have been murdered by someone very close to her, the crime then staged to look like an attempted sexual assault that went as far as her tennis panties being pulled down to her knees before her enraged assailant beat her to death.

According to the statement of one of Mrs. Finlay's tennis partners, Kim and Mrs. Finlay had gotten quite hostile toward each other over the summer, and Mrs. Finlay *had begun saying things like Chinese people should work in Laundromats, not marry people like her nephew.* Sykes sure as hell would have been on high alert if she had been the detective and someone had told her that, would have zeroed in on all of it, would have connected the dots, decided Kim and Mrs. Finlay pretty much hated each other and maybe when Kim dropped by the house after tennis that day—after yet another shopping spree charged to Mrs. Finlay's country club account—they got into an argument that went no place good.

"Still sounds mighty circumstantial to me," Rutherford the sheriff says from beside the showcase of pistols that is propping him up.

"The DNA isn't circumstantial," Win replies, and he keeps looking at Sykes, as if to remind the sheriff that the two of them are in this together.

"Don't understand why they didn't get the DNA back then. You sure something didn't get contaminated after twenty years?"

"They didn't do DNA testing back then," Win says, looking at Sykes, and she nods. "Just standard serology, ABO typing, which certainly indicated that the blood on the tennis clothing was Mrs. Finlay's. But what they didn't test twenty years ago were areas of clothing that might yield other biological information."

"Like what areas?" the sheriff asks, getting an impatient look on his face.

"Areas that rub against your skin, areas that might have sweat or saliva, other body fluids. Get it from all sorts of things. The inside of collars, under the arms, the brims of hats, socks, the inside of shoes, chewing gum, cigarette butts. We need highly sensitive DNA technology for tests like that. PCR. STR. And by the way, when DNA is contaminated, you don't get false positives."

Rutherford doesn't want to get into it, says, "Well, George and Kim aren't going to give you any trouble. And like I told you, I know they're home. Had my secretary call them up, pretend she was collecting money for the FOP hurricane fund. You ever seen anything like all these hurricanes? The Lord Almighty's unhappy with something, you ask me."

"Plenty to be unhappy about," Sykes says to him. "Plenty of ambition, greed, and hatred, the very same things that led to Mrs. Finlay's murder."

Sheriff Rutherford says nothing, won't look at her, has been addressing his every comment to Win. It's a man's world, probably explaining why there's all these hurricanes, punishment for women not staying home and doing what they're told.

"Before y'all head out," the sheriff says to Win, "I'd like to clear up the train part, because I'm still suspicious it was a homicide, like maybe there was some sort of organized crime involved, Dixie Mafia or something. And if that's so"—he slowly shakes his jowly head—"then maybe we should be approaching this different, bring in the FBI."

"No way it was a homicide." Sykes is adamant. "Everything I've found out about Mark Holland's case indicates suicide."

"And what's everything?" the sheriff asks Win, as if it's Win who just made that claim.

"Like the fact that when he was married to Kim, she went through his money and was cheating on him, having an affair with Mark's best friend, another cop. Mark had plenty of reason to be depressed and angry," she says, looking right at the sheriff.

"Might not have been enough for Barber to run with," Win adds, "but it should have caused him to ask a few questions about Kim's character and morals. Which he clearly did, since he contacted the medical examiner's office in Chapel Hill, then stapled a Polaroid photograph of Holland's remains to the personal-effects inventory from Mrs. Finlay's autopsy."

"A personal-effects inventory that had tennis clothes on it? Because the tennis clothes were size six, he made some Sherlock leap to a train fatality?" Rutherford peels open a stick of spearmint gum, winks at Win, says, "Guess I'll leave my DNA on it, huh?" Then, "Go on." Chewing. "Go on, then. I'm listening. Hook that up with the train fatality. Hope you can." Chewing.

"Ten," Sykes says. "The tennis clothes were size ten."

"Well, not that I'm an expert on women's attire, but I can't see any connection between this poor cop being run over by a train and this dead old lady's tennis clothes. You implying Detective Barber figured those clothes were too big to fit Mrs. Finlay?" He says all this to Win.

"I bet Barber didn't notice," Sykes says.

"Don't think I would have," the sheriff says to Win. "How 'bout you?" He winks at him again, chewing.

"Detective Garano's the one who *did* notice," Sykes says.

"Possibly a simpler answer is the bloody tennis clothes were what Barber submitted to the TBI labs for testing," Win suggests. "He had a copy of it, stapled it to the morgue photo. Tucked them inside his September MasterCard bill, maybe because that's where the previous month's charges were listed for his trip to the ME's office in Chapel Hill. People do things, don't think about them. Who knows."

"That sure is the truth," Sykes agrees, thinking of the case file Toby Huber stupidly stuck in the oven.

"A lot of details never make sense," Win goes on. "A lot of holes never get filled in. A lot of what is reconstructed probably looks very little like what really happens in those minutes, those split seconds, when a violent outburst ends someone's life."

"You some kind of philosopher or something?" Rutherford narrows his eyes, chews his gum.

Win gets up from his chair, looks at Sykes, gives her the signal.

"We just need a little time to give them the happy news, then you can pick them up," Win says to the sheriff.

At least he said "we," Sykes thinks. He didn't have to include her. *It's his case,* she thinks, but no matter how often she reminds herself of that, she feels disappointed, depressed about it, resentful. After all those dark places and boxes and phone calls and missed Academy classes and everything else, it certainly feels like her case, and it would feel pretty damn good to tell Kim and George Finlay they didn't get away with it, that they're about to find themselves in handcuffs and end up in a very different Big House from what they're used to—this one with razor wire.

"They're nice enough folks," Rutherford says to Win as they walk out to the parking lot, takes a good, long, disparaging look at Sykes's old VW Rabbit, same thing he did when she and Win first drove up. "Well, call me when you're ready," he says to Win. "A real shame locking them up." Chewing gum. "They've never caused any trouble around here."

"Doesn't look like they're going to get a chance to, either," Sykes says.

*

A FEW MILES AWAY is Little River Road, where many of Flat Rock's wealthy residents have big homes and estates, many of them summer homes, many of their owners from the far reaches of New York, Los Angeles, Boston, and Chicago.

Sykes pulls her car off the long, unpaved driveway, parks to one side, in the weeds so she and Win can show up with no advance warning. They get out and start walking toward the house that Vivian Finlay's nephew, George, and his *93 percent East Asian* wife, Kim, inherited from Mrs. Finlay after her murder. The well-off couple have been married twenty-two years, their wedding six months after Kim's first husband, Detective Mark Holland, committed suicide on lonely train tracks in a lonely part of North Carolina.

"Well, I know I would have," Sykes remarks, carrying on a conversation they've been having for the past ten minutes.

"It's easy to say twenty years after the fact," Win reminds her. "We weren't there."

"You mean you wouldn't have bothered checking out the tennis reservations?" Sykes says as they walk along the unpaved drive, getting closer to the house where George and Kim enjoy their privileged lives in their lovely home. "You know, just done the same damn thing I did?"

She has to remind Win yet again of how hard she's worked, of what an amazingly thorough and smart investigation she's conducted.

"If Barber had done that, he would have realized it

wasn't Mrs. Finlay who used the ball machine that day," Sykes goes on, has made this point maybe four times now, "not unless she signed in as a *guest*. All he had to do was ask questions."

"Maybe he felt about it a little bit the same way I do," Win suggests. "He didn't like dealing with a club that would never have him as a member."

She walks close to him. He puts his arm around her.

"So, she's going to jail?" Sykes asks, and she isn't talking about Kim Finlay.

She's thinking of Monique Lamont.

"Personally, I think she's been punished plenty," Win says. "But I'm not finished yet."

For a moment they are quiet as they walk in the sun, the driveway long and winding, trees everywhere. He can feel the heaviness in Sykes's heart, sense her pain and disappointment.

"Yeah, you've got a lot of unfinished business up there, all right," she says. "Guess you'll be leaving after you take care of these two." She stares in the direction of the house.

"We could use a few good CSIs in Massachusetts," he says.

She walks with her arm around him, holding him tight.

"You think the box of silver coins ever existed?" she asks, maybe just to change the subject, maybe to get her mind off where Win lives and works, off where he has his life, off how entwined his life is with Lamont's, no matter how much he denies it.

"Probably," he says. "I'm guessing Kim grabbed it on her way out the first time, after she killed her, trying to figure out how to stage it to look like a burglary/sex crime, disguise what in truth was probably an impulse crime. Blame it on a suspicious-looking black man. Worked like a charm, especially back then. People used to call the police on my dad. Happened a lot. He's in his own yard and gets reported as a prowler."

The sun is hot on their heads, the air cool, the roof of the house visible now, peeking above trees. They remove their arms from each other, walking apart, like colleagues again, talking about the case, Sykes wondering why Jimmy Barber never questioned what happened to Vivian Finlay's shoes and socks, wondering what Kim found to wear when she made her getaway after stripping off her bloody tennis clothes, wondering a lot of things.

Then the house is right there in front of them, George and Kim Finlay, now in their sixties, sitting in white chairs on the wide white porch, eating lunch.

Win and Sykes stare at the couple on the porch staring at them.

"They're all yours," he quietly says.

Sykes looks at him. "You sure?"

"It's your case, partner."

They follow the slate walkway, head to the wooden steps

that lead up to the porch, where George and Kim have stopped eating. Then Kim gets up from her chair, a stooped woman with graying hair pinned back, dark-tinted glasses, wrinkles that indicate she scowls a lot.

"Are you lost?" she loudly asks.

"No, ma'am, we're definitely not lost," Sykes says, she and Win stepping onto the porch. "I'm Special Agent Delma Sykes with the Tennessee Bureau of Investigation. This is Investigator Winston Garano, Massachusetts State Police. I talked to you on the phone the other day?" she says to George.

"Why, yes." George clears his throat, a small man, white hair, looks uncertain, pulls his napkin out of the front of his Izod shirt, doesn't seem sure whether he should stand or sit.

"The murder of Vivian Finlay has been reopened due to new evidence," Sykes says.

"What evidence could there possibly be after all these years?" Kim says, acts clueless, even tries to look distressed by the memory.

"Your DNA, ma'am," Sykes says.

15

He and Nana, and a secret mission, mid-October, the night starting out crisp and cool with not much of a moon.

Watertown, driving fast to an address where a client of hers said that dogfights were secretly being held in the basement on the weekends, horrible, violent fights, pugs, terriers, bulldogs, pit bulls, starved, baited, torn to pieces. Twenty dollars, the price of admission.

Win can still see the look on Nana's face as she pounded on the door, see the look on the man's face when she walked right into his dark, squalid house.

I have you between my fingers, she said, holding up two fingers, pinching them together. *And I'm squeezing. Where are the dogs? Because we're taking every one of them right now.* And she squeezed her fingers together as tightly as she could, right in his mean, soulless face.

Crazy witch! He yelled at her.

Go take a look in your yard, look at all those shiny new pennies everywhere, she said, and maybe time has embellished history, but as Win recalls it, the moment she mentioned the pennies and the man went to the window to look, a fierce wind kicked up from nowhere and a tree branch slammed against that very window and shattered it.

Nana and Win drove off with a carload of dogs—pitiful, mangled creatures—while he cried uncontrollably, tried to pet them, do something to make them not hurt and shake so much, and after they left them at the animal hospital, they drove home and it had gotten very cold, and the heat had been turned on inside the house, and Win's mother and father and Pencil were dead.

"Pencil?" Monique Lamont asks from her glass desk.

"A goofy mixed-breed yellow Lab, Pencil. Because as a puppy he was always chewing up my pencils," Win replies.

"CO poisoning."

"Yes."

"That's awful." It sounds so empty when Lamont says it.

"I felt it was my fault," he tells her. "Maybe the same

way you feel about what happened to you, that it's somehow your fault. Victims of rape often feel that. And you know that. You've seen it enough in your office, in court."

"I'm not a victim."

"You were raped. You were almost murdered. But you're right. You're not a victim. You were one."

"As were you."

"In a different way, but true."

"How old?" she asks.

"Seven."

"Geronimo," she says. "I've always wondered why *Geronimo*. Courage? Determination? Revenge for the deaths of his family? *The great Apache warrior.*"

She is her old self in a handsome black suit, sunlight lighting up every piece of glass in her office. Win feels as if he's in the middle of a rainbow, a rainbow that is hers. If she tells the truth, the whole truth, there is hope.

"Because you had to become the hero?" she is asking, trying to show warmth and hide her fear. "You had to become the warrior because you were the only one left?"

"Because I felt useless," he says. "Didn't want to do sports, compete, be on teams, do much of anything that might somehow measure me and show how useless I really was. So I kind of kept to myself, reading, drawing, writing, all sorts of solitary things. Nana started calling me Geronimo."

"Because you felt useless?" Lamont reaches for her sparkling water, a blank expression on her striking face.

Nana always reminded him, *You're Geronimo, my darling. Don't ever forget, my darling.*

And Win is saying to Lamont, "One of the many things Geronimo said is, *I cannot think that we are useless or God would not have created us. And the sun, the darkness, the winds are all listening to what we have to say.* So there you have it, what I have to say about myself. The truth, Monique." He adds, "Now it's your turn. I'm here to listen, but only if you plan on telling me everything."

She sips water, looks at him, deliberating, then, "Why would you give a damn, Win? Why really?"

"Fairness. The worst things that have happened aren't your fault."

"You'd really care if I went to prison?"

"You don't belong in prison. It wouldn't be fair to the other inmates."

Surprised, she laughs. But her mirth fades quickly. She drinks more water, her hands nervous.

Win says, "This isn't just about your running for governor, is it?"

"Apparently not," she says, keeping her eyes on him. "No, of course not. It was a twofold plan. My losing the Finlay homicide file and then its showing up on my property would have turned At Risk into a farce, turned me and my office into one, ingratiated Huber with the governor, the two of them in on that one together, I have no doubt. Either I'm murdered or I'm ruined or both, really. No one saying nice things at my funeral. Useless. I know that word, too, Geronimo." She pauses, looking at him. "Useless and foolish."

"The governor want you murdered?"

She shakes her head. "No. He just didn't want me to win the election. Jessie wanted the governor to be grateful to him—how the hell do you think he's gotten where he is in life? Favors. Manipulations. He wanted me dead and, oh, well, that certainly would have made life easier for Crawley, too, but no. Our dear governor wouldn't have the stomach for that. Jessie always wants everything in a big way. Especially money."

"Insider trading, Monique? Maybe buying shares in a high-tech DNA lab that's about to get a lot of attention?"

She reaches for her water bottle. It's empty. She pulls out the straw, drops it in the glass trash basket under her desk.

"PROHEMOGEN," Win then says. "DNA technology that genetically matches patients with drugs. The lab you picked for your media extravaganza may do ancestral profiles in criminal cases, but that's not where the money is."

She listens. She has that familiar look on her face when she is putting the case together.

"The money's in using genomics to help with the development of these next-generation superdrugs. Huge money, huge," Win says.

She doesn't answer, listens intently.

"The lab in California." He keeps going. "All the national attention you, the governor, will bring it because of this murdered old woman in Tennessee. Well, that's extremely helpful, now isn't it? You draw big attention to them and their lucrative biotechnology—give them that kind of free advertising—and guess what? Maybe their stock goes up. How much stock do you own?"

"That makes at least one thing obvious," she says. "Make it look as if I took the case home, was hiding it. But make sure it's found."

He looks at her for a long moment, says, "Pretty shrewd. Ruin you but save the day. The case file's found eventually. Publicity and more publicity. At your expense. Maybe the case is solved, maybe not, but a lot of publicity for that lab in California."

"It will get it anyway. Already is. The case is solved."

"The lab didn't do anything wrong. In fact, it did everything right. Helped solved the case."

She nods, distracted.

"Sad truth is, that murdered old woman didn't matter at all in any of this," Win says. "The powers that be didn't care."

Lamont is thinking, probably trying to move things

along in a direction that suits her, says, "I know you probably don't believe me, but I did care. I wanted her case solved."

"How much stock do you own?" Win asks again.

"None."

"You sure?"

"That idea would never have entered my mind. I knew nothing about the company, but in Jessie's position, he's privy to all sorts of biotechnology, all sorts of private labs springing up all over the world. I didn't know about this, about the California lab and its biotechnology. I just thought we were working a twenty-year-old murder case that turned into a very public crime initiative I called At Risk. Really."

"Huber the one you were with the night before you were attacked? Probably when your keys disappeared? You said you were out, went to work straight from wherever it was you were staying."

Win has a minidisc running on top of her glass desk. He is taking notes.

"We had dinner. I can't . . . I can believe a lot of things about him . . ."

"Motive." Win's not going to let her avoid the answer.

She takes her time, then, "Jessie and I are friends. Just as Jessie and you are friends."

"I seriously doubt it's quite the same."

"Earlier this year, he gave me some advice about my portfolio." She clears her throat, tries to steady her voice. "I made some money, realized what was going on a week later when I read in the paper that U.S. regulators had cleared the sale of a particular drug being developed at some lab, not the one in the Finlay case. Another one."

"Enough of a motive for him to set up your murder?"

"He's been getting insider tips in exchange for subcontracting out thousands of DNA kits to be analyzed for our database, for databases in other states based upon his recommendations. Major purchases of instruments for his labs, recommendations for other crime labs to buy the same things. It's been going on for years."

"He admitted all this to you?"

"After his stock advice, a lot of things began to add up." She glances at the recorder. "The more he told me, the more he implicated me. I'm guilty of insider trading. Next I'm guilty of conspiracy, of knowing what the director of the state crime labs is doing and I don't say a word. Not to mention . . ."

"Right. Your not-so-professional relationship."

"He loves me," she says with nothing in her voice as she stares at the recorder.

"Amazing way to show it."

"I ended it months ago, after he gave me the advice about the stock and I realized what he was into, what he had just gotten me into. What he is. I told him I didn't love him anymore, not that way."

"You threaten him?"

"I told him I wanted nothing more to do with his illegal activities, that they had to stop. And if they didn't, there would be consequences."

"You told him this when?"

"Last spring. Probably wasn't a smart thing to say," she mutters, staring hard at the recorder.

"You could have had a lawyer present," Win reminds her. "You said all this willingly. I didn't force you."

"Nice suit, by the way." She looks at his light gray suit, swallows, tries to smile.

"Emporio Armani, about three seasons out of date, seventy bucks. I didn't force you," he repeats.

"No, you didn't," she says. "And I'll take what comes."

"You'll testify against Huber?"

"It will be a pleasure."

Win picks up the recorder, pops out the disc, says, "Ever enter your mind you got enough glass in here to burn down your entire building?"

He selects a crystal paperweight, holds it up to the sun streaming through a window, focuses a white-hot dot on the disc. Lamont watches in amazement as a thin stream of smoke rises.

"What are you doing?" she says.

"You're living inside a tinderbox, Monique. Could burst into flames any minute. Maybe you should be more careful, take the heat off yourself, direct it elsewhere. Focus it very intensely where it belongs."

He hands her the ruined disc, their fingers lightly touching, says, "In case you get cold feet. Just pull this out and remember what I said."

She nods, tucks the ruined disc in a pocket.

"Another bit of advice. When someone else interviews you, like a grand jury, for example," he adds, "I suggest you leave out unnecessary details. The way I see it, most people are going to assume Huber was setting you up, conspiring with the governor, jealous, vindictive because you spurned him, greedy. On and on. I wrote down most of it. The relevant information." He holds up his notepad. "Just left out the misleading information. And you know what that information is. Such as any stocks Huber recommended, anything illegal he admitted to you that you never passed on. No proof. You could have chosen to make any investment you wanted, doesn't mean you got inside information, right? His word against yours."

She watches him, studies him, as he hits send on his cell phone.

"Sammy?" he says. "I want Huber brought in for questioning. Yup. The time has come. Get the warrant, we're going to search every place he owns. And our little buddy, Toby. Bring him in, too."

"With pleasure. Lay it on me," Sammy says.

"Attempted murder, conspiracy to murder, arson. And let's see." Win looks at Lamont, some of that old steely glint back in her eyes. "I'm sure the Feds will be delighted to hear all about his SEC violations."

"And then what? What about me?" Lamont asks Win as he ends the call. "You really think I'll be all right?"

"Funny how nothing changes," he says, getting up from his chair, smiling at her. "Funny how it's always about you, Monique."

THE FRONT

TO URSULA MACKENZIE,
who publishes me so brilliantly in the UK.

1

Win Garano sets two lattes on a picnic table in front of the John F. Kennedy School of Government. It's a sunny afternoon, mid-May, and Harvard Square is crowded. He straddles a bench, overdressed and sweaty in a black Armani suit and black patent-leather Prada shoes, pretty sure the original owner of them is dead.

He got a feeling about it when the saleslady in the Hand-Me-Ups shop said he could have the "gently worn" outfit for ninety-nine dollars. Next she pulled out suits, shoes, belts, ties, even socks. DKNY, Hugo Boss, Gucci, Hermès, Ralph Lauren. All from the same *celebrity whose name I can't tell you,* and it occurred to Win that not so long ago, a wide receiver for the Patriots got killed in a car wreck. One eighty, six feet tall, muscular but not a moose. In other words, about Win's size.

He sits alone at the picnic table, more self-conscious by the moment. Students, faculty, the elite—most of them in jeans, shorts, carrying knapsacks—cluster at other tables, deep in conversations that include very few comments about the dull lecture District Attorney Monique Lamont just gave at the Forum. *No Neighbor Left Behind.* Win warned her it was a confusing title, not to mention a banal topic for such a prestigious political venue. She's not going to appreciate that he was right. He doesn't appreciate that she ordered him here on his day off so she could boss him around, belittle him. Make a note of this. Make a note of that. Call so and so. Get her a coffee. Starbucks. Latte with skim milk and Splenda. Wait for her outside in the heat while she hobnobs inside the air-conditioned Littauer Center.

He sullenly watches her emerge from the brick building, escorted by two plainclothes officers from the Massachusetts State Police, where Win is a homicide investigator currently assigned to the Middlesex County District Attorney's detective unit. In other words, assigned to Lamont, who called him at home last night and said effective immediately, he's on leave from his regular duties. *I'll explain after my lecture at the Forum. See you at two.* No further details.

She pauses to give an interview to the local ABC affiliate, then to NPR. She talks with reporters from *The Boston Globe,* the AP, and that Harvard student, Cal Tradd, who writes for the *Crimson*, thinks he's from *The Washington Post*. The press loves Lamont. The press loves to hate her. No one is indifferent to the powerful, beautiful DA—today, conspicuous in a bright green suit. Escada. This year's spring collection. Seems she's been on quite the shopping spree of late, a new outfit practically every time Win sees her.

She continues talking to Cal as she walks confidently across the brick plaza, past massive planters of azaleas, rhododendrons, and pink and white dogwoods. Blond, blue-eyed, pretty-boy Cal, so cool and collected, so sure of himself, never flustered, never frowns, always so damn pleasant. Says something while scribbling on his notepad, and Lamont nods, and he says something else, and she keeps nodding. Win wishes the guy would do something stupid, get himself kicked out of Harvard. Flunking out would be even better. What a friggin' pest.

Lamont dismisses Cal, signals for her plainclothes protection to give her privacy, and sits across from Win, her eyes hidden by reflective gray-tinted glasses.

"I thought it went well." She picks up her latte without thanking him for it.

"Not much of a turnout. But you seemed to make your point," he says.

"Obviously, most people, including you, don't grasp the enormity of the problem." That flat tone she uses when her narcissism has been insulted. "The decline of neighborhoods is potentially as destructive as global warming. Citizens have no respect for law enforcement, no interest whatsoever in helping us or each other. This past weekend I was in New York, walking through Central Park, and noticed a backpack abandoned on a bench. Do you think a single person thought to call the police? Maybe consider there could be an explosive device inside it? No. Everyone just kept going, figuring if it blew up, it wasn't their problem as long as they didn't get hurt, I suppose."

"The world's going to hell, Monique."

"People have slipped into complacency, and here's what we're going to do about it," she says. "I've set the stage. Now we create the drama."

Every day with Lamont is a drama.

She toys with her latte, looks around to see who's looking at her. "How do we get attention? How do we take people who are jaded, desensitized, and make them care about crime? Care so much they decide to get involved at a grassroots level? Can't be gangs, drugs, carjackings, robberies, burglaries. Why? Because people want a crime problem that's, let's be honest, front-page news but happens to others, not to them."

"I wasn't aware people actually want a crime problem."

He notices a skinny young woman with kinky red hair loitering near a Japanese maple not far from them. Dressed like Raggedy Ann, right down to her striped stockings and clunky shoes. Saw her the other week, in downtown Cambridge, loitering around the courthouse, probably waiting to go before a judge. Probably some petty crime like shoplifting.

"An unsolved sexual homicide," Lamont is saying. "April fourth, 1962, Watertown."

"I see. Not a cold case this time but a frozen one," he says, keeping his eye on Raggedy Ann. "I'm surprised you even know where Watertown is."

In Middlesex County, her jurisdiction—along with some sixty other modest municipalities she doesn't give a damn about.

"Four square miles, population thirty-five thousand, very diverse ethnic base," she says. "The perfect crime that just so happens to have been committed in the perfect microcosm for my initiative. The chief will partner you up with his lead detective. . . . You know, the one who drives that monstrous crime scene truck. Oh, what is it they call her?"

"Stump."

"That's right. Because she's short and fat."

"She has a prosthesis, a below-the-knee amputation," he says.

"Cops can be so insensitive. I believe the two of you know each other, from the little grocery store around the corner where she works a second job. So that's a good start. Helps to be friends with someone you're going to spend a lot of time with."

"It's an upscale gourmet shop, and isn't just a second job, and we're not friends."

"You sound defensive. The two of you go out, maybe not get along? Because that could be a problem."

"Nothing personal between us, never even worked a case

with her," Win says. "But I would think you have, since Watertown has plenty of crime and she's been around as long as you have."

"Why? Has she talked about me?"

"Usually we talk about cheese."

Lamont glances at her watch. "Let's get to the facts of the case. Janie Brolin."

"Never heard of her."

"British. She was blind, decided to spend a year in the States, chose Watertown, most likely because of Perkins, probably the most famous school for the blind in the world. Where Helen Keller went."

"Perkins wasn't located in Watertown back in the Helen Keller days. It was in Boston."

"And why would you know trivia like that?"

"Because I'm a trivial person. And obviously you've been planning this *drama* for a while. So why did you wait until the last minute to tell me about it?"

"This is very sensitive and must be handled very discreetly. Imagine being blind and realizing there's an intruder inside your apartment. That horror factor and something far more important. I think you're going to discover she very well may have been the Boston Strangler's first victim."

"You said early April 1962?" Win frowns. "His alleged first murder wasn't until two months later, in June."

"Doesn't mean he hadn't killed before, just that earlier cases weren't linked to him."

"How do you propose we prove the Janie Brolin murder—
or the Strangler's other thirteen alleged murders, for that
matter—was committed by him when we still don't really
know who he was?"

"We have Albert DeSalvo's DNA."

"No one's ever proved he was the Strangler, and more to
the point, do we have DNA from the Janie Brolin case for
comparison?"

"That's for you to find out."

He can tell by her demeanor there's no DNA and she
damn well knows it. Why would there be, some forty-five
years later? Back then, there was no such thing as forensic
DNA or even a thought that there might be someday. So
forget proving or disproving anything, as far as he's concerned.

"It's never too late for justice," Lamont pontificates—or
Lamonticates, as he calls it. "It's time to unite citizens and
police in fighting crime. To take back our neighborhoods, not
just here but worldwide." Same thing she just said in her unin-
spiring lecture. "We're going to create a model that will be
studied everywhere."

Raggedy Ann is sending text messages on her cell phone.
What a whack job. Harvard Square's full of them. The other
day, Win saw some guy licking the sidewalk in front of the
Coop.

"Obviously, nothing about this to the press until the case
is solved. Then, of course, it comes from me. It's too hot for
May," she complains, getting up from the picnic table.

"Watertown tomorrow morning, ten sharp, the chief's office."

She leaves her barely touched latte for him to dutifully toss in the trash.

An hour later, Win is finishing his third rep on the leg press when his iPhone vibrates like a large insect. He picks it up, wipes his face with a towel, puts on the wireless earpiece.

"Sorry. You're on your own," Stump says, in response to the voice mail he left her.

"We'll talk later." He has no intention of discussing it in the middle of the Charles Hotel health spa, which he can't afford but is allowed to use in exchange for his security expertise and connections.

In the locker room, he takes a quick shower, changes back into his same outfit except for his shoes, which he swaps out for motorcycle boots. He grabs his helmet, his armored mesh jacket, and gloves. His motorcycle is parked in front of the hotel, a red Ducati Monster, protected by traffic cones, in his reserved spot on the sidewalk. He's tucking his gym bag inside the hard case, locking it, when Cal Tradd walks up.

Cal says, "I figured a guy like you would ride the Superbike."

"Really? Why would you figure that?" Before he can catch himself.

The last thing he wants is to engage the spoiled little bastard, but he's knocked off balance, would never have guessed

Cal would know anything about motorcycles, certainly not a Ducati 1098 S Superbike.

"Always wanted one," Cal says. "Ducati, Moto Guzzi, Ghezzi-Brian. But you start piano lessons when you're five, forget even a skateboard."

Win's sick and tired of the reminder. The mini Mozart, giving recitals by the time he was five.

"So when are we going to ride around together?" Cal goes on.

"What's so hard about the words *no* or *never*? I don't have ridealongs and I hate publicity. And I've told you this . . . let's see. About fifty times now?"

Cal digs in a pocket of his khakis, pulls out a folded piece of paper, hands it to him. "My numbers. Same ones you probably threw away last time I gave them to you. Maybe you'll call me, give me a chance. Just like Monique said in her lecture. Cops and the community need to work together. There's a lot of bad stuff going on out there."

Win walks off without so much as a *see you later*, heads toward Pittinelli's Gourmet Market, another place he can't afford. It took some nerve to wander in a couple months ago, see if he could work out an arrangement with Stump, who he'd heard of but never met. They aren't friends, probably don't even get along, but have a mutually beneficial arrangement. She gives him discounts because he happens to be state police and happens to be headquartered in Cambridge, where her market is located. Put it this way, it just so happens that

Cambridge cops no longer ticket Pittinelli's delivery trucks when they're in violation of ten-minute parking zones.

He opens the front door and runs into Raggedy Ann, on her way out, tossing an empty Fresca can into a trash bin. The freako acts as if she doesn't see him, the same way she did a little while ago at the School of Government. Now that he thinks of it, she treated him as if he were invisible the other week, too, when she was hanging around the courthouse, and he passed within inches of her, even said "excuse me." Close up, she smells like baby powder. Maybe it's all the makeup she's wearing.

"What's going on?" he says, blocking her way. "Seems like we keep running into each other."

She pushes past him, hurrying along the busy sidewalk, cuts through an alleyway. Gone.

Stump is stocking shelves with olive oil, the air pungent with the aroma of imported cheeses, prosciutto, salami. Some college kid is sitting behind the counter, lost in a paperback, the shop otherwise empty.

"What's with Raggedy Ann?" Win asks.

Stump looks up from her crouched position in the aisle, hands him a corked bottle shaped like a flask. "Frantoio Gaziello. Unfiltered, a little grassy, with a hint of avocado. You'll love it."

"She was just in your shop? And right before that, she was hanging around Lamont and me at the School of Government. And I've seen her around the courthouse, too. A little coincidental, maybe?" He studies the bottle of olive oil, looking for the price. "Maybe she's stalking me."

"I certainly would if I were some pitiful, deranged street person who thinks she's a rag doll. Probably from one of the local shelters," Stump says. "In and out, never buys anything except Fresca."

"Sure drank it fast. Unless she didn't finish it. Tossed the can in the trash as she was coming out of your store."

"Her MO. Looks around, drinks her Fresca, and leaves. Seems harmless."

"Well, she's starting to give me a creepy feeling. What's her name, and which shelter? I think it would be a good idea to run a background on her."

"I don't know anything about her except she's not right." Twirling her finger at her temple.

"So, how long you known about Lamont's assigning me to Watertown?"

"Let me see." She looks at her watch. "You left your voice mail an hour and a half ago? Let me do the math. I've known for an hour and a half."

"That's what I thought. Nobody's told you, so she makes sure from the get-go that you and I don't get along."

"I don't need some harebrained new hobby right now. She sends you to Watertown on some secret mission, don't come crying to me."

He crouches next to her. "You ever heard of the Janie Brolin case?"

"You can't grow up in Watertown and not have heard of that case, which was half a friggin' century ago. Your DA's nothing but a consummate, cold-blooded politician."

"She's your DA, too, unless Watertown PD's seceded from Middlesex County."

"Look," she says, "it's not my problem. I don't give a damn what she and the chief have cooked up. I'm not doing it."

"Since it occurred in Watertown, since there's no statute of limitations for homicides, technically it is your problem if the case is reopened. And as of now, looks like it has been."

"Technically, homicides in Massachusetts, with rare exception, such as Boston, are the jurisdiction of the state police. Certainly you guys remind us of that on a regular basis when you show up at the scene, take over the investigation, even if you don't know a damn thing about anything. Sorry, you're on your own."

"Come on, Stump. Don't be like this."

"We just had another bank robbery this morning." Arranging bottles on shelves. "Fourth in three weeks. Plus the hair salon breaks, car breaks, house breaks, copper thefts, hate crimes. Never stops. I'm a little busy for cases that happened before I was born."

"Same bank robber?"

"Same-o, same-o. Hands the teller a note, empties the cash drawer, call goes out over BAPERN."

Boston Area Police Emergency Radio Network. So local cops can talk to one another, assist one another.

"Meaning every cop car on the planet shows up, lights and sirens full-tilt. All of downtown looks like a Christmas parade. Ensuring our one-man Bonnie and Clyde knows exactly where we are so he can stay out of sight until we're gone," she says as a customer walks in.

"How much?" Win refers to the bottle of olive oil he's still holding.

More customers. Almost five p.m., and people are getting off work. Pretty soon, it will be standing room only. Stump sure as hell isn't a cop for the money, and he's never figured out why she doesn't retire from the department and have a life.

"It's yours at cost." She gets up, walks to another aisle, picks out a bottle of wine, gives it to him. "Just got it in. Tell me what you think."

A 2002 Wolf Hill pinot noir. "Sure," he says. "Thanks. But why the sudden kill-me-with-kindness act?"

"Giving you my condolences. Must be fatal working for her."

"While you're feeling sorry for me, mind if I get a few pounds of Swiss, cheddar, Asiago, roast beef, turkey, wild rice salad, baguettes? And kosher salt, five pounds would be great."

"Jesus. What the hell do you do with that stuff? Throw margarita parties for half of Boston?" As she stands up, so at ease with her prosthesis, he rarely remembers she has one. "Come on. Since I feel so sorry for you, I'll buy you a drink," she says. "One cop to another, let me give you a little advice."

They collect empty boxes and carry them to the store-room in back, and she opens the walk-in refrigerator, grabs two diet cream sodas, and says, "What you need to focus on is motive."

"The killer's?" Win says, as they sit at a folding table, walled in by cases of wine, olive oils, vinegars, mustards, choco-lates.

"Lamont's."

"You must have worked a lot of cases with her over the years, but she acts as if the two of you have never met," he says.

"Bet she does. I don't guess she told you about the night we got so ripped, she had to sleep on my couch."

"No way. She doesn't even socialize with cops, much less get drunk with them."

"Before your time," says Stump, who's older than Win by at least five years. "Back in the good ole days before an alien took over her body, she was a kick-ass prosecutor, used to show up at crime scenes, hang out with us. One night after a murder-suicide, the two of us ended up at Sacco's, started drinking wine, got so wasted we left our cars and walked to my place. Like I said, she ended up spending the night. We were so hungover the next day, both of us called in sick."

"You must be talking about someone else." Win can't envi-sion it, has a weird feeling in the pit of his stomach. "You sure it wasn't some other assistant DA, and maybe over the years you've gotten the two of them confused?"

Stump laughs, says, "What? I've got Alzheimer's?

Unfortunately, the Lamont you know never goes to crime scenes unless television trucks are everywhere, hardly ever sees a courtroom, has nothing to do with cops unless she's giving them orders, and doesn't care about criminal justice anymore, only power. The Lamont I knew may have had an ego, but why wouldn't she? Harvard Law, beautiful, smart as hell. But decent."

"She and *decent* don't know each other." He doesn't understand why he's suddenly so angry and territorial, and before he can stop himself, he nastily adds, "Sounds like you have a slight touch of the Walter Mitty syndrome. Maybe you've been a lot of different people in life, because the person I'm drinking a cream soda with is short and fat, according to Lamont."

Only thing short about Stump is her dark hair. And she's certainly not fat. In fact, now that he's paying attention, he has to say she's pretty damn buff, must work out a lot, has a great body, actually. Not bad looking. Well, maybe a little masculine.

"I'd appreciate it if you didn't stare at my chest," she says. "Nothing personal. I tell all the men that when I'm alone with them in the back of the shop."

"Don't assume I'm hitting on you," he says. "Nothing personal. I tell all the women that when I'm alone with them. Tell men, too, if the need arises. So to speak."

"Had no idea you were such a cocky dude. So to speak. Arrogant, for sure. But wow." She looks intently at him. Sips her soda.

Green eyes with flecks of gold in them. Nice teeth. Sensuous lips. Well, a little wrinkled.

"And here's another house rule," she says. "I have two legs."

"Goddamn. I haven't said a thing about your leg."

"That's my point. I don't have *a leg*. I have two. And I've seen you checking."

"If you don't want to draw attention to your prosthesis, then why do you call yourself Stump? For that matter, why do you put up with anybody calling you Stump?"

"I don't guess it might occur to you that I was called Stump before I had a bad day on my motorcycle."

He doesn't say anything.

"Since you're a biker boy, let me give you a tip," she says. "Try not to let some redneck in a pickup truck run you into a guardrail."

Win suddenly remembers his soda. Takes a swallow.

"And another word tip?" She tosses her empty can into a trash bin that's a good twenty feet away. "Stay away from literary allusions. I taught English lit before I decided to be a cop. Walter Mitty wasn't a lot of different people, he was a daydreamer."

"Why the nickname, if it's not about your leg? You've got me curious."

"Why Watertown? That's what you should be curious about."

"Obviously, because the murder occurred there," he says. "Maybe because Lamont knows you—even if she acts like she doesn't. Or at least she used to know you. Before you got short and fat."

"She can't stand that I saw her drunk, and know a lot about her because of what happened that night. Forget it. She didn't pick Watertown because of the case. She picked the case because of Watertown."

"She picked the case because it isn't just any old unsolved murder," Win retorts. "Unfortunately, it's one the media will love. A blind woman visiting from the UK is sexually assaulted and murdered. . . ."

"No question Lamont will milk it for all it's worth. But it's worth more than one thing. She has other agendas."

"Always does."

"It's also about the FRONT," Stump says.

Friends, Resources, Officers Networking Together.

"In the last month, five more departments joined our coalition," she goes on. "We're up to sixty, have access to K-nine, SWAT, antiterrorism, crime scene investigation, and most recently a helicopter. We're still making bricks without straw, but we're on our way to needing less and less from the state police."

"Which I think is great."

"The hell you do. State police hates the FRONT. Lamont most of all hates the FRONT, and what a coincidence. It's headquartered in Watertown. So she's siccing you on us, setting us up to look like the Keystone Kops. We have to have some superhero state police investigator come in and save the day so Lamont can remind everyone how important the state police is and why it should get all the support and funding. A wonderful bonus is she gets back at me, makes me look bad, because she'll never forgive me for what I know."

"What you know?"

"About her." It's obvious that's all Stump intends to say about it.

"I don't understand how our solving your old case makes you look bad."

"*Our* solving it? *Unh-uh.* I keep telling you. You're on your own."

"And you wonder why the state police doesn't like . . . Hell, never mind."

She leans forward, meets his eyes, says, "I'm warning you, and you're not listening. She'll make sure the FRONT looks bad whether the case is solved or not. You're being used in ways you don't even know. Being set up in ways you can't even imagine. But start with this: The FRONT gets big enough one of these days? Then what? Maybe you guys don't get to be bullies anymore."

"We're bound by state law just like you are," Win says. "It's not about bullying, and you'll never hear me say the system's fair."

"Fair? How about worst conflict of interests in the entire United States? You guys have complete control over all homicide investigations. Your labs process all evidence. Even the damn death investigators at the morgue are state police. And then the DA whose state police investigative unit works all this, soup to nuts, is the one who prosecutes the case. For you and yours truly here, that would be Lamont, who answers to the Attorney General, who answers to the governor. Meaning the governor de facto has control over all homicide investigations in Massachusetts. You're not dragging me into this. It's headed only one way—toward disaster."

"Doesn't appear your chief thinks so."

"Doesn't matter what he thinks. He has to do what she says. And he won't take the blame, will just pass it down the line. Trust me," Stump says, "get out while you can."

2

Lamont used her reelection last fall as an excuse to fire every member of her staff. Fresh starts are a compulsion of hers. Especially when it comes to people. Once they serve their useful purpose it's time for change, or, as she puts it, a *resurrection* from something that's no longer vital.

Although she doesn't waste energy on personal reflection, a remote part of her is aware that her inability to maintain long-term relationships might not serve her well as she ages. Her father, for example, was extraordinarily successful, handsome, and charming but died completely alone in Paris last year, his body not found for days. When Lamont went through his belongings, she discovered years of birthday and holiday gifts he'd never opened, including a number of expensive pieces of art glass from her. Explaining why he never bothered to have his secretary call or dictate a thank-you note.

The Middlesex County courthouse is a concrete-and-brick high-rise in the dreary, crime-ridden heart of Cambridge's government center, her office on the second floor. As she steps off the elevator and notices the detective unit's closed door, her internal weather turns overcast. Win won't be inside his cubicle anymore, not for God knows how long. His reassignment to Watertown will make it difficult for her to demand his presence whenever she pleases.

"What is it?" she asks, when she finds her press secretary, Mick, sitting on the sofa in her corner office, talking on his phone.

She makes her usual cutthroat motion, indicating for him to end the call instantly. And he does.

"Don't tell me there's a problem. I'm in no mood for problems," she says.

"We have a little situation," says Mick, still new at the job, but promising.

He's handsome, polished, shows well, and does what he's told. She settles behind her glass desk inside her glass-filled office. Her ice palace, as Win calls it.

"If the situation's *little,* you wouldn't be in my office, waiting to pounce on me the instant I walk in," she says.

"I'm sorry. I'm not going to say I told you so. . . ."

"You just did."

"I've been quite vocal about what I think of your reporter friend."

He means Cal Tradd. Lamont doesn't want to hear it.

"Let me find a way to say this delicately," Mick says.

It takes a lot to unnerve her, but she knows the warning signs. A tightness in her chest, a chilly breath on the back of her neck, an interruption in the normal steady rhythm of her heart.

"What has he said to you?" she asks.

"I'm more concerned about what you've said to him. Did you do something to make him spiteful?" Mike says bluntly.

"What the hell are you talking about?"

"Maybe you slighted him in some way. Such as giving that front-page story to the *Globe* last month instead of to him."

"Why would I give him a front-page anything? He works for a student newspaper."

"Well, can you think of any other reason he might have to get you back for something?"

"People never seem to need a reason."

"YouTube. Just posted a few hours ago. Frankly, I don't know what we're going to do about it."

"Do about what? And your job is to always know what to do about it—whatever it is," she retorts.

Mick gets up from the sofa, moves next to her, commandeers her computer, and logs on to the Internet, on to YouTube.

A video clip.

Carly Simon's "You're So Vain" as Lamont walks into a ladies' room, stops at a sink, opens her ostrich-skin handbag. Begins touching up her makeup in the mirror, primping, studying every angle of her face, her figure, experimenting with buttons on her blouse, which to button, which to unbutton. Pulling up her skirt, adjusting her pantyhose. Opening her mouth wide, examining her teeth. A voiceover from her own reelection campaign reciting "Clamping Down On Crime. Monique Lamont, DA for Middlesex County."

Instead of a handcuff snapping shut at the end of the ad, her teeth in the mirror do.

"Is this why you brought up Cal?" Severely. "Immediately assuming he's to blame? Based on what?"

"He's your shadow, practically stalks you. He's immature. It's something a college kid would do. . . ."

"Such a strong case you make." Sarcastically. "Good thing I'm the DA, not you."

Mike stares at her, wide-eyed. "You're going to defend him?"

"He couldn't possibly have done it," she says. "Whoever recorded this clearly was in the ladies' room. A female, in other words."

"And it would be easy enough for him to pass as a damn girl. . . ."

"Mick. He follows me like a puppy, was hanging around me the entire time I was at the School of Government. He had no time to suddenly become a cross-dresser or hide in the damn ladies' room."

"I didn't realize—"

"Of course you didn't. You weren't there. But you're right. The first order of business always is to find out who betrayed me." Pacing. "Most likely, some female student in a stall saw me through a crack in the door and recorded all this nonsense with her cell phone. The price of being a public figure. No one will take it seriously."

Mick stares at her as if she just fell off a shelf and shattered—like one of her pieces of art glass.

"Further," she says, "what matters is whether you look good. And I'm happy to say, I do." She replays the clip, reassured by her exotically beautiful face and perfect teeth, her shapely legs, her enviable bosom. "Make a note of it, Mick. That's how it works out there."

"Not exactly," he says. "The governor called."

She stops pacing. The governor never calls.

"About YouTube," Mick says. "He wants to know who's behind it."

"Let me see. I must have it written down somewhere."

"Well, it's an embarrassment no matter who did it. And when you look bad, he looks bad, since he's the one who . . ."

"What did he say, exactly?" she asks.

"I didn't talk to him directly."

"Of course you didn't talk to him directly." Angrily pacing again. "Nobody talks to him directly."

"Not even you." As if she needs to be reminded. "And after all you did for him," Mick adds. "You haven't seen him once. He never returns your phone calls. . . ."

"This might be our opportunity." She cuts him off yet again, her thoughts like pool balls, scattering across the felt, clacking into pockets. "Yes. Absolutely. The best revenge is success. So what do we do? We turn this YouTube debacle to my advantage. My chance to have an audience with His Highness and get his support for my new crime initiative. He'll be interested when he sees what's in it for him."

She instructs Mick to get the governor's chief of staff on the phone. Now. It's urgent she sit down with Governor Howard Mather immediately. Mick suggests she might have to "grovel," and she reminds him never to use that word unless he's talking about someone else. However, she concedes, if she finally acknowledges Mather as her mentor, that will have an impact. She really needs his advice. She's suddenly found herself in a PR nightmare. She fears it could reflect poorly on him and doesn't know what to do. Et cetera.

"That will be hard for him to resist," she adds.

"But what if he does? Then what do I do?"

"Stop asking me to do your job!" she erupts.

In a very different part of Cambridge is the run-down frame house where Win was raised by his grandmother, Nana. Overwhelmed by ivy, flowering shrubs, and trees, her yard has become a subdivision of bird- and bat houses, and feeders.

His motorcycle bumps and fishtails over the rutted, unpaved driveway, and he parks near Nana's ancient Buick. Helmet off, and his ears are filled with the fairylike music of wind chimes stirred by the breeze, as if magical sprites alight on trees and the eaves of Nana's home and decide not to leave. She says they drive off mean and niggling entities, which should include the neighbors, Win thinks. Selfish, bigoted, rude. Fighting over shared driveways and off-street parking. Staring suspiciously at the steady stream of people who show up at the house.

He pops the trunk of the old Buick, which of course Nana hasn't bothered to lock, places his motorcycle gear inside, opens her back door, steps over the line of kosher salt on the floor. She's sitting in her kitchen, busy laminating bay laurel leaves in wide strips of transparent tape, the TV tuned to a classical music station. Miss Dog—deaf and blind and technically stolen because Win sneaked her away from her abusive owner—is under the table, snoring.

He sets his gym bag on the kitchen counter, then a knapsack filled with groceries, leans down, kisses Nana's cheek, says, "As usual, your car wasn't locked. Your door wasn't locked, and your alarm isn't set."

"My darling boy." Her eyes are bright, her long, snowy hair piled on top of her head. "Tell me about your day."

He opens the refrigerator, the cupboards, putting away her

groceries, says, "Bay leaves don't deter burglars. That's why you have an alarm system and good locks. You at least locking up and setting the alarm at night?"

"Nobody's interested in an old woman who has nothing worth stealing. Besides, I have all the protection I need."

He sighs, does no good to nag her, pulls out a chair, rests his hands in his lap because there's no room on the table for them, virtually every inch occupied by crystals, candles, statues, icons, talismans, or lucky charms. She hands him two large laminated bay leaves, her silver jewelry clinking, a ring on every finger, bracelets up to her elbows.

"Put these in your boots, my darling," she tells him. "One in the left, one in the right. Don't do like you did last time."

"What might that have been?" He slips the laminated leaves in his pocket.

"You didn't put them in your shoes, and what did the Husk do?"

What she calls Lamont. An empty shell, nothing there.

"She gave you some awful job. A dangerous one," Nana says. "Laurel is the herb of Apollo. When you wear it in your shoes, your boots, you stand on victory. Make sure the tip points toward the toe, the stem toward the heel."

"Yeah, well, I just got another awful job."

"Full of lies," Nana says. "Be careful what you do, because it isn't about what she says."

"I know what it's about. Ambition. Selfishness. Hypocrisy. Vanity. Persecuting me."

Nana cuts off another strip of tape. "Justice is what I need in thought, word, and deed. I'm seeing a revolving sign and rubber marks on pavement. Skid marks. What's that about?"

He thinks of Stump's motorcycle accident, says, "Got no idea."

"Be very careful, my darling. Especially on your motor-cycle. I wish you wouldn't ride that thing." Laminating another bay leaf.

When the price of gas hit three dollars a gallon, he sold his Hummer and bought the Ducati. Then what a coinci-dence. About a week later, Lamont came up with a new policy: Only her investigators on call could take home their state police cars.

"For tonight anyway, you get your wish because I need to fill your old battleship with gas," he says to Nana. "Will bring it back tomorrow. Even though you've got no business behind the wheel."

He can't stop her. So at least he'll make sure she doesn't end up stranded on the roadside somewhere. Nana tends to forget about flat-footed realities, such as keeping her car filled with gas, checking the oil, making sure her registration is in the glove box, locking her doors, buying groceries, paying bills. Little things like that.

"Your clothes will be nice and clean. As always, my dar-ling." Indicating his gym bag on the kitchen counter. "What touches your skin and the magic begins."

Indulging her in another one of her rituals. She insists on

hand-washing his workout clothes in a special concoction that leaves them smelling like an herb garden, then wrapping them in white tissue paper and returning them to his gym bag. A daily swapping. Something about an exchange of energy. Drawing negativity out of him as he sweats, while drawing in the herbs of the gods. Whatever makes her happy. The things he does that nobody knows about.

Miss Dog stirs, rests her head on his foot. Nana centers a leaf on a strip of tape. She reaches for a box of matches, lights a Saint Michael the archangel candle in a colorful glass jar, and says, "Someone's poking a stick at something and will pay the price. A very high price."

"Poking a stick at something is her normal routine," he says.

"Not the Husk. Someone else. A nonhuman."

Nana doesn't mean an animal or a rock. Nonhumans are dangerous people incapable of love or remorse. In other words, sociopaths.

"One person comes to mind immediately," Win says.

"No." Nana shakes her head. "But she's in danger."

He reaches across the table, plucks Nana's car keys off the outstretched ceramic arm of a small Egyptian statue, says, "Danger keeps her from getting bored."

"You're not leaving this house, my darling, without putting those bay leaves in your boots."

He pulls off his motorcycle boots, slips in the bay leaves, making sure they're pointing the correct way, according to manufacturer's instructions.

Nana says, "Today is the day of the goddess Diana, and she rules silver and copper. Now, copper is the old metal of the moon. It conducts spiritual energy, just as it does heat and electricity. But beware. It's also used by bad people to channel hoaxes. That's why it's being stolen hand over fist these days. Because falsehoods rule. The dark spirit of hatefulness and lies dominates the planet right now."

"You've been watching too much Lou Dobbs."

"I love that man! Truth is your armor, my darling." She dips into a pocket of her long skirt, pulls out a small leather pouch, places it in Win's hand. "And this is your sword."

He unties the drawstrings. Inside are a shiny new penny and a small crystal.

"Keep them with you at all times," she says. "When put together, they form a crystal wand."

"Great," he says. "Maybe I can turn Lamont into a frog."

Not long after he leaves, Nana carries a box of kosher salt upstairs to her bathroom, where octagonal mirrors hanging in the corners direct negativity back to the sender.

> Evil this way bent
> Return whence it's sent!

She never goes to bed unclean, lest the unpleasantness of the day continue in her dreams. Unsettledness. She feels the presence of the nonhuman. A childish one filled with mischief and meanness, resentment and pride. She pours salt on the shower floor, turns on the water, and chants another spell.

> Rising moon and setting sun,
> My sacred work is never done.
> Breath and light for me are one.
> Warrior of justice, come!

The salt beneath her feet draws bad energy from her and washes it down the drain, and she ends her shower with an herbal brew of parsley, sage, rosemary, and thyme that she boiled in an iron pot this morning. She pours the fragrant water over her head to cleanse her aura, because her work brings her into contact with many personalities, not all of them good, especially this one. The nonhuman. A young one who is ranging about. It is close now and wants something of Nana's, something very dear to her.

"My most powerful instrument of magic is my very being," she says out loud. "I will pinch you between my two fingers!" she warns it.

In her bedroom, she opens a drawer and retrieves a small red-silk bag filled with iron nails, tucks it into the left pocket of her clean, white robe. She sits next to Miss Dog on the bed, writes in her journal by the light of white candles. Writes her usual musings about *Magick* and *Spells* and the *Work of the Mage*. The journal is thick, bound in Italian leather, and she has filled its pages, the pages of many journals for many years, writing in her large, looping script. Then a heavy fatigue, and candles out, and she has one foot into the land of sleep when she sits up with a start in the dark. She grabs the bag of nails out of her robe pocket and jangles them loudly.

Miss Dog, deaf and snoring, doesn't stir. Footsteps downstairs along the wooden hallway between the kitchen and the living room.

Nana jumps out of bed, jangles the nails again as she flies out the bedroom door.

"I will punish you by the rule of three times three!" she yells.

Footsteps moving fast. *Stomp-stomp-stomp-stomp-stomp.* The kitchen door slams shut. Nana looks out her window, sees a shadow running, carrying something. She hurries down the stairs and out of the house, and wanders about her overgrown property as wind chimes clatter and clang, agitated and angry. She feels the emptiness of what was just there. Then the sound of a car, and far down the street, taillights are the bright red eyes of the devil.

3

Inside the FRONT's mobile crime lab, Stump examines the note from the day's bank robbery, looking for something, anything, foiled again.

Raising latent fingerprints on paper isn't the sure thing depicted on all those cop shows, and in the real world, this bank robber has yet to leave a useful clue. She stops what she's doing as she hears a car pull up. Then her cell phone rings.

"It's me." Win's compelling baritone voice. "You giving tours? I'm outside your big-ass truck."

She pulls off her latex gloves, opens the tailgate. He climbs up the steps, squints in the bright lights as she lets him in, shuts the heavy doors, slam-dunks the used gloves in the trash, yanks a new pair out of a box.

"How did you know I was here?" she asks.

"You had a bank robbery today. Remember?" He moves close to the countertop where she's working. "And let me see. You aren't at your shop. So I called your dispatcher and asked where I might find you."

"You're offensive and presumptuous, and I'm not amused." Pulling on the latex gloves, having a bit of a struggle with them.

"What you got here?"

If there's one thing she detests, it's a guy who's so perfect, he looks like a friggin' Calvin Klein underwear ad and, if that's not annoying enough, assumes he can charm the birds out of the trees. Well, not this tough old bird. Besides, if she runs him off, she's only doing him a favor.

"What I've got is nothing," she says irritably. "It's as if he's wearing gloves, only I know he's not."

"You sure? Absolutely?" He moves closer.

She can smell him. The hint of a spicy, masculine cologne. Probably expensive, like everything else he's got.

"I'm sure this will shock you," Stump says, "but I recognize gloves when I see them." She rewinds the surveillance tape, says, "Help yourself."

The bank's glass front door opening. White guy—or could be Hispanic—acting normal, perfectly at ease, with baggy blue sweats, sunglasses, dark hair, a Red Sox baseball cap pulled low, smart enough to know where the cameras are and to divert his face from them. No other customers inside. Three teller windows, one occupied by a young woman. Smiles as he approaches, slips her the note. She stares at it, doesn't touch it, terror on her face. Fumbles with the cash drawer, fills a deposit bag. He runs out of the bank.

"Another look at his hands." Win leans closer.

She backs up the video, pausing it so he can get a good look at the robber's hands as he's sliding the note under the teller's window. She can feel Win's closeness, as if he heats up the air.

"No gloves," he agrees. "Same thing in the other robberies?"

"So far."

"That's a little strange."

The note from this morning's case is on clean butcher paper covering the counter, and he stares at it for a long time, as if he's reading an entire page of print, not just the same simple ten words the robber writes on every note.

EMPTY CASH DRAWER IN BAG. NOW! I HAVE A GUN.

She explains, "Neatly written in pencil on a four by six-inch sheet of white paper, torn from a notepad. Same as the other three cases."

"Watertown, Somerville, now Belmont," Win says. "All of

them members of the FRONT, unlike Cambridge, which has yet to join your private club, and . . ."

"And why do you think this is?" she interrupts. "Lamont's headquarters is in Cambridge, and she has her own private club called Harvard, which pretty much owns Cambridge. So could that possibly have something to do with why Cambridge hasn't joined the FRONT and probably never will?"

"I was going to add that your robber also hasn't hit Boston," Win says. "What's going through my mind is Watertown, Somerville, and Belmont border on Cambridge. And Boston is close by as well. Certainly there are a lot of banks in Cambridge, not to mention Boston, yet your robber's avoided both places. Coincidental?"

"Maybe they'll be next." She's got no idea where he's going with this. "If so, I guess yours truly here won't be helping out, since Cambridge and Boston cops do their own crime scene investigation, handle their own evidence."

"That's one point I'm trying to make," he says. "Boston PD has its own labs, and if we're honest about it, Cambridge gets priority with state police labs because of Lamont."

"And because Cambridge hasn't joined the FRONT, and *if we're honest about it,* departments that join us get punished for it. Get treated as if we've committed treason." Rudely. She doesn't know why he seems to bring out the worst in her.

"If I were a smart bank robber," Win continues, "I would

definitely pick targets where police resources are limited and the evidence analysis is going to take forever, assuming it's done at all."

"Well, that would be most of Middlesex County. So I'm missing your point."

"My point is maybe you should think about where he's not committing his crimes as opposed to where he is committing them. Let's just say this guy's avoiding Boston and Cambridge. Then why? Maybe for reasons I just cited. Or maybe because he lives in Boston or Cambridge. Is afraid someone might recognize him."

"So maybe you're the one robbing the banks. Since you've got that nice apartment in Cambridge."

"Says who?"

"I check somebody out when he's on my radar screen," Stump says. "You sure live like you rob banks."

"You don't know the first thing about how I live. You just think you do."

She points a latex-sheathed finger at the note, says, "Same spelling and punctuation, same block printing."

"You should wear cotton examination gloves. Latex can smear pencil, some inks. This piece of paper from the same notepad?" he asks.

"Wow. So you know about indented writing, too."

"You used electrostatic detection?"

"Holy smoke. And you know about ESDA, too. You're quite the brain trust. As if we have an ESDA, by the way," she says, annoyed. "And if we'd asked you guys? Well, maybe ten years later you'd get around to it. Anyway, oblique lighting did the trick. Each note shows the impressions of the last note written."

"The guy wants us to know it's him," Win says.

"Us? There's no us. How many times do I have to tell you? And you can quit trying to insert yourself into my life, because it's not going to work. I'm not helping you with your publicity stunt."

"I'm sure Janie Brolin wouldn't appreciate your considering her murder a publicity stunt."

Stump wishes he would go away. For his own damn good.

She says, "Why might this bank robber want us to, quote 'know it's him'?"

"Maybe he's showing off. Maybe he's some kind of thrill seeker—gets off on all this."

"Or maybe he's just plain stupid, doesn't realize each time he writes a note, he leaves indentations of it on the sheet of paper below it," she says.

"What about latent prints? Anything on the other three notes?"

"Nothing. Not one damn fingerprint, not even a partial."

"Okay, then he's not stupid," Win says. "Otherwise, he wouldn't keep getting away with it. Middle of the day. And no fingerprints. Not even partials. You used ninhydrin?"

It is an inexpensive, tried-and-true reagent used to develop latent fingerprints on porous surfaces such as paper.

The chemical reacts to the amino acids and other components of oils and sweat secreted from the skin's pores. She tells him it hasn't worked on any of the notes, nor have forensic light sources with various bandwidths and special filters.

"And the tellers aren't touching the notes," Win says.

"Just leave them right where they are. Bottom line? We've got nothing. And unless this dude's wearing magic gloves that are invisible to the naked eye, there's no logical explanation for why he isn't leaving a trace of his identity on what now is four notes. Even in cases where there's no usable ridge detail, people who don't wear gloves leave something. A finger mark. A smear. A partial print from the side of the hand or the palm."

"Surveillance videos in all four cases?" Win asks.

"Different clothing, but looks like the same guy to me."

"You mind if I ask you something?"

"Probably."

"Why did you become a teacher and then quit?"

"I don't know. Why are you wearing a gold watch? You fix some rich person's parking ticket, maybe let him off the hook for driving two hundred miles an hour in his Ferrari or something? Or maybe you really are a bank robber."

"My dad's. Before that, his dad's, before that, Napoléon's—just kidding, although he was fond of Breguets," Win says, holding out his wrist to show her. "According to family legend, stolen. Some of my esteemed relatives in the Old Country could have auditioned for *The Sopranos*."

"You sure as hell don't look Italian."

"Mother was Italian. Father was black, and a teacher. A poet, taught at Harvard. I'm always curious why people want to be teachers, and it's rare I come across one who felt the calling, went to all the trouble, then quit."

"High school. Lasted two years. The way kids are these days, I decided I'd rather arrest them." Opening cabinets, returning various bottles of chemicals, dusting powders, crime lights, camera equipment, her hands nervous and awkward. "Anyone ever tell you not to stare? It's impolite. You stare worse than a baby," she says, sealing the bank robber's note in an envelope. "Last resort would be to swab for DNA. But no point, in my opinion."

"If he's not leaving sweat, not likely he's leaving DNA, unless he's shedding a lot of skin cells or sneezing on the paper," Win says.

"Yeah. Try wasting state police lab time on that one. Two years now I've been waiting for results on that girl who got raped in the Boneyard. The cemetery near Watertown High School. Not about bones. About smoking joints. Three years I've been waiting for results on the gay guy who got beaten to a pulp on Cottage Street. And forget all the hair salon breaks, what's going down in Revere, Chelsea, on and on. No one's going to take anything seriously until people start getting murdered right and left," she says.

They step out on the truck's diamond-plate steel platform; she shuts the vertical rear doors, locks them. He walks her to her unmarked Taurus, dull paint job, lots of dings on the doors, and she gets inside, waiting for him to stare at her leg, waiting for him to ask some stupid question about how she drives with a fake foot. But he's subdued, seems oblivious, is gazing off at her two-story brick police department, old and tired and much too small. As is true of most departments in Lamont's jurisdiction, no room to work, no money, nothing but frustration.

She starts the car, says, "I'm not going near the Janie Brolin case."

"Do what you gotta do."

"Believe me, I am."

He leans closer to her open window, says, "I'm working it anyway."

Her hand shakes a little as she adjusts the fan, and cool air blows on her face. She says, "Lamont this, Lamont that. And you snap to attention, do whatever she says. Lamont, Lamont, Lamont. No matter what, she gets what she wants and every-thing turns out great for her."

"I'm surprised you'd say that after what she went through last year," Win says.

"And that's the problem," Stump says. "She'll never for-give you for saving her life, and she'll punish you for the rest of yours. Because you saw her . . . Well, forget it." She doesn't want to think about what he saw that night.

She drives off, watches him in the rearview mirror, won-ders where the hell he got that piece-of-junk Buick. Her cell phone rings, and her heart jumps as it occurs to her it might be him.

It's not.

"Done," says Special Agent McClure, with the FBI.

"I guess I'm supposed to celebrate," Stump says.

"Was afraid of that. Looks like you and I need to have another little face-to-face. You're starting to trust him."

"I don't even like him," she says.

It's twenty of ten when he parks across the street from the courthouse, surprised to see Lamont's car in her reserved space by the back door.

Just his luck she's decided to work late, and it would be just like her to assume his showing up to clear out some of his desk is a ruse. She's so vain, she'll be convinced his real intention is to see her, that he somehow knew she'd be here at this hour, that he can't stand the thought of not being across the hall from her anymore. What to do. He needs files for court cases, his notes, personal items. It occurs to him it would serve her right if he cleared out his entire office, make her wonder if he's ever coming back. He rolls down his window as his phone vibrates. Nana. Second time she's called in the past hour. This time he answers.

"You're usually asleep by now," he says.

His grandmother keeps odd hours, takes her superstitious shower right after it gets dark. Goes to bed, gets up around two or three in the morning, starts fluttering about the house like a luna moth.

"The nonhuman has stolen the essence of you," she says. "And we must work fast, my darling."

"She's been trying for years, still hasn't touched my essence." As he watches the back of the courthouse, the top floor lit up. The county jail. Can't get his mind off Lamont. "Don't you worry, Nana. My essence is safe from her."

"I'm talking about your gym bag."

"Don't worry about my laundry, either." He doesn't show his impatience, wouldn't hurt Nana for the world. "I probably won't be able to drop by tomorrow, anyway. Unless you need your car?"

"As I was on the threshold of sleep, the thing came in and I ordered it back out the door. You've gotten mixed up in far more than you bargained for," she says. "It took your gym bag to steal your essence! To wear you like its own skin!"

"Wait a minute." He focuses on the conversation. "Are you telling me someone broke into your house and stole my gym bag?"

"The thing came in and took it. I went out into the yard, then the street, and it drove off before I could pin it inside my magic circle."

"When was this?"

"Soon after it got dark," she says.

"I'm coming over."

"No, my darling. There's nothing you can do. I cleansed

the doorknob, cleansed the kitchen of the evil energy from top to bottom . . ."

"You didn't . . ."

"Eradicated its impure, evil energy! You must protect yourself."

She begins her litany of protective rituals. Kosher salt and equilateral crosses. Draw a pentacle over a photograph of himself. White candles all over the place. Octagonal mirrors on all of his windows. Hold the telephone against his right ear, never the left, because the right ear draws bad energy out, while the left ear draws it in. Finally, she exclaims, *"Something bad's going to happen to the one who did this!"* And her Nana laugh, a good-hearted cackle as he ends the call.

She's always been unusual, but when she gets "on her broom," as he puts it, she unnerves the hell out of him. Her bouts of premonition and clairvoyance, her spates of casting curses and spells, resurrect old feelings of foreboding, distrust, maybe even blame. Magic Nana. What good was she when it came to the worst thing that's ever happened to him? All those promises about what the future held. He could go anywhere, be anything, the world was his to seize. His parents didn't want another child because he was so special, he was enough. Then that night, and Magic Nana never saw it coming and certainly didn't prevent it.

That chilly night when she took her adoring grandson on one of her secret missions, and she had not the slightest sense that something was terribly wrong. How was that possible?

Not even the faintest foreshadowing, not even when they got home and opened the door and were greeted by the most absolute silence he's ever experienced in his life. He thought it was a game at first. His parents and his dog in the living room, pretending to be dead.

After that he didn't go on any of Nana's secret missions, has never had any interest in the same mystical guidance so many other people seem to need. All while he was growing up, this parade of strangers in and out of the house. The bereft, the helpless, the desperate, the frightened, the sick. All paying her whatever they could, whatever their commodity might be. Food, hardware, clothing, art, flowers, vegetables, handiwork, haircuts, even medical care. It never has mattered what or how little, but it has to be something. Nana calls it an "equal exchange of energy," her belief that an imperfect ebb and flow of giving and receiving is what causes everything that's wrong in the world.

Without a doubt, it's the root of what's wrong between Win and Lamont. There sure as hell's no quid for her quo. He stares at her retractable-hardtop black Mercedes, as shiny as volcanic glass, about a hundred and twenty grand, forget preowned. She doesn't care what she pays, is too proud to ask for discounts, or more likely enjoys the rush of being able to afford sticker price, afford whatever she wants. He imagines what that must be like. To be a lawyer, an attorney general, a governor, a senator, to have money, to have an extraordinary wife and children who are proud of him.

It will never happen.

He couldn't get into law school, business school, a doctoral program—Ivy League or otherwise—not even if he were a Kennedy or a Clinton. Couldn't even get into a decent college, his application to Harvard probably laughed at, didn't matter that his father had been a professor there. Good thing his parents weren't around when his high-school guidance counselor commented that for such a "bright boy," Win had the lowest SAT scores she'd ever seen.

Lamont suddenly emerges from the courthouse back door in a hurry, briefcase, keys in hand, wireless earpiece pulsing blue as she talks on her cell phone. He can't hear what she's saying, but it's obvious she's arguing with someone. She gets into her Mercedes, speeds right past without noticing him, has no reason to recognize Nana's car. He has a funny feeling, decides to follow her. He stays several cars behind her on Broad Street, then on Memorial Drive along the Charles River, back toward Harvard Square. On Brattle Street, she tucks her Mercedes in the driveway of a Victorian mansion worth six, maybe eight, million, he guesses, because of the location and size of the lot. No lights on, looks unlived-in and poorly maintained except that the grass is mowed.

He drives around the block, parks a couple streets away, grabs a small tactical light he always keeps in Nana's glove compartment. He trots back to the house, notices the grass and some of the shrubbery are wet. The irrigation system must have been on earlier. A curtained window dimly lights up, a barely discernible glow, barely wavering. A candle. He moves silently and out of sight, freezes when he hears a back door opening, shutting. Maybe her, maybe someone else. She's not alone. Silence. He waits, contemplates barging into the house to make sure Lamont's all right, has a bad feeling of déjà vu. Last year. Her door ajar, the gas can in the bushes, and then what he discovered upstairs. She would have died. Some people say what happened to her was worse than death.

He continues to wait. The house is dark, and not a sound comes from it. An hour passes. Just when he's about to do something, he hears the back door shut, then footsteps. He ducks behind a tall hedge, watches a dark shape turn into Lamont as she walks alone to her car, carrying something. She opens the passenger door and the interior light goes on. What appears to be sloppily folded linens. She tosses them on the seat. He watches her drive off, no sign of whoever she had been with inside the house. Bizarre thoughts race through his mind. She's involved in something illegal. Drugs. Organized crime. Her recent shopping sprees—maybe she's on the take. His new assignment— maybe there's more to it than another one of her political charades. Maybe there's a reason she doesn't want him in her office, want him around.

He remains in his hiding place a little longer, then starts exploring the perimeter of the house, his tactical light brightly cutting across damage to the siding where down-spouts appear to have been forcefully removed, and along the roofline, more damage, the gutters gone. Copper flashing with a green patina, suggesting the missing downspouts and gutters might have been old oxidizing copper. Through a window by the back door, he can see the burglar-alarm panel. Green light, not armed. He uses the tactical light to tap out a pane of glass, reaches his hand inside, careful not to cut him-self, and unlocks the door. He studies the alarm panel. Obsolete, inactive, green light indicates only that power's on. The house smells musty, the kitchen in shambles, appliances ripped out, tarnished copper plumbing parts scattered over the floor.

He walks in the direction of the room he's fairly certain Lamont was in earlier, the beam of light cutting across the dusty hardwood flooring. Footwear impressions everywhere, some of them quite visible, perhaps from people walking through wet grass before entering the house. He crouches, takes a closer look at impressions that have no tread pattern, the familiar teardrop shape left by high-heel shoes. Lamont. Then others. Larger, round-toe, mesh tread pattern, and unmistakable stripe-shaped impression on the heel. Prada or a Prada knockoff. For a confused instant, he wonders if he left them. Not possible. For one thing, he's still wearing his motorcycle boots. He realizes, uncannily, that he forgot his Prada shoes, left them in his gym bag, which now, according to Nana, has been stolen.

There are other shoewear impressions, similar in size but different treads, maybe running shoes, hiking boots, maybe left by multiple people. Or maybe the same two people have been in here multiple times, obviously not always wearing the same shoes. He uses the tactical light for side lighting, takes photographs with his iPhone from three different angles, using a nine-millimeter cartridge from his pistol for a scale. He estimates the size of the Prada or Prada-like shoes is a ten, maybe ten and a half, about his size. He looks around some more, shining the light across ornate light fixtures, crown molding, cornices, and castings, probably original to the house. He finds the room he's looking for, what appears to have been a parlor in the long-ago past.

Footprints everywhere, some of them appearing to be the same as the ones in other areas of the house, and in the middle of the floor is a bare mattress. Nearby is a thick candle, the wax around the wick melted and warm, and an unopened bottle of red wine, a 2002 Wolf Hill pinot noir, same pinot, even the same vintage that Stump gave him earlier today when he talked to her at Pittinelli's. The same pinot, same vintage, of the bottle he accidentally left in his gym bag along with his Prada shoes.

He takes more photographs, returns to the kitchen, and notices something on a countertop that strikes him as peculiar: The torn cardboard and plastic packaging from a disposable camera—a Solo H_2O with a flash. Maybe some insurance investigator taking pictures of the damage to the house. But rather unprofessional to use a disposable camera. He opens cupboards, rummages, finds an old stew pot, two foil pans. Careful how he touches them, he places the bottle of wine in the pot, the candle in one foil pan, and the disposable camera package in the other. One last sweep with his light, and he notices a window that isn't latched, notices disturbed dust on both sides of the glass. More photographs using side lighting, but he doesn't see any ridge detail, just smudges. A lot of peeling paint has been knocked off the sill and the outside of the sash. Could have been done by someone opening the window from the outside and maybe climbing through it.

Stump sounds distracted when she answers her phone. When she realizes it's him, she seems taken aback.

"I thought I made it clear you're on your own," she says authoritatively, as if she might arrest him.

"The 2002 Wolf Hill pinot," he says.

"You're calling me at this hour to tell me what you think of the wine?"

"You said you just got it in. Has anybody bought it? And do any other stores carry it around here?"

"Why?"

Her tone is different, as if she's not alone. An alarm is going off inside him. Be careful what you say.

"Price shopping." He thinks fast. "Uncorked it when I got home. Amazing. Thought I'd get a case of it."

"You're really nervy, you know that?"

"So I was kicking back, started thinking. Maybe you should try it with me," he says. "At my place. I cook a mean veal chop."

"I don't believe in eating baby calves," she says. "And I've got no interest in having dinner with you."

4

Nana's Buick shakes and coughs as the engine turns off, and the driver's door screeches open like a prehistoric bird.

Win pockets the key, wonders why Farouk the landlord is sitting on the back steps, lighting a cigarette. Since when does he smoke, and he's breaking his own rule. No smoking, no lighting matches or grills, not so much as a spark is allowed on the grounds of his nineteenth-century brick apartment building, a former school, impeccably maintained and rented to privileged people. Or in Win's case, to someone who earns his keep. It's past midnight.

"Either you just started a nasty new habit or something's up," says Win.

"An ugly shorty was looking for you," Farouk says, a dish towel under him, probably so he doesn't get dirt on his ill-fitting white suit.

"She calls herself my shorty?" Win says. "Or is that what you're calling her?"

"She say it, not me. I don't know what it is."

"Gang slang for girlfriend," Win says.

"See! I knew she was a gangster! I knew it! That's why I'm this upset! I don't want peoples like that, try very hard to keep things the right way." In his heavy accent. "These peoples you see in your job, they come here, I have to ask you to move out! My tenants will complain and I will lose my leases!"

"Easy going, Farouk . . ."

"No! I let you here for this unbelievable good price to protect me from bad peoples, and then they come here, these very ones you're supposed to keep away!" He jabs his finger at Win. "Good thing no one but me sees her! I'm very upset. Peoples like that show up here, and you let me down. You have to move."

"What did she look like, and tell me exactly what happened." Win sits next to him.

"I come home from dinner and this white girl come from nowhere like a ghost . . ."

"Where? Here in back? Were you sitting out here smoking when she showed up?"

"I got very upset and so I go to visit José across the street to have a beer and see if he know anything about the shorty, ever seen her, and he said no. So he give me a cigarette or two. I only smoke when I get very stressed, you know. I don't want you to have to move, you know."

Win tries again. "What time was it when she showed up, and where were you? Inside your apartment?"

"I just was dropped off from dinner, so I'm thinking maybe nine o'clock, and you know I always come in from back here, and as I walk up these steps, there she is like a ghost out of a movie. Like she was waiting. I never seen her before and have no idea. She say to me, 'Where's the policeman?' I say, 'What policeman?' Then she says, 'Geronimo.'"

"She said that?" Few people know his nickname. Mostly cops.

"I swear," Farouk says.

"Describe her."

"It's hard to see, you know. I should get lights. A cap on, big pants and short. Skinny."

"What makes you think she's involved in gang activity? Aside from my telling you what a shorty is."

"The way she talk. Like a black person even though she white. And very rough talk, street talk, said a lot of bad words." He repeats a few of them. "And when I say I don't know a policeman named Geronimo, because I protect you always, she cuss me some more and say she knows you live here, and she hand me this." He slides an envelope out of his jacket pocket.

"How many times I got to tell you not to touch things if

they're suspicious?" Win says. "That's why I had to take your fingerprints a couple years ago. Remember? Because you touched something else some wacko left me?"

"I'm not one of these *sissies* on TV."

Farouk is hopeless with acronyms, thinks CSI is pronounced "sissy." Thinks DNA is *D&A,* refers to drugs and alcohol testing.

"You can get prints, other evidence off paper," Win reminds him, knowing it won't do any good. Farouk never remembers, doesn't care.

Certainly this isn't the first time someone has delivered unsolicited communications to the building or has simply shown up uninvited. The downside to Win's living here so long is it's impossible to keep his address a secret. But typically, his unexpected visitors are nonthreatening. A woman he's met somewhere. Now and then, someone who's read about a case, saw something, knows something, and asks around until he or she gets Win's address. More often, some paranoid soul who wants police protection. Sure, people leave him notes, even alleged evidence, but Win's never seen Farouk this upset.

Win takes the envelope, using his fingertips to hold it by two corners, returns to Nana's car, manages to collect his evidence, carry it without dropping anything. Farouk smokes and watches.

"You see her again, you call me right away," Win says to him. "Some nutcase comes looking for me, don't bum cigarettes and sit out here in the dark for hours, waiting for me to show up."

"I don't want those gang peoples. Don't need drugs and shootings around here," Farouk exclaims.

The building is a walk-up, no such thing as elevators back in the Victorian days of reading, writing, and arithmetic. Win carries the pot and pans up three flights of stairs to his apartment—two former classrooms that were connected during the renovation. Added were a kitchen, a bathroom, a window-unit air conditioner. Since he lived here during the construction, helped supervise and keep an eye on the place, he got his way about a number of things, such as preserving the original fir floors, wainscotting, vaulted ceilings, even the chalkboards, which he uses for grocery lists, other reminders of errands he needs to run, and phone numbers and appointments. He sets the evidence on a table, shuts the heavy oak door, locks it, dead bolts it, looks around the way he always does to make sure nothing is amiss, and his mood sinks lower.

After a day of Lamont and Stump, he feels worse about himself than usual, is depressingly aware of the Oriental rug, the Thomas Moser table, the leather sofa and mismatched chairs, and shelves of remaindered books he got for almost nothing and has such a hard time reading. Everything undesirable or secondhand, from junk shops, yard sales, eBay,

Craigslist. Flawed, damaged, unwanted. He slides out his pistol, places it on the dining-room table, takes off his jacket and tie, unbuttons his shirt, sits at his computer, and logs on to a people-search database, enters the address for the Victorian house in Cambridge. He prints out the last thirty-five years of owners and their possible relatives. Other searches reveal the most recent real-estate transaction was this past March when the run-down property was purchased for six-point-nine million dollars by a limited liability company called FOIL. In uppercase. Must be an acronym. He Googles it.

Nothing much. Just a few hits: a San Diego rock band, an educational site called First Outside Inside Last, Freedom of Information Law, Forum of Indian Leftists, a board game that has to do with words and wit.

He can't imagine how any one of them might be connected to a Victorian mansion on Brattle Street, and it crosses his mind to call Lamont and demand an explanation, tell her he knows where she was earlier tonight, that he saw her. Maybe scare her into confessing to whatever she was doing there. He envisions the room with the mattress, the candle, evidence that photographs were taken. He thinks about the vandalism, signs of what appear to be copper theft. And he obsesses over the bottle of wine, the Prada shoe impressions. If someone is setting him up, who and why? And how is it possible Lamont's not involved?

He covers the dining-room table with butcher paper, puts on latex gloves. Pours an ampoule of iodine crystals in a Ziploc bag, places the envelope inside it, seals the bag, and gently shakes it. A minute or two, and he removes the envelope, blows on it, not worried about DNA—the underside of the sealed flap is the best source for that. His warm, moist breath causes a chemical reaction with the iodine. Several finger-prints appear on the paper, turning black as he continues to blow on them. He slits open the envelope, slides out a folded sheet of plain white paper. Neatly printed on it in pink Magic Marker is *Tomorrow morning. Ten o'clock. Filippello Playground. Yours truly, Raggedy Ann.*

Next day, three p.m., London time.

At New Scotland Yard, Detective Superintendent Jeremy Killien gazes out the window at the revolving triangular steel sign in front of the legendary steel building. Usually, the sign's slow spins help him concentrate. But he's nicotine-deprived and irritated. As if he doesn't have enough to do, and then the commissioner drops a bloody bomb on him.

Killien's fifth-floor office, in the heart of the Specialist Crime Directorate, is overwhelmed by the iconography of his life. Books, file folders, the layered civilizations of paperwork that he'll excavate someday, the walls a polite and prestigious crowd of photographs. Margaret Thatcher, Tony Blair, Princess Diana, Helen Mirren—each posing with him in it. He has the expected shadowbox of police caps, patches, and in a corner, a mannequin dressed in a Victorian uniform worn by a bobby

whose collar number, 452H, meant his beat was Whitechapel
during the era of Sherlock Holmes and Jack the Ripper.

Hell, one lousy cigarette. Is it so much to ask? For the past
hour Killien's tried to ignore the urge, and is outraged all over
again that after decades of donating his life to the
Metropolitan Police Service, he no longer can smoke at his
desk or inside the building, has to creep out of the building on
the service lift to the enclosed courtyard with its loading bay
that stinks of rubbish and get his fix like some homeless
person. He opens a drawer, helps himself to another piece of
mint-flavored nicotine gum, calms down a bit as his tongue
begins to tingle.

Dutifully, he returns to the perusal of this unsolved Massachusetts homicide from 1962. Bizarre. The commissioner
must be off his trolley to take on such a thing. An unsolved
forty-five-year-old murder that didn't even occur in the UK?
Winston "Win" Garano, also goes by the nickname Geronimo.
No doubt because of his mixed race. A handsome fellow,
Killien will give him that. Mocha skin, wavy black hair, the
strong, straight nose of a Roman emperor. Thirty-four years
old, never married, both parents died when he was seven. A
faulty heater, carbon monoxide poisoning. Even killed his dog,
Pencil. Odd name for a dog.

Let's see, let's see. Raised by his grandmother, Nana . . .
Oh, this is a good one. Calls herself a "woman of the craft." A
witch. Deplorable driving record. Parking violations, running
red lights, illegal U-turns, speeding, license suspended and

reinstated by payment of fines. Good Lord, oh, here we go. Arrested three years ago, charges dropped. Seems she flung nine hundred and ninety-nine newly minted pennies on Massachusetts governor Mitt Romney's yard. A better one yet. Wrote Vice President Dick Cheney's name on parchment, placed it inside a bag of "dog poop," buried it in a cemetery. Caught in the act both times, was putting a curse on them. Well, no crime in that. She should have gotten a reward.

It appears Win Garano has been removed from his normal duties, assigned to the Watertown case. Sounds suspicious. Sounds like punishment. Sounds like he's done something to alienate his boss. Monique Lamont, district attorney for Middlesex County. Despite strong support from the public, she withdrew from the 2006 gubernatorial election, switched to the Republican party, and placed herself back on the ballot for reelection to her current position. Won by a wide margin. Never married, no current significant relationship. Killien stares for a long time at a photograph of her. Dark hair, dark eyes, quite stunning. Prominent family of French descent.

His phone rings.

"Have you had a chance to review the Massachusetts situation?" the commissioner asks him right off.

Situation? That's an unusual way to put it. Killien opens a manila envelope, slides out more photographs, police and autopsy reports. Takes a second for him to realize to his astonishment that the victim is Lamont. Raped and almost murdered last year.

"Hello? Are you there?" The commissioner.

"Looking at it even as we speak, sir," Killien replies, clearing his throat.

The attack took place in the bedroom of her Cambridge, Massachusetts, home, her assailant shot to death by this same detective, Win Garano. What was he doing inside her bedroom? There it is. Concerned by her demeanor on the phone, drove to her house, found the back door ajar, interrupted the assailant and killed him. Crime scene photographs of the would-be murderer on Lamont's bedroom floor, blood everywhere. Photographs of Lamont, of her injuries. Ligature marks around her wrists, her ankles. Suck marks on her fully exposed . . .

"Are you listening to me?" The commissioner's commanding voice.

"Of course, sir." Killien looks out the window at the revolving sign.

"The victim, as I'm sure you're well aware by now, was British. From London," the commissioner says.

Killien hasn't gotten that far, and if he says as much, the commissioner will give him stick about it. Killien avoids answering the question by asking a different one. "This wasn't thoroughly investigated by the Met at the time?" He moves paperwork around on his desk. "I don't see anything. . . ."

"We weren't contacted, apparently. There didn't seem to be a British interest, apparently. The victim's boyfriend was American, was the main suspect, and even if there was the slightest suspicion she may have been the work of the Boston Strangler, there wouldn't have been a reason to involve us."

"The Boston Strangler?"

"The district attorney's theory."

Killien spreads out photographs taken at the hospital, where she was examined by a forensic nurse. He imagines the cops seeing Lamont like this. How can they look at their powerful DA ever again and not imagine what's in these pictures? How does she cope?

"Of course I'll do whatever you wish," he says. "But why the sudden urgency?"

"We'll discuss it over a drink," the commissioner says. "I have an event at the Dorchester, so meet me there five sharp."

Meanwhile, in Watertown, Filippello Park is deserted.

Nothing but empty picnic tables beneath shade trees, vacant playing fields, and cold barbecues. Win figures the *playground* Raggedy Ann referred to in the card she left with Farouk is probably the tot lot, so he waits on a bench near sliding boards and a splash pool. No sign of anybody until eight minutes past ten, when he hears a car on the bike path. There are only two types of people outrageous enough to drive on bike paths: cops or idiots who should be arrested. He gets up as a dark blue Taurus parks, and Stump rolls down her window.

"Understand you're supposed to meet someone." She looks furious, as if she hates him.

"You chase her off?" he says, none too friendly himself.

"You shouldn't be here."

"Believe it's a public park. And what the hell are you doing here?"

"Your meeting's been canceled. Thought I'd drop by to let you know in person. Was considerate about it, even after what you did."

"What I did? And who the hell told you—"

"You show up uninvited at the mobile lab," Stump interrupts. "Spend an hour with me, pretending to be a nice guy, even helpful. Call later and ask me on a date, and all the while you're burning me!"

"Burning you?"

"Shut up and get in. I recognized your car wreck over there. You can get it later. Don't think you have to worry about anybody stealing it."

They creep along the bike path, her dark glasses fixed straight ahead, her dress casual bordering on sloppy, but deliberate. Khaki shirt, untucked, baggy, to hide the pistol on her hip or at the small of her back. Her jeans are loose-fitting, a faded soft denim, frayed in spots, and long, probably to conceal an ankle holster. Most likely her left ankle. Could be on her right ankle, he has no idea. Is ignorant about prosthetics, and he follows the contours of her thighs, wondering what she does to keep the right one as muscular as the left, imagines she must manage leg extensions, maybe on a specially designed machine, or she might wrap weights below the knee and do extensions that way. If it were him, no way he'd let his thigh completely atrophy just because some other part of him was missing.

She suddenly stops the car, yanks up a lever under her seat to shove it back as far as it will go, and props her right foot up on the dash.

"There," she snaps at him. "Get an eyeful. I'm sick of your not-so-subtle voyeurism."

"Great hiking boots," he says. "LOWAs with Vibram out-soles, shock-absorbing, amazing stabilization. If it wasn't for the brim of the prosthesis socket just above your kneecap—which is visible through your jeans, by the way, only because your leg is bent and halfway in the air—I wouldn't know. I'm not the one having the problem. Curious, yes. Voyeuristic, no."

"You left out manipulative, because that's what you are—a goddamn manipulator who must do nothing but cruise designer-clothing stores, men's catalogs. Because all you care about is the way you look, and no wonder. Since that's all there is to you. And I don't know what you're up to, but this isn't the way to start. First, you were supposed to meet the chief at ten. So already you're demonstrating your lack of respect."

"I left a message."

"Second, I don't appreciate you messing with people who are none of your business."

"What people?"

"The lady you bullied into meeting you at the park."

"I sure as hell didn't bully anyone. She left a note at my apartment building late last night, signed it Raggedy Ann, told me to meet her at the playground this morning." He doesn't realize how ridiculous it sounds until he's said it.

"Stay away from her."

"Thought she was just some crazy from a local shelter. Now suddenly you have a personal relationship."

"I don't give a damn what you thought."

"How did you know I was meeting her?"

Stump shoves the seat forward, starts driving again.

"You know what?" he says. "I don't have to put up with this. Turn around and drop me off at my car."

"Too late for that. You're getting your way. Gonna spend a little time with me today. And maybe by the end of it you'll take my recommendation and go back to your day job and get the hell out of Watertown."

"Oh, before I forget. I was burglarized last night." He's not about to mention Nana, that actually she was burglarized, not him. "Now I find out some fruit loop who dresses like a rag doll is lying about me. Then, magically, you show up instead of her."

"What burglary?" Stump sets aside her hard-ass act for a minute. "You mean your apartment?"

"No. The friggin' Watergate."

"What was stolen?"

"Some personal belongings."

"Such as?"

"Such as I'm not giving you details because right now I don't trust anybody. Including you."

Silence. They turn on Arlington, then Elm, then pull into a remote parking lot of the Watertown Mall, where she backs into a space between two SUVs.

"Car breaks," she says, as if their previous conversation didn't happen. "These jerks tie magnets to strings, drag them along a door to lift up the lock. Or poke a hole in a tennis ball, slam it against the lock so the forced air pushes it open. Of course, the big thing now is these portable navigation systems."

She opens the glove box, digs out a Magellan Maestro 4040 that has a broken adhesive disk. Plugs the charger into the cigarette lighter, wraps the cord around the rearview mirror. The crippled GPS dangles like fuzzy dice.

"People are stupid enough to leave them in their vehicles, in plain view. In my case, I was stupid enough to leave this one in my car, which is used by other cops when I'm off duty. A little different from what you're used to, I imagine? Crown Vics with GPS systems built in, cell phones with unlimited minutes. You know what happens when I reach my limit of minutes? I've got to pay the phone bill myself. And forget a take-home car."

"If I had a take-home car, you think I'd be driving that car wreck, as you so diplomatically described it?"

"Whose is it, anyway? Doesn't go with your designer suits and gold watch."

He doesn't say.

"See that old lady unlocking her minivan?" Stump goes on. "I could throw her to the pavement, be gone with her pocketbook before you could blink. To her, that'd probably be the worst thing that's ever happened in her life. To big shots like you, it's not even reportable."

"Clearly, you don't know me."

"Oh, I know plenty, because I know what you just did." Her dark glasses look at him. "You're worse than I thought. What'd you do? Ride around to local shelters until you found her so you could scare her to death?"

"I told you. She initiated . . ."

"Maybe she did. After you followed her around, terrifying her, taking advantage of her compromised mental state." Stump's antagonism is becoming less convincing.

He's not sure why, but he senses she's putting on a performance and isn't a particularly skilled actor.

"Who is she?" he asks. "And what's with the Raggedy Ann charade?"

"It's who she needs to be. Maybe believes it, maybe she doesn't. Who knows? Doesn't matter."

"It matters. There's a difference between psychotic and eccentric." He watches more shoppers return to their cars, not a GPS thief in sight.

Stump says, "She claims you threatened her. Claims you

told her if she didn't meet you in the park this morning, you'd make sure she got locked up every time she stepped out her door."

"She give you some plausible explanation for why I could threaten her?"

"You wanted sex."

"If you believe that, maybe you're the one who's psychotic," he says.

"Why? Because a guy like you could have anyone he wants, so why would he want an unattractive nobody like her?"

"Come on, Stump. If you've checked me out as thoroughly as you say, you know damn well I don't have that kind of reputation."

"Sounds like you don't know what people say about you, don't know the speculations."

"People say all kinds of things about me. But what are you referring to, exactly?"

"What really happened in Lamont's bedroom that night."

He's speechless, can't believe she just said that.

"How do I know the truth?" Stump says.

"Don't push me too far." He says it quietly.

"Just telling you, the speculation's out there. It's everywhere. People—especially cops—who think you were already in Lamont's house when the guy broke in. Specifically, already in her bedroom. Specifically, you could have protected her without killing him, but that might have resulted in people knowing your dirty little secret."

"Take me back to my car."

"I have a right to know if the two of you have ever had . . ."

"You don't have a right to anything," he says.

"If I'm going to have any respect for you . . ."

"Maybe you should start worrying about my having any respect for you," he says.

"I need to know the truth."

"So what if we did? How 'bout that? She's single. I'm single. We're both consenting adults."

"A confession. Thank you." Coldly.

"Why is it so important to you?" he asks.

"It means you're living a lie, you're nothing but a con artist, a phony. That you sleep with the boss, and that leads directly to why she's sent you to Watertown. Must be something in it for you. Especially if you're still sleeping with her. And you probably are. I have no use for people like you."

"No, I think the truth is you're trying really hard to have no use for me," Win says. "What? It reinforces your view of the universe if I'm garbage?"

"Narcissist that you are, you would think that."

"We didn't," he says. "There. Are you satisfied?"

Silence, as she starts the car, refusing to look at him.

"And I could have, if you really want to know," he adds. "I don't say that to brag. But after the fact, she was . . . how to put this? Very vulnerable."

"What about now?" Stump starts entering an address into her jerry-rigged GPS.

"After what happened to her? She'll always be vulnerable," he says. "Problem is, she'll never know it, just walk into one bad mistake after another. For all her brashness, Lamont runs like hell from herself. For all her smarts, she has no insight."

"That's not what I meant. What about now?"

"Not even close. Where are we going, by the way?"

"I need to show you something," Stump says.

5

The Dorchester Hotel is for heads of state and celebrities, not for the likes of Killien, who can scarcely afford a cup of tea there.

A Ferrari and an Aston Martin are being valet-parked in front as a taxi unceremoniously deposits him in a cluster of kaffiyeh-clad Arabs, who aren't interested in getting out of his way. *Probably related to the Sultan of Brunei who owns the damn place,* Killien thinks as he enters a lobby of marble columns and gold cornices, and enough fresh flowers for several funerals. One advantage to being a detective is he knows how to walk into a place or situation and act as if he belongs.

He buttons his wrinkled suit jacket, takes a left, enters the bar, makes a point of appearing indifferent to the red art glass, the mahogany, the purple and gold silk, the Asians, more Arabs, a few Italians, a couple of Americans. Doesn't seem to be a single Brit except the commissioner, sitting alone at a small, round table in a corner, his back to the wall, facing the door. After all is said and done, at heart the commissioner's still a cop, albeit a well-heeled one because he's made good choices in life, including the baroness he married.

He's drinking whisky, neat, probably Macallan with a sherry finish. Silver dishes of crisps and nuts nearby look untouched. He's impeccable in gray pinstripes, white shirt, dark red silk tie, his mustache neatly trimmed, blue eyes typically vague, as if he's preoccupied, when in fact he doesn't miss a thing. Killien's barely in his chair when a waiter appears. A pint of stout will do. Killien needs to keep his wits about him.

"I need to fill you in about this American case," the commissioner begins, not one for small talk. "I know you're wondering why it's a priority."

"Certainly I am," Killien says. "Haven't a clue what this is all about, although what I've seen so far is rather curious. For example, Monique Lamont . . ."

"Powerful and controversial. Quite stunning, I might add."

Killien thinks of the photographs. The commissioner would have looked at them as well, and he wonders if his boss shares his same rather unsettling reaction. It's not proper to look at photographs associated with a violent crime and allow one's attention to wander beyond the woman's wounds, into areas that have nothing to do with good policing. And Killien can't stop thinking about the pictures, envisioning her supple . . .

"Are you with me, Jeremy?" the commissioner asks.

"Yes, indeed."

"You seem a bit foggy."

"Not a-tall."

The commissioner says, "So. Several weeks ago, she rang me up, asked if I was aware that a possible victim of the Boston Strangler was a British citizen. Said the case had been reopened, and suggested the Yard get involved."

"Frankly, I don't know why we would do more than make a couple of inquiries behind the scenes. Sounds political to me."

"Of course. She already has extravagant publicity planned, including a BBC special that she guarantees would air if we participate, and so on and so on. Rather presumptuous, as if we need her backing for a BBC endeavor. She's quite bold."

"I don't know how we can help her prove such a theory, since there's no certainty as to the identity of the Boston Strangler. And probably never will be," Killien says.

The commissioner sips his whisky. "Her political agenda is unimportant. I know her type all too well. Ordinarily, her attempt to drag us into such a matter would be politically ignored. But it seems there's an angle she's unaware of, and that's why you and I are having this conversation."

The waiter appears with the pint of stout. Killien takes a big swallow.

"When she first approached the Yard about her very old case, as a courtesy, if nothing else, I had the matter looked into, which included finding out something about her. Just the routine checks," the commissioner continues. "And we've come up with a disturbing bit of information—not about the case, which frankly matters very little to me. But about Monique Lamont herself, and cash transactions and donations that have come to the attention of the US Treasury Department. Turns out her name is in the Defense Intelligence Agency's database."

Killien abruptly sets down his pint of stout. "She's suspected of funneling money to terrorists?"

"Indeed."

"Right off, what comes to mind is some bureaucratic blunder. Perhaps she suddenly made large wire transfers for legitimate reasons," Killien suggests.

Happens more often than people realize. Based on what he read in her dossier, like the commissioner, she's got millions she didn't acquire on her own, likely moves around a lot of money, pays cash for big purchases in America and abroad, makes generous donations to various organizations. Then he remembers something else he just reviewed. Last fall she suddenly changed political parties. In and of itself, that might well have motivated whoever felt betrayed or offended to seek revenge.

"Of most concern, it seems," the commissioner is saying, "is a sizable contribution she recently made to a children's relief fund in Romania. A number of these groups, as you know, are fronts for terrorist fund-raising. The one she gave to, in particular, is suspected of trafficking in orphans, supplying them to Al-Qaeda so they can be used as suicide bombers and such."

He tells Killien there was quite a lot in the press about the donation, about Lamont's compassion for orphans, which leads Killien to suspect that if the relief fund really is a terrorist front, it's doubtful Lamont knows. If she knew, why would she hold a press conference about it? Doesn't matter. You don't have to have intent or awareness to be guilty of a crime.

And the commissioner says, "She's on a no-fly list but is probably unaware of it since she hasn't tried to book a commercial flight in the past several months. When she does, she'll begin to realize she's being watched. Which is why we need to look into this immediately."

"If her assets have been frozen, certainly she would know it."

"CIA, FBI, DIA leave numerous accounts off the freeze list so possible terrorist funding can be monitored. It's likely she has no idea."

This piques Killien's own private fears. You never know who's riffling through your bank account, e-mails, medical records, or favorite sites on the Internet, until one day you discover your assets are frozen or you can't get on a plane, or agents show up at your business or flat and haul you in for questioning, perhaps deport you to a secret prison in a country that denies it uses torture.

"What's all this got to do with the murder of Janie Brolin and our sudden urgency to look into it?" he inquires.

The commissioner motions for the waiter to bring another whisky, says, "It gives us an excuse to look into Monique Lamont."

The State House dome shines over Boston like a gold crown, and as Lamont stares through the dark tinted window of the state police black Expedition, she wonders why twenty-three-karat gilt instead of twenty-four.

A pointless bit of trivia that most assuredly will irk Governor Mather, who touts himself as quite the historian. She's in a mood to throw him off balance as much as possible this morning. To pay him back for snubbing her, and at the same time to remind him of her immense value. Finally, he'll hear her out and realize the brilliance of her crime initiative, the Janie Brolin case, and its immense international implications.

The aide escorting Lamont is chatty. Lamont isn't. She walks with purpose, quite familiar with the hallway, the council chamber, the cabinet room, the waiting room of portraits and handsome antiques, and, finally, the inner sanctum. All that should have been hers.

"Governor?" the aide says from the doorway. "Ms. Lamont is here."

He's behind his desk, signing documents, doesn't look up, She walks in.

She says, "If anyone will know the answer to this, you will, Howard. The State House dome. Why twenty-three-karat instead of twenty-four?"

"I guess you need to ask Paul Revere that." Distracted.

"He covered it in copper," Lamont says.

The governor signs something else, says, "What?"

"In case you're ever asked, I know you wouldn't want to misspeak. Paul Revere covered the dome in copper to make it watertight." She helps herself to a heavy chair upholstered in lavish damask. "The dome wasn't gilded with gold leaf until about a century after that. And I'm fascinated you chose a portrait of William Phips." She studies the severe oil painting hanging over the marble fireplace behind Mather's desk. "Our esteemed governor of Salem witch trial fame," she adds.

One of the perks of being governor is picking the portrait of your favorite Massachusetts governor to hang in your office. It's common knowledge that Mather would have chosen a portrait of himself had it been painted yet. The pious, devil-hating William Phips stares askance at Lamont. She surveys more antiques, the stucco ornaments decorating the walls. Why is it men, especially Republican men, are so crazy about Frederic Remington? The governor has quite a collection of bronzes. *Bronco Buster* on his rampant horse. *Cheyenne* on a galloping horse. *Rattlesnake* about to bite a horse.

"I appreciate your taking the time to see me, Howard."

He muses, "Twenty-three-karat gold gilding the State House dome instead of twenty-four. News to me, but anyway, symbolic, isn't it? Perhaps to remind us that government isn't quite pure."

But the governor is—a pure conservative Republican. White, early sixties, pleasant beatific face that belies the heartless hypocrite behind it. Balding, portly, avuncular enough so as not to appear overbearing or dishonest, unlike Lamont, who is assumed to be ball-breaking and deceitful because she's beautiful, brilliant, enlightened, exquisitely dressed, strong, and quite vocal about her support and even tolerance of those less fortunate than herself. Simply put, she looks and sounds like a Democrat. And would still be one—in fact, would be governor—were it not for her entrusting her welfare to a direct descendant of that witchcraft hysteric Cotton Mather.

"What should I do?" Lamont begins. "You're the strategist. I admit I'm somewhat of a neophyte when it comes to politics."

"I've given this YouTube development some thought, and you may be surprised by what I have to say." He puts down his pen. "I happen to view it not as a liability but a possibility. You see, Monique, the plain-and-simple truth is, I'm afraid your switching to the Republican party hasn't had the desired effect. The public, more now than before, views you as the quintessential liberal, ambitious woman. The sort who doesn't stay home, raise children . . ."

"It's been quite public that I love children, have a sincere and demonstrable concern about their welfare, especially orphans . . ."

"Orphans in places like Lithuania . . ."

"Romania."

"You should have picked local orphans. Ones right here in America. Maybe a few displaced by Hurricane Katrina, for example."

"Maybe you should have suggested that before I wrote the check, Howard."

"Do you get where I'm going with this?"

"Why you've avoided me since you were elected. I suspect that's where you're going."

"You must recall the talks we had prior to the election."

"I remember every word of them."

"And apparently started ignoring every word of them after all was said and done. Which I consider ungrateful and unwise. So now you've come to me in your moment of need."

"I'll make it up to you, and know exactly how . . ."

"If you're going to be a successful Republican leader," he talks over her, "you must represent conservative family values. Be a proponent of them, a crusader for them. Antiabortion, anti–gay marriage, anti–global warming, anti–stem cell research . . . Well . . ." Fingertips touching, lightly tapping. "It's not for me to judge, and I don't care what people do in their personal lives."

"Everybody cares what people do in their personal lives."

"I'm certainly not naïve when it comes to emotional trauma. As you know, I served in Vietnam."

This route was not the one she expected, and she begins to bristle.

"After what you went through, it stands to reason you would emerge as someone who has more to prove. Aggressive, angry, driven, perhaps a bit unbalanced. Fearful of intimacy."

"I didn't realize that's what Vietnam did to you, Howard. It saddens me to realize you might be afraid of intimacy. How's Nora, by the way? I still can't get used to thinking of her as the First Lady." Dumpy old housewife with the IQ of a clam.

"I wasn't sexually violated in Vietnam," the governor says matter-of-factly. "But I knew of POWs who were." He stares off to one side, like the painted Governor Phips. "People have compassion about what happened to you, Monique. Only a monster would be insensitive to that terrible event last year."

"Event?" Anger flares. "You call what happened an *event*?"

"But realistically?" He mildly goes on. "People don't give a damn about our problems, our mishaps, our tragedies. We hate weakness. It's human nature. It's animal instinct. We also don't like women who are too much like men. Strength, courage are fine within bounds, as long as they're manifested in a feminine fashion, so to speak. What I'm suggesting is, this YouTube video's a gift. Primping in the mirror. Trying to look alluring in a way men appreciate and women can relate to. Exactly the image you need right now to reverse this strengthening tide of unfortunate speculation that what happened damaged you as a potential leader. Yes, you evoked a lot of public sympathy and admiration at first, but now it's fast moving the other way. You're coming across as distant, too tough, too calculating."

"I had no idea."

"The danger of the Internet is obvious," he continues. "Everyone can be a journalist, an author, a news commentator, a film producer. The advantage is just as obvious. People like us can do the same thing. Turn the table on these self-appointed . . . If I used the word that comes to mind, I'd be as vulgar as Richard Nixon. You might want to consider making your own video and posting it anonymously. Then, after much public speculation, get some loser geek out there to take credit."

Which is exactly what Mather does. She figured that one out a long time ago.

"What sort of video?" she inquires.

"I don't know. Go to church with an attractive widower who has several young children. Perhaps address the congregation with deep emotion, talk about your change of heart—a Road to Damascus conversion experience—that's made you passionately pro-life and a proponent of amending the Constitution to ban gay marriage. Talk about the plight of people and pets displaced by Hurricane Katrina to deflect attention away from your helping orphans who aren't Americans."

"People don't post things like that on YouTube. It has to be a candid moment that's embarrassing, controversial, heroic, something funny. Like that bulldog riding a skateboard . . ."

"Well"—impatiently—"fall down the steps when you're leaving the pulpit. Maybe some usher or, better yet, the pastor, rushes to your rescue and accidentally grabs your breast."

"I don't go to church. Never have. And the scenario is degrading. . . ."

"And examining your cleavage in a bathroom isn't?"

"You just said it wasn't. Said it was alluring. Indicated it was compelling and caused people to remember I'm a desirable woman and not some sort of cold-blooded tyrant."

"This is not a good time to be stubborn," he warns. "You don't have three years before the machinery cranks up again. It's already started."

"Which is why I've asked repeatedly to talk to you about another matter." She seizes the opportunity. "An initiative that you really need to hear about."

She opens her briefcase, pulls out a synopsis of the Janie Brolin case. Hands it to him.

He skims it, shakes his head, says, "I don't care if Win what's-his-name solves it. You're talking front-page news for a day, maybe two, and by election time, no one will care or even remember."

"This isn't about one case. It's about something much bigger. And I must emphasize that this can't be made public yet. It absolutely can't. I'm taking you into my confidence, Howard."

He folds his hands on top of his desk. "Don't know why I would make it public, since it's of no interest to me. I'm more interested in helping you with your self-destruction."

A double entendre if ever there was one.

"That's why I've taken the time to advise you," he says. "To put a stop to it."

What he wants to put a stop to is her. He despises her, always has, and became her supporter last election only to serve a very simple purpose. The Republicans needed to win every office they possibly could, especially the governorship, and the only way to ensure that was to weaken the Democratic party at the last minute by Lamont's withdrawing from the race. Her doing so for "personal reasons" was a front. Behind it, she and Mather made a deal she now knows he had no intention of keeping. She'll never be a Republican senator or member of congress and, most of all, never serve in his cabinet should he reach his goal of winning the presidency before he's dead. She fell prey to his machinations because, frankly, at the time, she wasn't thinking clearly.

"Now I want you to listen to me," the governor is saying. "This is a foolish, frivolous endeavor, and you don't need more bad publicity. You've already had enough for a lifetime."

"You don't know the facts of the case. When you do, you'll have a different opinion."

"Make your opening statement, then. Change my mind."

"This isn't about a forty-five-year-old unsolved homicide," she says. "It's about allying ourselves with Great Britain to solve one of the most infamous crimes in history. The Boston Strangler."

The governor scowls. "What the hell's Great Britain got to

do with some blind girl getting raped and murdered in Watertown? What has Great Britain got to do with the Boston Strangler, for God's sake?"

"Janie Brolin was a British citizen."

"Who gives a damn unless she was bin Laden's mother!"

"And she very likely was murdered by the Boston Strangler. Scotland Yard is interested. Very, very interested. I've talked to the commissioner. At great length."

"Well, now, that's hard to believe. Why would he even get on the phone with some DA from Massachusetts?"

"Perhaps because he's sincere about what he does, is very secure in who he is," she subtly retaliates. "And keeping in mind it's very much to the advantage of Great Britain and the US to forge a new partnership now that there's a new Prime Minister, and hopefully, soon enough, a new president who isn't . . ." She remembers she's now a Republican, and should watch what she says.

"Partnership in what to do about Iraq, terrorists, yes," Mather retorts. "But the Boston Strangler?"

"I assure you, Scotland Yard is enthusiastic, fully engaged. I wouldn't be pushing ahead if that part hadn't fallen into place."

"I still find it hard to believe. . . ."

"Listen, Howard. The investigation's under way. It's already happening. The most extraordinary criminal justice coalition in history. The UK and US fighting together to right a terrible wrong committed against a defenseless blind woman—a nobody in a nothing place called Watertown."

"Well, the whole thing's preposterous." But he's interested.

"If my plan succeeds—and it will—you'll be directly credited, which not only shows you're a crusader for justice and have a heart but pushes you into the international arena. You'll be *Time* magazine's man of the year."

It will be a cold day in hell before she gives him the credit. And if anyone's going to be man of the year, it will be her.

"As intriguing as it might be to think this blind British girl was murdered by the Boston Strangler," the governor says, "I don't see how the hell you're going to prove it."

"It can't be disproved. That's what ensures success."

"You'd better be right about this," he warns. "If it's an embarrassment, I'll make sure it's yours. Not mine."

"That's why we must keep this out of the press right now," Lamont reiterates.

He'll leak it immediately.

"We go public only if it's successful," she says.

He won't wait.

"Which, as I've said, I'm confident it will be," she adds.

Of course, he reads between the lines. She can see his thoughts in his beady eyes. Shallow, cowardly dolt that he is. He'll want the media to be all over this now, because in his limited way of thinking, if her initiative fails, it will be the last straw for her and she probably won't recover. If it succeeds, he'll step forward after the fact and take the credit—which (and this is what he fails to see) will simply serve to make him look like the dishonest, cynical politician he is. The only winner at the end of the day is going to be her, by God.

"You're right," the governor says. "Let's keep it quiet for now, wait until it's a fait accompli."

Revere Beach Parkway, speeding past Richie's Slush with its candy-cane striped roof, heading to Chelsea.

"Not to be confused with the Chelsea in London," Stump says.

"That another fancy literary allusion of yours?" Win says.

"No. Just a beautiful, really hip part of London."

"Never been to London."

The Massachusetts Chelsea, two miles from Boston, is one of the poorest cities in the commonwealth, has one of the state's largest populations of undocumented immigrants, and the highest crime rate. Multilingual, multicultural, crowded and run-down, people don't get along, and their differences often land them in jail or leave them dead. Gangs are a scourge that robs, rapes, and kills simply because it can.

"An example of what happens when people don't understand each other," Stump says. "I read somewhere there are thirty-nine languages spoken around here. People can't communicate, at least a third of them are illiterate. They misinterpret, and next thing you know, someone gets beaten up, stabbed, shot down in the street. You speak Spanish?"

"A few key phrases, such as *no*. Which is Spanish for *no*," he says.

The landscape continues to deteriorate, one block after another of run-down houses with bars on the windows, lots of check-cashing joints, car washes, as Stump drives deeper into the city's dark, depressing heart while the GPS dangling from the rearview mirror tells her to turn this way and that. They enter an industrial area that in the heyday of the Mob was the ideal drop-off for dead bodies, a squalid, scary square mile of rusting sheds, storage facilities, landfills. Some businesses are legitimate, Stump tells him. Many of them are fronts for drugs, fencing stolen goods, and other shady activities such as "disappearing" cars, trucks, motorcycles, small aircraft.

"Even a yacht once," she adds. "Guy wanted the insurance money, claimed the boat was stolen, trailered it up here and had it crushed into a cube."

His iPhone again. He checks caller ID. Number *Unknown*. Lamont's number comes up that way. He answers, and *Crimson* reporter Cal Tradd's voice is in Win's ear.

"How did you get this number?" Win says to him.

"Monique said I should call you. I need to ask you about the Janie Brolin case."

Goddamn her. She promised nothing was going to be released to the media until the case was solved.

"Look, this is important," Cal goes on. "I need to verify you're on special assignment, and there's a Boston Strangler connection."

"Go screw yourself. How many times I got to tell you I don't talk to reporters. . . ."

"Have you been listening to the radio, watching TV? Your boss is furious. Someone leaked all this, and my suspicion is it's the governor's office. I won't name names, but suffice it to say, I know some of the idiots who work down there. . . ."

"I'm not verifying anything." Win cuts him off, hangs up on him, says to Stump, "It's all over the news."

She says nothing, is busy driving and swearing at the GPS. It tells her to make a legal U-turn.

6

Stump parks in an alley where they have a good view of DeGatetano & Sons, a scrapyard with mountains of twisted metal behind fencing topped with razor wire.

She says, "You see where we are?"

"I saw where we are before we got here. You must think I spend all my time hanging out in Cambridge coffee shops," Win says.

Tough-looking customers are pulling up in trucks, vans, and cars, all loaded with aluminum, iron, brass, and, of course, copper. Eyes are furtive, guys filling grocery carts, pushing them inside the machine shop, vanishing into a noisy darkness.

"An unmarked Taurus in an alleyway?" she goes on. "We

may as well be a Boeing 747. Maybe we should pay attention to our surroundings, because they're sure as hell paying attention to us."

"Then maybe you shouldn't be so conspicuous," he says.

"That's what deterrents do. They're conspicuous."

"Right. Like chasing off cockroaches. Scare them from one corner to the next until they end up at the corner they started from. Why did you bring me here?"

"Chasing off cockroaches is exactly the impression I want people to have—want them to think I'm after petty thieves. Construction workers, installers, contractors, these dirtbags who pilfer metal from construction sites. Some of it scrap, a lot of it not. Bring it here, no IDs, no questions asked, paid in cash, the clients they rip off have no idea. Remind me never to remodel or build a house."

"If you're in and out of here on a regular basis, how come you need the GPS?" he says.

"Okay. So I have a terrible sense of direction. Don't have one at all." The way she says it, it sounds like the truth. "And I'd appreciate it if you kept that to yourself."

Win notices a thin person in baggy clothes, a baseball cap, climbing out of a pickup truck piled high with copper roofing, pipes, dented downspouts.

"Disorganized crime is what I call it," Stump says. "Unlike the old days when I was growing up in Watertown. Everybody knew each other, would be eating in the same restaurant with the Mafia—same guys who remember your grandmother at

Christmas or buy you ice cream. Truth be told? They kept the streets clean of scumbags. Burglars, rapists, pedophiles? They'd end up in the Charles River with the heads and hands cut off."

The thin person he's watching is a woman.

"Organized crime was a good thing," Stump continues. "At least they had a code, didn't believe in beating up old ladies, carjackings, home invasions, molesting little kids, shooting you in the head for your wallet. Or for no reason at all."

The thin woman pushes two empty carts toward her truck.

"Copper. Currently going for about eight grand a ton on the Chinese black market." Stump abruptly changes the subject, looking where Win's looking. "You beginning to understand why I brought you here?"

"Raggedy Ann," he says. "Or whatever her real name is."

She's filling a cart with scrap copper.

"Super Thief," Stump says.

"That whack job?" Win says in disbelief.

"Oh, she's a thief, all right. But not the one I'm after. I want the guy who's doing the major hits. Stripping buildings of plumbing pipes, downspouts, roofing. Ripping off miles of wire from power lines, construction sites, breaking into telephone trucks. Maybe his real deal is drugs—taking the money and buying oxys, then reselling them on the street. These days going for around a dollar a milligram. Drug crimes lead to other crimes, finally lead to violence. Including murder."

"And you think your Super Thief's unloading the stolen copper here," Win assumes.

"Somewhere around here, yes. At this particular fine establishment? Probably one of many he uses."

He watches Raggedy Ann, says, "An informant, I assume."

"Now you're getting it," Stump says.

Raggedy Ann pushes her cart, doesn't seem the least bit uncomfortable, as if she belongs in the dangerous world of Chelsea scrapyards.

"What makes you think it's the same person doing the major hits?" Win asks.

"A detail consistent in most of the big jobs. I believe he's taking pictures. We've recovered the packaging from disposable cameras, always the same brand. A Solo H-two-oh. Waterproof with a flash, go for about sixteen bucks in the store—if you can find them. And on the Internet for six or seven. He leaves them at the scene in plain view."

The mansion on Brattle Street. The vandalism, the missing copper downspouts and gutters, the ripped-up copper plumbing, and the Solo H_2O disposable camera box in the kitchen of a house where Win found evidence he fears was planted, evidence that might lead to him. He almost tells Stump about his stolen gym bag, but doesn't. How the hell does he know who's doing what? He's caught in a web of connections, and the spider at the center is Lamont.

He says, "Any prints on the camera packages you're finding?"

"No luck. The typical reagents didn't work on the paper,

and superglue didn't develop any prints on the plastic. But just because you can't see a print doesn't mean it isn't there. Maybe the labs will have some luck, because they certainly have more space-age instruments than I do. If they ever get around to it."

He almost asks if she's ever heard of an LLC called FOIL, but he doesn't dare. Lamont spent more than an hour inside that abandoned Victorian mansion. Who was she with? What was she doing?

"Let me ask you something, for the sake of speculation," he says. "Why would your copper thief take photographs at his crime scenes?"

"The first thing that comes to mind," she replies. "He gets off on it."

"Sort of like your bank robber who maybe gets off on leaving the same type of note every single time? Gets off on flaunting himself, letting everybody know he's the same guy doing all of them and not leaving a fingerprint or even a partial, even though you can see in the surveillance tapes that he's not wearing gloves?"

"Are you suggesting it might be the same guy doing all of this? The bank robberies and the copper thefts?" she asks skeptically.

"Don't know. But perpetrators who flaunt their crimes and taunt the police aren't your average bear. So to have two crime sprees in the same geographic area at the same time, and both have what appear to be the MO I'm describing, is extremely unusual."

"Didn't realize you're a profiler, in addition to all of your other talents."

"Just trying to help."

"I don't need your help."

"Then why am I sitting here? You could have told me this Raggedy Ann weirdo is an informant so I'd understand why I should stay away from her. You didn't need to show me."

"Seeing is believing."

"You going to tell me her name, or am I supposed to call her Raggedy Ann for the rest of my life?"

"You won't know her for the rest of your life. I can promise you that. I'm not telling you her name, and here are the rules." Stump looks across the street. "You've never seen her before, and she's never seen us and has no interest. We're down here because I just happened to drop by. No big deal. As I've explained, I do it from time to time."

"I assume you're going to act as if you don't know her, either."

"You assume right."

Raggedy Ann pushes the cart inside the shop.

"The guy who runs this yard is Bimbo—biggest juicehead in Chelsea. Thinks he and I are pals. Come on," Stump says.

Eyes are on them from every direction as they get out of the car and cross the street. The shop is filthy and loud, men cleaning and separating metal, cutting it up, stripping it of nuts, bolts, screws, nails, insulation. Tossing it in piles, clinking and clanking. Raggedy Ann parks her cartful of copper on a floor scale, same kind used in morgues to weigh bodies, and a man emerges from a pigsty of an office. He's short, with heavily gelled black hair and a steroid body, bulky as a bale of hay.

He says something to Raggedy Ann and she drifts back out of the shop. He motions to Stump, says, "So, how's it doing?"

"Want you to meet a friend of mine," she says.

"Yeah? Well, I've seen him somewhere before. Maybe in the paper," Bimbo says.

"That's because he's state police, and he's been in the paper, on TV, because he had to kill a guy last year."

"I sort of remember that. The guy who did the DA."

"He's okay or he wouldn't be here," Stump says of Win.

Bimbo is staring at him, then decides, "You say he's okay, I believe you."

"Seems like he had a little problem in Lincoln. Two nights ago. Another hit, and you know what I'm saying," Stump says.

"A lot of stuff coming in," Bimbo says. "What got hit?"

"Huge house, four million dollars. Right before they were going to hang the drywall, someone comes in and rips out all the wiring. Now the builder's got to hire round-the-clock security so it doesn't happen again."

"What do you want?" Bimbo shrugs his huge shoulders. "Copper don't talk to me. I got in a lot of wire the last two days, already at the smelter."

Raggedy Ann pushes in another cart loaded with scrap copper, parks it on the scale. She pays no attention to Stump, to Win. They don't exist.

Bimbo says to Stump, "I'll keep my eye out. Last thing I want is that kind of thing going on. I run a clean business."

"Right. A clean business," Stump says, as she and Win walk off. "The only thing not stolen around here is the damn pavement."

"You just gave me up to that dirtbag," Win says angrily, as they climb back into her car.

"Nobody down here cares who you are. As long as Bimbo doesn't. And now he's cool with you, thanks to me."

"Thanks nothing. You don't get to give me up to anybody without my permission."

"You're now on the FRONT's turf. You're a guest, and the house rules are ours, not yours."

"Your turf? Am I hearing a different song? Seems like as recently as this morning you didn't want me on your turf. In fact, you've told me more than once to get lost."

"My introducing you to Bimbo's part of the game. It tells him you're with me, so if he sees you again—or anybody else does, no big deal."

"Why would he ever see me again?"

"Always a good chance somebody will get murdered down here. So it's your jurisdiction. I just got you a passport. You don't have to thank me. And just in case you didn't understand what I meant about Raggedy Ann? Now you know I'm serious. Avoid her."

"Then tell her to quit writing me notes."

"I have."

"You said she's a thief. That's how she got the copper?"

"The copper you just watched her unload wasn't stolen. I've got a contractor friend who does me a favor. I give her enough scrap to get her to Bimbo's once, twice a week."

"Does he know she's an informant?"

"That would kind of defeat the purpose."

"I'm asking if he or anyone suspects it."

"No reason to. She's into everything, has been for years. A shame. Came from a really good family but like a lot of kids, got into drugs. Heroin, oxys. Eventually started tricking, stealing, to support her habit. Did two years in prison for stabbing some guy who was pimping her—mistake was not killing the SOB. She gets out of prison and was right back at it. I got her into a meth clinic, into protected housing. Long and short of it, she's valuable to me and I don't want her dead."

As they drive past more rusting sheds, bump over railroad tracks, her cell phone rings several times. She doesn't answer it.

"I lost one a couple of Christmases ago," she goes on. "Got burned by a task force cop who had sex with her, decided to name her in an affidavit so no one would believe her if she ratted him out. So he rats her out first. Next thing, she's got a bullet in her head."

297

Her cell phone rings again, and she pushes a button to silence it. Four times now since they left the scrapyard, and she doesn't even look at the display to see who it is.

The state police forensic labs have a simple but basic protocol: Evidence you submit should be incontrovertibly associated with crime.

What Win has in several brown paper bags isn't incontrovertibly associated with anything except his own fears, his own sense of urgency. If Lamont is involved in something sinister and is implicating him, he intends to find out privately before he does anything about it. Imaginative guy that he is, it's the *why* part of the equation that has him completely bewildered and unnerved. Why would someone break into Nana's house and apparently steal nothing but his gym bag? Why would this person even know about Nana in the first place, or that Win stops by her house almost daily to check on her, or that he routinely leaves his gym bag because of her laundry magic, or that she routinely fails to lock her doors or set her alarm, making it simple to enter, grab, and run?

Inside the lab building, an officer named Johnny mans the front desk, engrossed in whatever he's looking at on his computer screen.

"How ya doing?" Win says.

"You seen this?" Pointing at the screen. "Friggin' unbelievable."

He plays the YouTube clip of Lamont in the ladies' room. It's the first Win's heard of it, and he analyzes it carefully. Green Escada suit, Gucci ostrich-skin pocketbook, and matching high-heel shoes, obviously filmed at the John F. Kennedy School of Government. He recalls that minutes after her lecture, she sent him away to get her a latte, and for about an hour, she was out of his sight. Irrelevant, he reasons. It wouldn't have been a big deal for someone to hide in the ladies' room as long as the person had thought this whole thing out, and obviously, someone put a lot of thought into it. Preplanning. A recon to see when she was going into the ladies' room, making sure it was empty before hiding in a stall. A woman. Or someone dressed like one. Could have been a man, if no one was looking.

"Was a lousy thing to do," Johnny is saying. "Someone did that to my wife, I'd kill 'em. Looks like you got a mess on your hands, though. Mick was in the director's office not even an hour ago, about the . . . What's her name? The murdered lady from the blind school that's all over the news."

"Janie Brolin."

'That's the one."

"Lamont probably sent Mick down here because she's worried about any alleged evidence, although I can't imagine anything relating to the case still exists. Regardless, she'd want to make sure none of the scientists talk to reporters," Win says. "That's what I think, anyway."

"So don't I." A Massachusetts native's weird way of saying

So do I. "To give her credit? Wow." Shakes his shaved head, watching Lamont on YouTube again. "She's so cold, you forget she's hot, you know what I'm saying? She's got some set of . . ."

"Tracy around?" Win says.

"Let me buzz her." Can't take his eyes off Lamont in the ladies' room.

Tracy's in, and Win follows a long corridor, bypasses evidence intake, walks into Crime Scene Services, where she's seated at her computer station, looking at two enlarged fingerprints on a split screen, arrows pointing to minutiae she's visually comparing.

"We're having a little argument," she says, not looking up.

Win sets down his paper bags.

She points to the left side of the screen, then to the right. "Computer counts three ridges between these two points. I'm counting four. As usual, the computer isn't seeing what I'm seeing. My fault, was in a hurry, didn't clean it up first, took a shortcut and ran it through auto Encode. Anyway, what can I do for you? Because whenever you drop by with little brown paper bags, it's a clue."

"A sort of official case, and another case that isn't official at all. So I'm really just asking for a favor."

"Who, you?"

"Can't tell you the details."

"Don't want to know. Ruins my objectivity and reinforces my basic belief that everybody's guilty."

"Okay. One Fresca can I fished out of the trash the other day. One Raggedy Ann note and envelope, don't laugh. Prints on the envelope. Could be from my damn landlord, whose prints you have in the database for exclusionary reasons, since he's touched stuff in the past. I didn't mess with the note, and the sender isn't really in doubt, but I'd like these items checked, including DNA under the envelope's flap and on the Fresca can, if you can beg, borrow, and steal from your DNA pals. We've also got a candle and a bottle of wine, a very nice pinot, may have my prints on it. Maybe the lady in the wineshop, whose prints will also be in the database for exclusionary reasons, since she's also a cop. I've got photographs of shoe impressions, and the nine-mil cartridge I used for a scale. Didn't have a ruler handy, sorry."

"And what is it you want me to do with these shoe impressions?"

"Hang on to them for now, in case we recover something to compare them with." Such as his pair of stolen Prada shoes, should they ever surface.

"Finally," he says, "there's the packaging from a disposable camera."

"We've gotten in a number of them of late from different departments, all Middlesex County."

"I know, and the cops think you can't be bothered."

"I really can't be bothered," she says. "Their crime scene guys haven't found anything on them, and send them in anyway, in hopes we have a magic wand, I guess. Maybe they watch too much TV."

"You talking about the FRONT's crime scene guys?"

"Probably," she says.

"Well, that would be one guy, who's a woman, and she doesn't believe in magic wands," Win says. "And since my disposable camera package is the same kind as the ones you've already gotten, how about we make them a priority, a *do-it-now* sort of thing. And I have an idea."

"Whenever you come in here with your trick-or-treat bags, it's a *do-it-now* sort of thing, and you always have ideas."

"What would you expect a copper thief to have all over his person, including his hands?" Win asks.

"Dirt. Since he's probably touching dirty old oxidized gutters, roofing materials, all kinds of crap at construction sites . . ."

"Forget dirt. I'm talking about what might not be visible," Win says. "I'm talking microscopic."

"You want to examine these damn camera boxes under a microscope?"

"No," he says. "Luminol. I want you to check as if you're looking for blood."

He's ordering an iced coffee at Starbucks when he feels somebody behind him. Glances around. Cal Tradd.

At least he has the decency not to strike up a conversation in a public place. Win pays, grabs napkins, a straw, heads outside and waits by his car, waits for an overdue confrontation. In a few minutes, Cal appears, sipping one of those coffee drinks that looks like an ice-cream sundae. Piled high with whipped cream, chocolate, a cherry on top.

"You following me?" Win asks. "Because I'm feeling followed."

"I'm that obvious, huh?" Licking whipped cream, wearing nice sunglasses. Maui Jim's, about three hundred bucks. "Actually, I was heading to the police department. Probably just like you are. Otherwise, I don't think you'd be jarring your already jangled nerves with several shots of espresso at a Starbucks in little ole Watertown. Anyway, noticed your car."

"Really? How'd you know it was mine?"

"I know your apartment building. Matter of fact, almost rented a place there my freshman year. Second floor, the south end, overlooking that teeny-tiny square of blacktop in back where Farouk lets you park your Ducati, your Harley, your Hummer, this thing"—indicating the Buick—"whatever you happen to be riding or driving."

Win stares at him, sunglasses to sunglasses.

"Ask Farouk. He'll remember me," Cal says. "Skinny little blond kid whose overly protective mother decided her precious, fragile boy couldn't possibly live in your former school building. Not that the location's dangerous, in reality. But you know how people make judgments based on a person's appearance, demeanor, socioeconomic status. And here I am—rich, a musician, a writer, straight A's, faggy-looking. A walking hate crime waiting to happen." Dips his tongue back into the whipped cream. "I saw you that ill-fated day, by the way. No reason you'd remember. But we were leaving and you trotted by, jumped in your unmarked Crown Vic and sped off. And my mom said, 'Good God in heaven, who's that gorgeous man?' Small world, huh?"

"Save your six-degrees-of-separation crap for someone else. I'm not talking to you," Win says.

"I didn't ask you to talk. You'd be better off listening." Watching traffic go by on Mt. Auburn Street, a major thoroughfare that connects Watertown to Cambridge.

Win opens his car door.

Cal sucks on the straw, says, "I've been working on an investigative series about copper thefts—an international problem, huge, as you well know. There's this nutcase woman. Cunning in some ways, stupid in others, and overall, crazy."

Raggedy Ann, Win thinks.

"I've seen her around in places and situations that have my antenna up—way up," Cal continues. "There's this guy Bimbo. A real Ali Baba scumbag. I've interviewed him a couple times. So maybe three hours ago, I show up at his den of thieves to talk some more, and there she is, collecting cash from him. Same weirdo I've seen around Harvard Square, dressed all freaky like Raggedy Ann. Same weirdo I've seen hanging around Monique on a number of occasions."

"Hanging around her? How so?" Win leans against the car, crosses his arms.

Cal shrugs, sips his chocolaty coffee. "Places where she's

given talks, doing press conferences, outside the law school, the courthouse. I've seen this weirdo lady at least half a dozen times in the past few weeks, always dressed in tights, clunky shoes. I didn't think much about it until I recognized her at the scrapyard today. Dressed completely differently, in baggy clothes, a baseball cap. Selling scrap copper. I just thought you'd want to know."

"You ask what's-his-name about her?"

"Bimbo? Sure did. Said the expected. Didn't know anything. Translated, she's selling stolen stuff, right?"

"Then what?"

"Followed her for a while. She has this Woodstock-era VW van, curtains in the windows, probably sleeps in the damn thing. We're not even across the Mystic River when I get this feeling somebody's following me. Another van. This one a construction-type van, maybe one I'd seen earlier at Bimbo's. So I got the hell out of Dodge, got off in Charlestown."

"You mean the intrepid reporter gave up the chase?"

"These copper thugs in Chelsea, you kidding me?" Cal says. "Screw with them and you end up in a car trunk with your throat cut."

7

A sergeant lets Win into a cramped, dank space, dimly lit, nothing inside but old metal filing cabinets and shelves stacked with dusty logbooks and boxes. The Watertown Police Department's records room is a former bank vault, one floor below the jail.

"I don't guess you have some sort of reference system for what's in here," Win says.

"Oh, I'm sorry. The librarian's out sick today and her ten assistants are on vacation. You find what you want, pull the record. No photocopying. No pictures. You can take notes. That's it."

The air is thick with dust and the smell of mold. Already Win feels his sinuses closing up.

"How about I find what I need and you put me upstairs someplace. Maybe in the detective division," Win says. "An interview room would work."

"Jeez, more bad news. The UN's in town, tying up the conference room. The records got to stay in here, meaning if you want to look at them, you got to stay in here."

"This the only light?"

Fluorescent light tubes, one dead, the other losing its will to live.

"Can you believe it? All our maintenance guys are on strike." The sergeant disappears with his big ring of keys.

Win turns on his tactical light, swipes it over shelves of large logbooks, decades of them going back to the twenties. No way. Without photocopies, he'll never get through these reports, would be like bushwhacking his way through a jungle without a machete. Under ordinary circumstances, given plenty of time, he manages to sort through dense pages of information, or, best of all, he's *so busy* he has one of the clerks in the unit read aloud on CD, which he downloads into his computer as an audio file. Amazing what he listens to as he drives, works out in the gym, jogs. By the time he goes to court, he's memorized every pertinent detail.

He climbs a stepladder, pulls down the log for 1962, looks for a work space, resorts to an open file drawer, places the log on top of it, starts flipping through pages, starts sneezing, his eyes itching, miserable. April 4, and he finds the handwritten entry for Janie Brolin's murder. He jots down the location of the crime—meaning her address, since she was murdered inside her apartment—and that one simple fact completely changes the scenario. He can't understand it. Nobody noticed? The Boston Strangler? You've got to be kidding. He keeps going through drawers. Cases aren't filed alphabetically but by an accession number that ends with the year. Her case is WT218-62. He scans labels on file drawers, opens what should be the right one, finds records jammed together so tightly he has to take out sections of them at a time or he can't see what's there.

He pulls the Brolin case, then riffles through dozens of files in the same drawer, having learned long ago it's not uncommon for information from one file to accidentally find its way into another. After an hour of itching, sneezing, his mouth tasting like dust, he comes across an envelope wedged in the back of the drawer, and written on it is the Brolin case number. Inside is a yellowed newspaper clipping about a twenty-six-year-old man named Lonnie Parris, struck by a car while crossing the street near the Chicken Delight on Massachusetts Avenue in Cambridge. A hit-and-run that occurred in the early-morning hours of April 5—the day after Janie Brolin's murder. That's it. Just an old newspaper clipping.

Why the hell would a hit-and-run have the Brolin case number on it? He can't find the file for the Lonnie Parris death, probably because it's a Cambridge case. Frustrated, he tries his iPhone, can't get on the Internet or even make a call from down here in this cave. He leaves the records room, trots up a flight of stairs, finds himself in the jail's booking room. Cameras, a Breathalyzer, property lockers, and handcuffs dangling from nails along the walls to make sure prisoners behave while waiting their turn to be fingerprinted and have their mug shots taken.

Dammit, no signal in here, either. He steps behind the desk to try the landline phone but doesn't know the code to dial out.

"Stump? That you?" A loud voice startles him.

The jail cells, some inmate. Female. Probably held until she can be transferred to the jail on the top floor of the Middlesex County courthouse.

"I've had enough now, okay, already?" The voice again. "That you?"

Win walks past empty cells, heavy metal doors open wide, catches the faint ammonia stench of urine. The fourth cell door is shut, and posted on it is Q5+. The code for suicide risk.

"Stump?"

"I can get her for you," Win says, peering through the small mesh window, not believing what he sees.

Raggedy Ann sits cross-legged on a slab of a bed inside a cinder-block cell not much bigger than a closet.

"How you doing?" he says. "You need something?"

"Where's Stump? I want Stump!"

On the wall next to the door is a collect telephone for prisoners. It has a direct line out, and across from it on a windowsill is a bottle of hand sanitizer.

"I'm hungry!" she says.

"What they got you locked up for?"

"Geronimo," she says. "I know you."

Now he's hearing her accent, remembers what Farouk said about the so-called shorty. A white woman who talked "black."

"You know me? How's that? Except for our running into each other now and then," he says, nicely enough.

"I don't got nothing to say to you. Get out of my face."

"I can get you something to eat, if you want," he says.

"Cheeseburger, fries, and Diet Coke," she says.

"Dessert?" Win asks her.

"I don't eat nothing sweet."

Fresca, Diet Coke, nothing sweet. Kind of unusual for a junkie, he thinks. Most recovering heroin addicts can't get enough sugar. At least one good thing about looking through a metal mesh–covered window, he can study her without being obvious. Same baggy clothes she had on at the scrapyard. Her sneakers still have their laces. Unusual for a suicide risk. Of course, the jail cell has no towel racks, no window with bars, not even handles on the stainless-steel sink. Nothing to loop a belt, shoelaces, or even clothing around if you wanted to hang yourself.

Without her freakish rag doll getup, she looks more like a street urchin who might be pretty were it not for her curly red hair sticking up everywhere, her nervous mannerisms. Plucking at her fingers. Wetting her lips. Rapidly tapping one of her feet. No matter what he's heard about her, he can't help feeling pity. He knows that people don't grow up fantasizing about being a drug addicted prostitute or a homeless person who eats out of garbage cans. Most tormented souls who end up like Raggedy Ann started out with bad genetic loading, or abuse, or both, and their subsequent debilitating problems are hell on earth.

He picks up the receiver of the red wall phone, wipes it down with the hand sanitizer, and places a collect call.

The operator tells Stump that Win Garano is on the line and will she accept charges.

"You're calling me collect?" she says. "Where are you?"

"Your jail." His voice. "I don't mean in it."

She tenses up. "What happened?"

"Dropped by your records room. My cell phone wouldn't work in there. Looked for a landline and guess who's staying at your charming little B and B?"

"What's she told you?"

"She needs to see you. Wants a cheeseburger. Excuse me." Obviously to Raggedy Ann. "How you want that cooked?" A murmur. Then back to Stump. "Medium, hold the mayo. Extra pickles."

"I'm rather busy at the moment. I realize you've probably forgotten I moonlight as a successful businesswoman." Stump holds the phone between her shoulder and ear, places a block of Swiss on the slicer.

It's that time of day when customers come in all at once, and there's a long line at the deli counter. One impatient woman is waiting to be rung up, and two more people are walking in. Pretty soon—thanks to Win—she's going to lose control over every aspect of her life. *Damn him.* Wandering into the jail. If that isn't her bad luck. All he seems to bring her is bad luck.

"She's also getting cranky," Win adds.

"I'll be right there," Stump says to him. To the pushy woman at the deli counter, she says, "Be with you in just a minute."

"What's a good wine with smoked salmon?"

"A dry Sancerre or Moscato d'Asti. Third aisle." Back to Win. "Just tell her I'm on my way, and then get out of there and wait for me. I'll explain."

"You want to give me a hint?"

"Safekeeping. Had a little problem after I dropped you off at your car."

Never occurring to her, of course, that he intended to end up at her department, in the records room. Even if she'd known, she wouldn't have assumed he might take a tour of the damn jail.

"Wait a minute. She's saying something to me. Oh, yeah. Add fries, and I forgot the Diet Coke." His voice.

The feeling it gives her. The feeling he gives her, and it's getting worse. She doesn't know what she's going to do. It wasn't supposed to be like this. It was supposed to be relatively simple. He would show up at the department, work Lamont's

case, and leave. Even the chief said this trumped-up investigation wasn't Stump's problem and not to worry about it or get
involved. *Jesus God.* In the beginning, this was all about
Lamont. Win was a minor character and now has gotten
bigger than the great outdoors.

"Meet me in the parking lot in twenty, thirty minutes,"
Stump says to him.

He's inside Nana's car, waiting, when a red BMW 2002 pulls
up next to him.

"I'm impressed," he says, as Stump rolls down her window.
"Nineteen seventy-three, looks like the original paint job and
bumpers. Verona red? Always wanted one of these. Black
leather looks original, too. Only the seals and window felt look
new. From here, I mean. You had this since you were what?
Five, maybe six?" He notes the Wendy's bag in the backseat,
adds, "So what happened to land your special friend in jail for
safekeeping?"

"Soon as she left Bimbo's, she went to Filene's."

"How does she get around? Been meaning to ask."

"Piece-of-junk Mini Cooper. She ended up at Filene's,
shoplifted some makeup and a Sony Walkman."

"That makes her a suicide risk?"

"Q-five-positive status signals the department to check on
her, but she's unstable, easily set off. In other words, just the
sort you prefer to avoid."

"Anybody ever mention you're a lousy liar?" Win says. "Filene's doesn't carry electronics. Not possible she shoplifted a Walkman. And I don't think she drives a Mini Cooper."

"Why can't you pick up signals? Quit interrogating me about things that are none of your concern."

"I pick up on signals just fine. Especially when they're as subtle as a sonic boom. Here's a hint. Don't fabricate details about places you've never been, like big discount department stores that don't have private, spacious dressing rooms and a small, discreet staff. Not that I'm assuming you take off your prosthesis when you try on jeans, slacks, for example. But if nothing else, you probably have a few select places you frequent—probably small places, boutiques, maybe, where they know you."

"There was a problem after we left the scrapyards," Stump says. "She attracted attention from the wrong person, someone who followed her."

"Got any ideas?" To see if maybe, just maybe, Stump might tell the truth.

"Said some van, like a construction van. She was scared maybe some bad dude from the scrapyards got suspicious, followed her. She freaked out, called me, and I had her pulled by a marked car and arrested."

"Charged with what?"

"Said I had a warrant for her arrest, and she called to turn herself in. Said she'd been charged with selling stolen copper."

"You said it wasn't really stolen. Was like flash money.

And you can't arrest somebody without a hard copy of a warrant. . . ."

"Look. The point was to ensure her safety. End of story. I had her locked up. If she really was being followed, then whoever was doing it had ample opportunity to see her pulled, cuffed, put in the back of the patrol car. I'll let her out once it's dark."

"This mean she's done at the scrapyards?"

"If she doesn't go back at some point, it will confirm the suspicion there might be something up with her. That maybe she's working with the police. Assuming it's true that someone from the scrapyards was following her."

He passes on what Cal told him.

"Great. All I need is a damn reporter screwing with things," she replies. "These people are ruthless. He'd better watch out he doesn't get himself killed. What are you doing down here?"

She looks good in her red BMW, and her face is pretty in the late-afternoon light.

He says, "My, how quickly we forget. My mundane assignment of solving a forty-five-year-old homicide that might be connected to the Boston Strangler. Even though I know it can't be."

"Amazing if you've already determined that. In fact, I'd call it miraculous. You divine it, or what?"

"A glance at your records. You know much about the history of the Mafia in this quaint town of yours?"

"As I've mentioned before, my quaint town was a better place in the heyday of the Mob. Don't quote me."

"The apartment complex she lived in was on Galen Street, about a two-minute walk from Piccolo's Pharmacy, which isn't there anymore, of course."

"And?"

"Southside. Huge Mob neighborhood. Most of the apartments and houses all around Janie Brolin were occupied by Mob guys. All kinds of stuff going on, whatever you wanted. Numbers, jewelry, prostitution, illegal abortions, all around Piccolo's Pharmacy, Galen and Watertown streets. Why do you think there was no crime down there in the days of yore? I mean none."

"Where the hell do you get all this?" She cuts the engine of her BMW. "You see some movie or something?"

"Just things I've heard over the years, a few books here and there. You know, I'm in the car a lot. Listen to them on tape, CD, have an okay memory. Janie Brolin was murdered on April fourth. A Wednesday. Wednesdays were collection day, all kinds of people showing up to get paid by the bookies. Always the same day, eyes and ears all over the place. So you should think about that. Why was she an exception to the rule, the only murder—ever—in Southside during the early sixties, especially on collection day. Plus the Feds doing their thing. So ask yourself. The cops, the Feds didn't know who killed the girl? You really believe that?"

Stump gets out of her car, says, "You'd better not be making this up."

"Gives me the feeling the cops were in on it. As in a cover-up. You know the old saying, Don't screw with a Mafia guy unless you've got one with you."

"Translated?"

"Collusion. A team effort. Not a sexual homicide at all, period. You remember who was president in 1962?" he says.

They start walking toward the police department.

"Damn," she says. "Now you're really spooking me."

"Right. JFK. Before that he was a senator in Massachusetts, born right over there in Brookline. You know the theories about his assassination. The Mob. Who knows? Probably never will. But my point is, some Boston Strangler lowlife wouldn't have dared step foot anywhere near Janie Brolin's apartment. And if he was so stupid he didn't know any better, he would have ended up in the Dorchester Bay, dismembered, an ax buried in his chest."

"You've got my attention," Stump says.

An hour later, both of them are in the records room, going through Janie Brolin's case file. She's using his tactical light, and he's taking notes.

"Your clout and we can't go to your office or something?" Win says, his eyes and throat itching again.

"You don't understand. There are four of us in one small office, not including the house mouse." Meaning the administrative officer. "Everybody hearing everything the other person's saying. Cops talk. Do I need to tell you that?"

"Okay. The weather." Win flips back through his notes. "Anything about the weather on April fourth?"

"Not on any of these reports." Stump has Janie Brolin's file open, doing what Win did earlier, using a drawer as a table because there's nowhere else to work.

"What about newspaper articles?" he asks.

She looks at a few. Old, sharp creases from having been folded for more than forty years.

She says, "A mention that when the police arrived at her apartment around eight a.m., it was raining."

"Let's go over what we know so far. Janie's boyfriend, Lonnie Parris, groundskeeper/maintenance guy for Perkins, picked her up for work every morning at seven-thirty. This particular morning, he shows up, she doesn't answer the door, it's not locked. He comes in, finds her dead, and calls the police. When the cops arrive, Lonnie's gone. Has fled the scene, immediately making him a suspect."

"Why would he call the police? If he's the one who killed her," Stump wonders.

"Back to the facts as stated in these reports. Another question." He looks through photographs. "It's supposedly raining by the time the cops arrive. They're all over the scene. Or should be. You notice anything unusual about that?"

Stump looks at the photographs, and it doesn't take her long to observe. "The carpet. A cream color that shows dirt. It's raining and all these people in and out? Why is the carpet clean?"

"Exactly," Win agrees. "Maybe not as many cops in there as we're supposed to believe? Maybe somebody cleaned up the place just enough to get rid of incriminating evidence? Let's keep going."

"Postmortem took place at a funeral home? That's unusual, too, isn't it?" Stump says.

"Not back then." Flipping a page of his legal pad.

"Cause of death, asphyxiation from being strangled with a ligature, which was the bra tied around her neck." She reads on. "Petechiae of the conjunctivae. Hemorrhage over the back of the larynx and soft tissue over the cervical spine."

"Consistent with strangulation," Win says. "What about other injuries? Bruises, cuts, bite marks, broken fingernails, broken bones, whatever."

Stump scans the report, studies diagrams, says, "Looks like she had bruises around her wrists. . . ."

"You mean ligature marks. From her wrists being tied to the chair legs."

"Not just those," Stump says. "It also says there are marks around her wrists *consistent with fingertip bruises.* . . ."

"Suggesting he grabbed her wrists or gripped them tightly." Win keeps making notes. "She struggled with him."

"Not possible they're postmortem? From him dragging the body, moving it when he positioned it?"

"Someone grabbed her wrists while she still had a blood pressure," Win says. "You don't bruise when you're dead."

"Same kind of bruises around her upper arms," Stump

says. "And also her hips, buttocks, ankles. It's like everywhere he touched her, it turned into a bruise."

"Keep going. What else?"

"You're right about broken fingernails," she says.

"Defensive. She may have scratched him," Win says. "I hope they swabbed under her nails. Although they didn't do DNA testing back then. But they could have checked for ABO blood types."

The reports are there. Swabs were taken of various orifices. Negative for seminal fluid. Nothing from under her nails, Stump tells him. Maybe they didn't look. Forensic investigations were different back then, to put it mildly.

"What about a tox report?" Win asks, writing in his unique shorthand. Abbreviations and spelling that only he can decipher. "Any mention of alcohol, drugs?"

A few minutes of going through the file and she finds a report from the chemical laboratory on Commonwealth Avenue in Boston. "Negative for drugs and alcohol, although this is interesting." She holds up a police report. "States in the narrative that she was suspected of drug use."

"No drugs in the apartment?" Win frowns. It makes no sense. "What about alcohol in the apartment?"

"Looking," she says.

"Anything on her autopsy report that might indicate she had a history of alcohol abuse, drug abuse?"

"No mention that I can find."

"Then why would someone suggest she might have a

history of drug use? What about her trash? Anything found in her trash? What about her medicine cabinet? What was removed from the scene?"

"Here we go," Stump says. "A used syringe with a bent needle in a wastepaper basket. In the bathroom. And in the medicine cabinet, a vial of an unknown substance."

"Certainly the vial must have gone to the lab. The syringe, as well. No report on those?"

"Evidence, evidence . . ." Talking to herself, looking through the files. "Yes, the syringe and vial were submitted. Negative for drugs. Says the vial had, and I quote, 'an oily solution in it with unknown particulate.'"

"Keep going," Win says, writing as fast as he can. "What else was recovered from the scene?"

"Her clothes," Stump reads. "Skirt, blouse, stockings, shoes . . . You can see them in the photos. Her purse, wallet. A keychain with a Saint Christopher's medal—glad he protected her—and two keys. One an apartment key, the other a key to her office at Perkins, it says here. Those things were by the door, on the floor. Dumped out of her purse."

"Let me look again." Win takes all of the photographs from her, spends some time studying each one.

The scene, the morgue. Nothing he didn't notice earlier, except the scenario is making less sense to him. Her bed was made, and it appears she was dressed for work when she was attacked. A vial found, a used syringe, an unknown substance. Negative drug and alcohol screen.

"Dermatitis on her torso. A rash," Stump reads. "Maybe some sexually transmitted disease? Examination conducted by a Dr. William Hunter, Harvard's Department of Legal Medicine."

"Used to do the medico-legal investigations for the state police," Win says. "Back in the late thirties, the forties. Started by Frances Glessner Lee, this amazing woman into forensics way before her time. Unfortunately, the department she funded doesn't exist anymore."

"You think any of the evidence would still be left?" Stump asks. "Maybe at the Boston ME's office?"

"Wasn't around back then," Win says. "Not until the early eighties. Pathologists at Harvard worked cases as a public service. Any existing records would be at Countway Medical Library at Harvard. But they don't warehouse evidence. And digging around in there could take years."

He looks at photographs taken in Janie Brolin's bedroom. Ransacked drawers, clothing scattered on the floor. Perfume bottles, a hairbrush on top of a dresser, and something else. A pair of dark glasses.

Puzzled, he says, "Why do people who are blind or visually impaired wear dark glasses?"

Stump replies, "I guess to alert others that they're blind. And for self-conscious reasons—to cover their eyes."

"Right. It's not about the weather. About it being sunny," Win says. "I'm not saying that blind eyes aren't sensitive to light, but that's not why blind people wear dark glasses, including indoors. Here." He shows Stump the photograph. "If she were dressed for work, waiting to be picked up, and was ready to go, then why were her dark glasses in her bedroom? Why wasn't she wearing them? Why didn't she have them with her?"

"It was raining, a dark, gloomy day . . ."

"But blind people don't wear dark glasses because of the weather. You just said it yourself," he says.

"Maybe she forgot them for some reason. Maybe she was in the bedroom when someone showed up, interrupted her. Could be a number of reasons."

"Maybe," he says. "Maybe not."

"What are you thinking?"

"I'm thinking we should go get something to eat," Win says.

8

Nine p.m. The FBI's field office in Boston. Special Agent McClure uses the Cyber Task Force's network sniffer to capture Internet traffic of interest.

Specifically, data that fit the profile of e-mail sent from Monique Lamont's IP address and received from another address, also in Cambridge. She's been busy of late, and McClure has to surf through all of her communications, even if they couldn't possibly have anything to do with terrorism and the suspicion she's funding it through a Romanian children's-relief fund that may very well be connected to a nonprofit organization called FOIL. The FBI is becoming increasingly convinced there's a growing terrorist cell in Cambridge, and Lamont is financially supporting it.

Wouldn't surprise McClure in the least. All those radical students—Harvard, Tufts, MIT—who believe the Constitution ensures that they can do and say pretty much anything they want, even if it's anti-American. For example, holding demonstrations to oppose the war in Iraq, rallying for separation of church and state, disrespecting the flag, and, most personally offensive to the Bureau, vehement attacks on the Patriot Act, which rightly allows the very thing McClure is this moment doing: spying on a private citizen without a court order so other private citizens can be protected from other terrorist attacks or the fear of them. Understandably, there are misfires. Bank accounts, medical records, e-mails, telephone conversations that turn out to be unfortunate violations of people who turn out to have no terrorist involvement whatsoever.

The way McClure views it, however, is that almost everyone who is spied on is guilty of something. Like that John Deere salesman in Iowa a few months back who suddenly came up with enough cash to pay off the fifty thousand dollars he owed various credit-card companies. When his account was automatically flagged, further investigation revealed he had a second cousin whose college roommate's nephew married a woman whose sister's stepdaughter was, for a while, the lesbian lover of a woman whose best friend was a secretary at the Embassy of the Islamic Republic of Iran in Ottawa. Maybe the John Deere salesman wasn't involved in terrorism, but as it turned out, he was buying marijuana allegedly for medical purposes because of alleged nausea due to chemotherapy treatments.

McClure reads an e-mail sent to Lamont in real time.

I won't withdraw this easily. How can you, after all you've invested in the only true and pure passion you've ever had in your life? Problem is, you want it until it no longer suits, as if it's yours alone to walk away from, and guess what? This time you're into something you can't control. I'm capable of causing destruction that will exceed anything you could possibly imagine. It's time I show you exactly what I mean. The usual place, tomorrow night at ten. —Me.

Lamont replies.

Okay.

Special Agent McClure forwards the e-mail to Jeremy Killien at Scotland Yard, and writes:

Project FOIL reaching critical mass.

The hell with it, McClure thinks twice. Who cares what time it is over there? Scotland Yard guys can be yanked out of bed the same way FBI agents can. Why should Killien get special consideration? In fact, it would be a pleasure to annoy

Detective Superintendent Sherlock. The damn Brits. What have they done except focus on Lamont because of her latest publicity stunt, which caused them to find out she's under investigation, which in turn forced the Bureau to step things up so the Yard doesn't take the credit. It wasn't the Brits who first flagged her as a potential terrorist threat, after all, and now they think they can storm in and steal the Bureau's thunder.

McClure makes the call.

A couple of British-sounding rings, and Killien's sleepy British voice.

"Read your e-mail," McClure says to him.

"Hold on." Not exactly gracious about it.

McClure can hear Killien carrying the portable phone into another room. Hears keys clicking, muttering "damn bloody slow" and "almost got it up. Well, that didn't come out right, did it. There we are. Good God. Don't like the sound of that."

"I think we need to move on it," McClure advises. "Don't see how it can wait. Question's whether you want to be here. On such short notice. I understand it's not . . ."

"No option there," Killien interrupts. "I'll make my arrangements straightaway."

Win apologizes for serving tomatoes that aren't homegrown.

"As if I don't know. I happen to be an expert in produce," Stump says, sitting some distance from him in his living room. "In fact, you'll probably think this is an awful confession for me to make, but my real job is my market. My father started it from nothing, and it would break his heart if I let him down. But about tomatoes. An insider's tip. Best ones are from Verrill Farm, but we've got a couple months to go, depending on how much rain we get. I love being a cop, but the market loves me back."

The lights are low, his apartment filled with the tantalizing aroma of hickory-smoked bacon. Fresh tomatoes or not, the BLT Win fixed tastes about as good as anything she's ever eaten, and the French Chablis he opened is crisp and clean and perfect. Stump looks out at a typical Cambridge view. Old brick buildings, slate roofs, and lighted windows. When he suggested getting something to eat, she assumed he meant a late-night dinner, was excited and unnerved when he suggested his place. She should have said no. She watches him eating his sandwich and sipping his wine, and feels even more certain that she should have said no. When he lit a candle on the coffee table and turned out the lights, she knew for a fact she'd just made a tactical error.

She sets down her place, says, "I really should be going."

"Not polite to eat and run."

"You can call me tomorrow if you need more help. But . . ." She starts to get up but seems to be made of stone.

"You're scared of me, aren't you?" he says in the soft, moving light. "Were scared of me long before I got thrown into this case and then pulled you down with me."

"I don't know you. And I tend to be wary of the unfamiliar. Especially if I try to put together pieces and they don't fit."

"What pieces?"

"Where do I start?"

"Wherever you want. Then I'll get to all your pieces that don't fit." His eyes pick up the candlelight.

"I think I need another glass of wine," she says.

"Was just about to do that." He refills their glasses, the leather couch creaking as he moves close.

She smells him, feels his arm barely brushing her sleeve, feels his presence like gravity. Pulling her in.

"Um. Well." Sips her wine. "Start with this. Why do they call you Geronimo?"

"Not sure who *they* are. But why don't you venture a guess. This should be good."

"A mighty warrior. Always on the warpath. Maybe someone who makes potentially fatal leaps. Remember when we were kids? You jump off the high dive and yell 'Geronimo'?"

"Didn't have access to a pool when I was a kid."

"Oh, no. You're not going to give me some discrimination sob story, are you? I happen to know that when you were a kid, people of color were allowed in public schools."

"Didn't say it was about discrimination. I just didn't have access to a pool. The *they* you're talking about is my grandmother. She's the one who nicknamed me Geronimo. Not because of his warrior status or fatal leaps or whatever but because of his eloquence. He said, 'I cannot think that we are useless or God would not have created us. And the sun, the darkness, the winds are all listening to what we have to say.'"

Something catches in her chest. "I don't see the connection," she says.

"Between those words and the person sitting next to you? Maybe I'll tell you, but it's your turn. Why Stump? Honestly speaking? I can't think of any good reason for anybody to call you Stump."

"The World War Two Navy destroyer, USS *Stump*," she says.

"I thought that might be it."

"Seriously. My father came here to escape Mussolini, every horror you can think of when you conjure up that monstrous period of history. One that I hope to hell is never repeated, or I'll believe our entire civilization is damned."

"I worry we're already damned. Worry about it more every day. I'd probably move if there was a good place to run."

"Imagine how the old-timers feel. My dad watches the news three, four hours a day, says he keeps hoping if he watches long enough, things will get better. He's depressed. Sees a psychiatrist. I pay out of pocket because . . . Well, don't get me started on health coverage and all the rest of it. When I was a kid, he started calling me Stump because of the war hero the ship was named after. Admiral Felix Stump, known for his gallantry, his fearlessness. The ship named after him had the motto: 'Tenacity: Foundation of Victory.' My father always said the secret to success is simply not giving up. Kind of a cool thing to tell a little girl."

"When you had your motorcycle accident, didn't it ever occur to you to change your nickname?"

"And how do you do that?" She looks at him, and for reasons she can't fathom, what he just said hurts. "People have called you Stump most of your life and suddenly you tell them, 'Hey, now that half my leg's been amputated, don't call me Stump anymore.' It would be like not calling you Geronimo anymore because you got whacked out and leapt off your balcony or something, paralyzed yourself."

"I'm not reading into this that you might have had suicidal thoughts when you crashed your motorcycle into a guardrail, am I?"

Reaching for her wine, she says, "I don't guess Lamont's ever mentioned my accident. Since she never's really mentioned me, according to you."

"She's never mentioned you, according to her. Never once except the other morning when she said I'd be working with you. Which, by the way, wasn't true at that time, because you had no intention of helping."

"There's good reason why she doesn't talk about me," Stump says. "And there's good reason why she'll probably always regret I didn't die in that accident."

Win is quiet for a moment, looking out the window, drinking his wine. She feels his distance, as if the air between them just got cooler, and anxiety and guilt rush back at her with force. What she's doing is wrong. What she's done is wrong. She gets up from the couch.

"Thanks," she says. "I'd best head out."

He doesn't move. Just stares out the window. The candle-light moving on his profile makes her ache.

"If you need any further help with reports, other paper-work, well, I'm happy to. Anytime," she says.

He turns his head, looks up at her. "What?"

"I'm saying it's not a problem. No big deal." Her feet don't want to move. "You forget who you're talking to." Why doesn't she shut up. "I know when someone has a hard time reading. Another one of those pieces that doesn't fit. Yet one more way you fool people." She's suddenly on the verge of tears. "I don't know why you feel you have to lie about it. To me. I've known it for about as long as I've known you. All those times you come in my shop, ask clever questions to disguise the fact that you can't read the ingredients on a damn jar of marinara sauce. . . ."

He stands up, moves close to her, almost menacingly.

"You've got to get past it, that's all," she says, and it crosses her mind that he might hurt her.

Maybe she's goading him into it. Because she deserves it, after what she's done.

"Then both of us are lame," he says.

"That's a terrible word. Don't ever use it around me. Don't ever use it around yourself," she says.

He grips her shoulders, is inches from her face, as if he's about to kiss her, and her heart pounds so hard it throbs in her neck.

"What happened between you and Lamont?" he says. "You asked me the same question. Now I'm asking you."

"It's not what you think."

"How the hell do you know what I think?"

"I know exactly what you think. Exactly what somebody like you would think. All guys like you think about is sex. So if something happens that someone can't talk about, it has to be about sex. Well, what she did to me is about sex, all right."

She pulls him down to the couch, forces his hand on her lower leg, knocks it against her prosthesis, and it makes a hollow sound.

"Don't," he says, almost on top of her, the light of the candle gently shaking the darkness. "Don't do this," he says, sitting up.

"The night we were at Sacco's. She drank at least a bottle of wine by herself, went on about her father, this aristocrat, rich, some internationally prominent lawyer, and how she never meant anything to him and how much she feared it had messed her up, made her act out in ways she didn't really understand and was sorry about later. Well, there's this guy, and he's been staring at her, flirting with her all night. She ends up bringing him back to my house, and they go at it in my bedroom. I'm the one who slept on the couch."

Silence. Win starts rubbing the back of her neck.

"He was this loser, this stupid, crude, ignorant loser, and as luck would have it, a convicted felon she'd sent to prison a few years earlier. Of course, she didn't remember. All the people who go through her court, so many damn cases you can't remember faces, names. But he remembered her. Which is why he hit on her in the bar to begin with."

"She did something stupid," Win says quietly. "And you were there to see it. Is it really such a big deal?"

"It was to pay her back. To screw her good, as he put it. To screw her worse than she screwed him, he was yelling that morning on his way out my door. Then what does she do? She pulls his case, does a little digging, finds out he's in violation of his parole. Goes back to jail for six months, a year, I don't remember. One day, he and a couple of his redneck buddies see me filling my Harley at a Mobil station on Route Two, follow me, and he starts whooping at me out his window, yelling, making sure I saw his face right before he ran me into the guardrail."

Win pulls her against him, rests his chin on top of her head. "She know?" he asks.

"Oh, sure. Couldn't do anything about it, though, now could we? Or it would come out in court how I first met the guy. How my thinking it was safer to let the two of them have sex in my bedroom instead of her disappearing with some jerk she'd just met in a bar. How my treating her like a friend, in other words, ultimately lost me a leg."

He touches it, traces it with his finger, over her knee, rests his hand on her thigh, says, "It's not about sex. Not the way you mean it. She couldn't ruin that part of you if she tried."

*

335

The pathologist who performed the autopsy on Janie Brolin lives on a narrow inlet of the Sudbury River, in an odd little house on an odd property as overgrown as Nana's.

The patio in back is missing bricks and almost completely covered with ivy. An old wooden canoe is stranded in a yard scattered with bright yellow daffodils, violets, and pansies. Win rings the bell, showing up unannounced, and already his day is starting out badly because of good news from the labs. Tracy found prints.

His idea of trying luminol paid off in one respect—a latent print fluoresced on the disposable camera package he found in the Victorian mansion, meaning whoever touched the cardboard had a copper residue on at least one of his fingers. Copper and blood both fluoresce when sprayed with luminol, a common crime scene problem that in this instance worked to Win's advantage. Unfortunately, the copper-residue print doesn't match anyone in the AFIS database. As for other prints? The ones on the wine bottle came back to Stump and Win, and as for Farouk, he left several partials on the envelope he touched. The Fresca can and note from Raggedy Ann both have prints that match one another but don't match anybody in AFIS, either.

Stump lied.

Now's not the time to think about it, he tells himself as he rings Dr. Hunter's doorbell again.

How could she? In his arms, in his bed, staying with him until four a.m. He just made love to a lie.

"Who is it?"

Win identifies himself as state police.

"Come around to the window and give me proof," a strong voice says through the door.

Win moves to one side of the porch, holds his credentials up to the glass. An old man in a three-wheel mini-scooter peers at the creds, then at Win, seems satisfied, drives back to the door, and lets him in.

"Safe as it is around here, I've seen too much. Wouldn't trust a girl scout," Dr. Hunter says, driving into a wormy chestnut living room that overlooks the water. On a desk is a computer and a router, piles of books and papers.

He parks across from the fireplace, and Win sits on the hearth, looking around at photographs, many of them younger versions of Dr. Hunter with a pretty woman who Win supposes was his wife. A lot of happy moments with family, friends, a framed newspaper story with a black-and-white picture of Dr. Hunter at a crime scene, police everywhere.

"I have a feeling I know why you're here," Dr. Hunter says. "That old murder case suddenly in the news. Janie Brolin. Must say, I couldn't believe it when I first heard. Why now? Then, of course, our friendly local DA is known for, shall we say, her surprises."

"Ever enter your mind way back then that the Boston Strangler did it?"

"Utter nonsense. Women raped and strangled with their own clothing, their bodies displayed, and all the rest? It's one thing to use a scarf or stockings and tie them in a bow, quite another to use the victim's bra, which in my experience usually happens when the killer was sexually assaulting her, shoving and tearing at her clothing, and the bra is the most obvious and convenient ligature because of its general vicinity to the neck. I should add that Janie wasn't the sort to let anybody in her house for any reason whatsoever unless she was absolutely certain who it was."

"Because she was blind," Win supposes.

"I'm not far from it myself. Macular degeneration," he says. "But I can tell a lot by a person's voice. More than I used to. When one of your senses gets worse, the others pitch in and try to help it out. Journalists were more circumspect in 1962, or maybe her family just wouldn't talk or the press wasn't interested. I don't know, but what was left out of the papers, as best I recall, was Janie Brolin's father was a doctor in London's East End and no stranger to crime, patched up victims of it on a regular basis. Her mother worked in a pharmacy that had been robbed a couple of times."

"So Janie wasn't naïve," Win says.

"Feisty, street-smart, which is one of the reasons she had the pluck to take a year abroad, all by herself, and come to Watertown."

"Because of Perkins. She was blind and wanted to work with the blind."

"That's the speculation."

"You ever talk with her family?"

"Her father, just once and very briefly. As you well know, not everybody wants to talk to the pathologist. They can't deal with our part in it, mainly ask the same question time after time."

"If their loved one suffered."

"That's it," Dr. Hunter says. "Rather much the only thing her father asked me. He wanted a copy of the death certificate but not the autopsy report. Neither he nor his wife came over here. The body was returned to London along with what few personal effects she had. But he didn't want to know the details."

"Unusual for a doctor."

"Not for a father."

"What did you say when he asked?"

"I said she suffered. I never lied. You can't lie."

Stump enters Win's mind.

"You tell someone what he wants to hear, that his loved one didn't suffer, and then what happens if the case goes to court and the defense finds out you said that?" Dr. Hunter says. "He catches you in a lie—albeit a well-intended one. And your credibility's impeached. Now, then. I'll give you what I've got. Isn't much."

His chair quietly hums as he drives toward a doorway. "Dug up what I could find when I heard about all this on the news. Figured somebody was going to ask, and I figured right." In the hallway. "All this mess in my closets, under beds . . ." Fades out. Then comes back. "A few things from those days because we knew better back then."

He parks his scooter, a Bankers Box on his lap, keeps talking. "In the first place. Harvard really wasn't all that gung-ho about having a department of legal medicine or they'd still have one. There were a few of us pathologists who liked the investigative part, were only too happy to do autopsies, be crime doctors, as some people called us. But we held on to our own records, to whatever we deemed important or wanted to use for teaching purposes, knowing full well that when we went out the door, there wasn't going to be anybody left who gave a damn about our legacy. By the way. You see her on YouTube?"

Lamont. Which makes Win think of Stump again.

"Can't believe what people do these days," Dr. Hunter says. "Glad I'm not your age. Happy to be trekking along on the downslope. Not much to look forward to except home movies made by strangers, and, well . . . one of my grand-daughters's in Iraq. And I'm supposed to be in a retirement home with a lot of my friends, those left, anyway. Been on the list five years, my number recently came up. Can't afford it because I can't sell my house. Not so long ago, people were fighting over it." He indicates the computer on his desk over-looking the river. "I call it a cyber-pandemic. Once the floodgate opens, and you know the rest."

"I'm sorry. . . ."

"Monique Lamont, I mean. The second one's worse than the first. Go log on." A wave of his hand, indicating the computer again. "I get Google alerts for all sorts of things. The

DA, crime, city council, because I like to keep up with what's going on in Middlesex County. Since I happen to live in it."

Win goes over to the computer, logs on to the Internet, doesn't take him long to find the latest video clip making the rounds.

The Commodores singing, "Ow, she's a brick house . . ." As Lamont in a hard hat, other officials, and construction workers inspect tons of collapsed concrete ceiling slabs inside a tunnel near Boston's Logan Airport.

Then a voice-over from one of her old campaign ads: "Getting to the bottom of it, demanding justice." As Lamont stoops over, inspects a section of a twisted steel tieback, her fitted skirt hikes up to her buttocks.

Dr. Hunter says, "Obviously, from that road construction disaster last summer, the Big Dig, when that tunnel collapsed and crushed that car, killed the woman passenger. Never was a fan of Monique Lamont, but now I'm starting to feel sorry for her. It's not right to do that to somebody. But that's not why you're here. If I knew the answer to Janie Brolin, the case would have been solved when I was working it. My opinion now is the same as it was. A domestic homicide staged to look like a sexual homicide."

"Staged by her boyfriend. Lonnie Parris?"

"They'd been heard arguing in the past, if my memory serves me well. Reports from neighbors of the two of them going at each other. So that morning, maybe he comes to pick her up for work. They get into it. He strangles her, then stages it to look like some sexual predator did it. Flees the scene and has the misfortune of having a close encounter of the vehicular kind."

"All I found about him was a newspaper article, couldn't find his case file. Assume Cambridge has it, since it was a Cambridge case. Did you do his autopsy?"

"I did. Multiple trauma. What you'd expect if you were run over."

"Run over? As opposed to being struck while you're upright?"

"Oh, he was run over, for sure. More than once. Some of his injuries were postmortem, indicating to me he'd been dead on the road for a while, long enough for a couple more cars to run over him before somebody finally felt a bump, decided it might be a good idea to get out and check. This was early in the morning. Dark out."

"Possible he might already have been dead before he was run over?"

"You mean staged to look like an accident? It's possible. All I can tell you is he wasn't stabbed and he wasn't shot. He certainly suffered massive trauma, especially to his head, while he was alive."

"I just find it interesting that he called the police from Janie's apartment after supposedly walking in and finding her murdered," Win says. "Then he disappears before the police show up. And not even twenty-four hours later, he's dead in the middle of a road. Not hit while he was standing. But run over because he was already on the pavement."

"We did the best we could. Didn't have the wizardry you do these days."

"We don't have wizardry, but certainly there are capabilities that didn't exist when you were working these cases, Dr. Hunter. I'm wondering"—pointing at the Bankers Box—"what you've got."

"Mostly the same old records in here you've probably already seen. The Cambridge records included. But the best stuff—well, it would have been somewhat unseemly for me to walk out the door with it when I retired. Specifically, pathological specimens. When the Department of Legal Medicine was disbanded in the eighties, our specimens stayed behind, no doubt were thrown out eventually. I wish I still had Janie Brolin's eyes. Quite fascinating. Used to pass them around in wet labs. It was anybody's guess."

"What about her eyes?" Win asks.

"As you might expect, during her autopsy, I shone a bright light into her eyes, wondering if I might discover anything on gross examination that would account for her blindness. And I discovered strange shiny brownish specks over the corneas, what I suspect was the sequela of a disease process that caused her blindness. Or maybe she was suffering from some undiagnosed neurological degeneration that might result in an altered distribution of pigmentation. To this day, don't know. Well, not useful for your purposes, anyway. A medical curiosity that's more to my taste."

"May I?" Win gets up, walks over to the Bankers Box.

"Be my guest."

Win carries it back to the hearth, takes off the lid. The expected paperwork and photographs, and a plastic airtight food container.

"Been around a long time, hasn't it?" Dr. Hunter says. "Tupperware. That and Ball glass jars. Staples in the morgue."

The lid is labeled with the case number that by now is so familiar: WT218–62. Inside are a syringe with a bent needle and a small vial that Win holds up to the light.

An oily residue in it, and what looks like tiny flecks of tarnished copper.

9

After a quick stop at the labs to drop off the syringe and vial, he checks on Nana.

"Brought your car back," he says loudly. "Door unlocked. Alarm off. At least I can take some comfort in consistency. Because everything else is chaos, Nana."

All this as he carries groceries into her kitchen, not realizing she has a visitor. Poor Mrs. Murphy from Salem. Quite the irony that Nana has clients from what is literally called "The Witch City," where the police department emblem features a witch flying on a broom. No joke.

"I didn't realize you were with someone." He sets down the bags, starts putting things away.

Groceries from a real grocery store, where he paid full price.

"How you doing, Mrs. Murphy?" he asks.

"Oh, not so good."

"Looks to me like you've lost some weight."

"Oh, not so much." The ever-morose Mrs. Murphy, all three hundred pounds of her.

Has a glandular condition, she says. It's no better, she says. Does everything Nana tells her, and for a while, not so bad. Then the psychic vampire shows up again, drains her life force while she's asleep, and she's too depressed and tired to exercise or to do anything but eat.

"I know," Win says. "I work for a psychic vampire. It's hell."

Mrs. Murphy laughs, slapping her huge thighs. "You're such a funny one. Always cheer me up," she says. "I told you to get away from her, though. You seen her movies? Oh, whatever they're called. Same thing the presidential candidates are doing. You-Two or something. Anyway, I keep up with you and that big case you're suddenly doing. I remember that case, don't you?" Nodding at Nana. "It was like someone doing that to Helen Keller when she was young, only, of course, nobody killed Helen Keller. Thank God."

"Thank God," Nana agrees.

"I remember thinking it was like Alfred Hitchcock. Not an original thought. A lot of people said that at the time. Sort of like *Wait Until Dark*, where you imagine this poor blind girl struggling to dial the phone, struggling to get help, and she can't even see the phone, much less the killer. Not knowing which direction to run because she can't see anything. How terrifying is that? Well, I'll be going so you can spend some time with your boy," Mrs. Murphy says to Nana.

Win helps Mrs. Murphy out of her chair.

"Such the gentleman, that one." She opens her pocketbook, pulls out a twenty-dollar bill, leaves it on the table, points her finger at Win. "I still got that daughter of mine, you know. Lilly's a fine one—and not dating anybody at the moment."

"I'm so busy right now, I'm not fit for a lady, especially one as fine as your daughter."

"Such a gentleman." She says it again, enters a number on her cell phone, says to whoever answers, "I'm coming out now. What? Oh, no. It's better if I wait in the driveway. I'm too tired to walk around the block, honey."

She leaves, and Nana opens the refrigerator, takes a look at what Win just bought.

"All sorts of wonderful things, my darling," she says, opening a cupboard, checking in there, too. "What's happened with your friend?"

"It was easier to stop at Whole Foods. That roasted chicken is right off the rotisserie, and the wild rice salad—you need some grain. Has nuts and dried cranberries. I filled your car with gas, checked the oil, you're all set."

"Sit down for a minute," Nana says. "See this?" Points to a

large gold locket she's wearing around her neck, one of about ten other chains with charms and symbols he doesn't understand. "I have a piece of your hair in this locket from when you were a baby. And now I've added a piece of my hair. Maternal energy, my darling. Your grandmother protecting her grandson. There are angels walking the earth. Don't you fear."

"If you run into one, send her my way." He smiles at her.

"What happened with your friend?"

"What friend, and what makes you think anything happened?"

"The one who's caused a darkness in your heart. It's not what you think it is."

"Nothing's ever what I think it is," he says. "That's what makes life interesting, right? Gotta go."

"England," she says.

He stops in the doorway. "That's right. Janie Brolin was from England." It's been all over the news.

Lamont and Scotland Yard, the dynamic duo. Who knows? Maybe they'll save what's left of the world.

"No," Nana says emphatically. "It's not about that poor girl."

Outside, he puts on his motorcycle gear while Mrs. Murphy watches, her big fake-leather pocketbook looped over the crook of a corpulent arm.

"You look like one of those shows," she says. "*Star Trek*. I used to love Captain Kirk. Now he does those travel commercials. Isn't that an irony? Captain Kirk doing travel commercials, I guess staying in hotels where *no man's stayed before.*" Laughing. "For ninety-nine dollars. Nobody sees the irony except me."

Win puts on his helmet, says, "You want to hop on the back and I'll give you a ride?"

She guffaws. "Don't make me wet my pants! My Lord in heaven. A whale like me on a itty-bitty jet ski."

"Come on." He pats the back of the seat. "Hop on. I'll take you to your car."

Her face goes slack. Then something soft and sad in her eyes, because he means it.

"Well, there's Ernie," she says as a Toyota turns into the driveway.

Lamont's in her office when he gets off the elevator.

Doesn't take a detective to figure that out. Her car's in its reserved parking place, her office door's shut, and he can hear the faint murmur of voices behind it. She's probably talking to her latest Ken-doll press secretary. Win walks into the investigative unit, barely speaks to his colleagues, who give him a curious look, since he's supposed to be on leave solving a case of international importance. Mainly what he needs right now is his comfort zone, his phone, and his computer. He sets Dr. Hunter's files on the desk, checks his grandfather's allegedly stolen watch. It's almost nine p.m. in London. He goes on the Internet, finds a general information number for Scotland

Yard, tells the lady who answers he's a homicide detective in Massachusetts and really needs to speak to the commissioner. It's urgent.

That goes over like the proverbial lead balloon. Sort of like calling the White House and asking for the president. After much to-do, he gets a pleasant enough woman in the investigative division, finds out the man he wants is Detective Superintendent Jeremy Killien. Problem is, he's out of the country.

"You know where he can be reached?"

"Left for the United States. That's all I know. If you call back tomorrow during office hours, perhaps one of the commissioner's administrative assistants can be of service." She gives him a direct number.

Can't be about the Brolin case. No way some detective superintendent from Scotland Yard would be flying all the way here about that. Win sits and thinks, shakes three Advils from a bottle, has a wicked headache and that detached, slow-motion feeling he gets when he's sleep-deprived, not working out or eating enough. He starts on Dr. Hunter's files, most of what's in them the same information he and Stump looked at in the records room. Well, he's not going to ask her to help him with anything now, and he goes through notes, other paperwork, sentence by sentence, page by page, comes across a name that stops him cold.

J. Edgar Hoover.

Other names, Mafia names that are vaguely familiar,

scribbles in Dr. Hunter's almost unreadable hand, sketchy references to a conversation he had on April 10 with a journalist who worked for the Associated Press. Win logs on to the Internet, initiates one search after another. The reporter won several awards for a number of series he wrote about organized crime. Win starts printing out stories. Reading them is slow going, and, as he expected, the journalist died years ago, so forget talking to him.

At almost five p.m., his phone rings.

It's Tracy from the labs.

"Nothing helpful from DNA. No matches in CODIS. But you were right," she says.

He asked her to take samples from the syringe and vial, and to examine them with the scanning electron microscope and X-ray analysis so they could magnify the particulate in the oily residue and also determine its elemental composition. Assuming the strange brownish flecks are inorganic—like copper.

"They're metal," she confirms.

"What the hell would have copper in it? She was injecting particles of copper into herself?"

"Not copper," Tracy says. "Gold."

What begins to emerge is a portrait of a violent tragedy that, like almost all others Win has worked, is rooted in randomness, bad timing, a seemingly insignificant incident that ends a person's life in an astonishingly brutal way.

Although he'll never prove it, because there's no one left to say, it appears that less than forty-eight hours before Janie Brolin was murdered, she set the fatal event in motion by the simple act of stepping outside her apartment door to continue an argument with her boyfriend, Lonnie Parris. Win gets up from his desk, realizes he's been at it for almost five hours. He passes empty cubicle after empty cubicle, everyone gone. On the other side of the floor are the district attorney's offices, and the door to Lamont's suite. She's there. He can feel her intense, selfish energy. He knocks, doesn't wait for an answer, walks in, shuts the door behind him.

She's standing behind her spotless glass desk, packing her briefcase, looks up at him, an uneasy expression flitting across her face. Then she's her inscrutable self again, in a smoky blue suit and a greenish-black blouse, a subtle mismatch that is so Armani.

Win helps himself to a chair, says, "I need a few minutes."

"I don't have them." Shutting her briefcase, loud snaps as she fastens the clasps.

"I think you might want the information before I pass it along to Scotland Yard, to Jeremy Killien. And by the way, when you recruit other agencies into my investigation, it would be polite to let me know."

She sits, says, "You're well aware the Yard's involved."

"Right, now I am. Because I heard about it in the news you leaked."

"I didn't leak it. The governor did."

"Gee. Wonder how he found out. Maybe someone leaked it to him first."

"We're not discussing this," she says, as only she can. Never a comment, always a command. "Obviously, you have news about our case. Good news, I hope?"

"I don't think anything about this case could be good news. For you, it's probably not good news, and if Jeremy Killien weren't on his way to the US or already here, I'd advise you to let him know he probably doesn't need to waste Scotland Yard's time on . . ."

"He's on his way here? And how might you know that?"

"One of his colleagues told me. He left for the States. Don't know when and don't know why."

"Must be for some other reason. Not because of our case." She doesn't sound so sure of that. "I can't imagine him coming here and not discussing it with me first."

She switches on an art glass lamp, the window behind her dark. Lights in surrounding buildings are blurred by fog. It's going to rain, and Lamont hates rain. Hates it so much he once suggested she might have a seasonal affective disorder. One Christmas he even bought her a light box that's supposed to mimic the sun and lift your mood. Didn't work. Annoyed the hell out of her. Bad weather is bad timing for bad news.

"Janie Brolin most likely suffered from rheumatoid arthritis, probably had since she was a child," Win begins. "Maybe because her father was a doctor, it seems she resorted to a rather innovative treatment of sodium aurothiomalate. You familiar?"

"No." Impatiently, as if she's got someplace to go and is uptight about it.

"Gold salts. Used to threat chronic arthritis. Hard to say what dosage. Could have been ten to fifty milligrams weekly. Could have been less at longer intervals, administered by injection. Possible side effects include blood disorders, dermatitis, a proclivity to bruise easily—which might explain the excessive bruising all over her body. Plus corneal chrysiasis . . ."

Lamont shrugs, one of her "you've lost me" looks. Her way of treating him as if she's bored and he's stupid. She's getting more tense by the moment, intermittently glancing up at the Venetian glass clock on the wall across from her desk.

"Gold deposits in the corneas, which don't cause visual disturbances—in other words, don't impair your vision. But upon examination with a light, you see these minute brownish metallic flecks. What she had on autopsy," Win says.

"So what?"

"So everything adds up to her not being blind but having photosensitivity, another possible side effect from gold therapy. And people with sensitivity to light tend to wear dark glasses."

"And so what?"

"And so she wasn't blind."

"And so what?"

"And you just don't want to hear it, do you?"

"Hear your tangled thoughts? I don't have time to work my way through them."

"I believe Janie Brolin was a Mob hit. As was her boyfriend, Lonnie Parris. Her apartment was in the heart of Watertown's Mafiaville. She was fully aware of what was going on around her because she wasn't blind, meaning she sure as hell would have seen who was at her door the morning of April fourth, meaning it probably was someone she trusted enough to let in. Not necessarily her boyfriend, Lonnie Parris, who no more murdered her than the Boston friggin' Strangler did. I think by the time Lonnie showed up to drive her to Perkins, she was already dead. He walked in and found her."

Lamont says, "I'm waiting for whatever you're basing all of your assumptions on. In fact, I'm waiting for any of this to make sense."

"Two days earlier. April second," Win says. "A Mob underboss who happened to live across the street from Janie used contacts at the Registry of Motor Vehicles to get a license plate run so he could get the address of a certain juror who was a holdout in a not-guilty verdict. One of the underboss's boys was on trial for murder. In addition to being unhelpful, this juror also made an unfortunate comment, insulted this same underboss. Look it up. Plenty was written about it in the press."

Lamont. That stare of hers. As unwavering as a cat's.

"The inappropriate remark implied this Mob underboss and J. Edgar Hoover had a ménage à trois with another high-ranking FBI official. By the way, not that such things

355

hadn't been said before. But in this instance, the underboss in question—Janie's neighbor—had a couple of his guys show up at the juror's residence, abducted him, brought him back to the underboss's house. Not about persuading him to change his mind as much as it was about revenge. He ends up dead. His body goes in the car trunk, never to be seen again. That much is known from other cases later on, subsequent testimony from informants, et cetera."

"And has to do with what?"

"Has to do with the fact that on that particular night, April second, according to notes I've come across, various reports, and so on, Janie and her boyfriend were heard arguing in her apartment. This argument led outside, culminating in his storming off in his car."

"Maybe I'm just obtuse," Lamont says.

"She was home the night the juror was murdered across the damn street and loaded in a car trunk, Monique. And she wasn't blind. And anybody who knew her would have been aware of that. We'll probably never know exactly what happened, but it's more than possible that on the morning of April fourth, one of the Mob guys showed up at her place. Probably a neighbor, someone she was acquainted with. She opens her door, and that's it. Murdered, staged to look like a sexual homicide and a burglary. Without knowing he's part of the scenario, Lonnie shows up, walks in, makes this horrible discovery, calls the police. Boom. Mob guys show up, grab him, and off he goes."

"Why?"

"He probably saw the same thing Janie saw on April second. He was a liability. Or a scapegoat. Make it look as if he killed her and fled, and then accidentally gets hit by a car. Problem is, he wasn't hit. He was run over. How did that happen? He pass out while crossing the street in the early-morning hours after Janie was killed?"

"Drunk?"

"Tox was negative for drugs and alcohol. Good plan. Her death is explained. His death is explained. The end."

"The end? That's it?"

"That's it. Your Boston Strangler theory? As much as it breaks my heart? Forget it. Better call the governor. Better call the Yard. Better call a press conference. Since your international case has already been in the news from here to the moon. And England's got nothing to do with this except it lost a nice young woman to some Mafia dirtbags who happened to be her neighbors while she was enjoying a year in the States. She would have been better off blind."

"And that never came out at the time of the investigation? That she wasn't really blind?" Lamont asks.

"People make assumptions. Maybe nobody asked or cared or thought it was relevant. And then there's the cover-up factor. The police obviously cooperating with the Mob, since it appears that's what this is about."

"If she wasn't blind, why the hell would she work with them?" Lamont asks.

"The blind, I assume you mean."

"Why? If she wasn't?"

"She had a disease that caused her suffering every day. Changed her life. Limited it in some ways. Made her try harder, more courageous, too. Miracles and the Midas Touch. And nothing really worked. Why wouldn't she care about the pain and suffering of others?"

"Wasn't worth it. That's for damn sure," Lamont says. "Still a big story. It's all about how you spin it. Let's don't be coy. Better it doesn't come from a press release or press conference, which nobody really trusts, the public doesn't. Especially these days." She smiles as her next brainstorm hits. "A college reporter."

"You're not serious."

"Perfect. Absolutely serious," she says, getting up, grabbing her briefcase. "Not from me but from you. I want you to get with Cal Tradd."

"You're going to place a story like this in the friggin' *Crimson*? A student newspaper?"

"He investigated it, worked with you, with us, and what a great story. Becomes a story about a story. Just the sort of thing people love with this 'everybody's a journalist, everybody's the star in his own movie' craze. Reality TV, YouTube. Average Joe saves the day. Yes, indeed. And, of course, the general media will pick it up, will go all over the place, and everybody's happy."

Win walks out after her, slides his iPhone off his belt,

remembers the piece of paper in his wallet. Gets it out, unfolds it, is entering Cal's cell phone number when he notices something as the elevator doors close, taking Lamont down to the lower level of the courthouse, to her car. He holds up the piece of white notepaper, tilts it this way and that, can barely see indented letters, the faintest shadow behind the telephone numbers Cal wrote in a very neat hand.

A *T,* and *AG,* and what looks like a *W* followed by an exclamation point. He runs back into his office, grabs a sheet of printing paper, a pencil, remembering his conversation with Stump inside the mobile crime lab, their examination of the note used in the most recent bank robbery. A note exactly like three others in three earlier bank robberies. Neatly written in pencil on a four- by six-inch sheet of white paper, and he uses a ruler, draws a rectangle four by six inches—same size as the piece of paper Cal gave him. Win works it out, lining up the indented letters with what he remembers about the bank robbery note Stump showed him.

EMPTY CASH DRAWER IN BAG. NOW! I HAVE A GUN.

The image on the surveillance tape. The robber was about Cal's height but looked heavier. No problem. Wear several layers of clothes under your baggy warm-up suit. Darker skin. Dark hair. A million ways to do that. Including mascara— oldest trick in the book, and washes off in minutes. A quick search of the National Criminal Information Center, NCIC.

Cal Tradd. His date of birth and absence of a criminal record, explaining why there are no prints or DNA on file—not that he's ever left either, it would seem, except, perhaps, a coppery print on a disposable camera package that luminol reacted to as if the print were left in blood.

Bank robberies and copper thefts from all over this area. Excluding Cambridge, where Cal goes to school. And Boston, where he's from, Win thinks.

He tries Lamont, and his call rolls over to voice mail on the first ring. Either on the phone or she has it turned off. He tries Stump. Same thing. He doesn't leave a message for either one of them as he runs out of the courthouse, grabs his motorcycle gear out of the hard case, speeds off. A light rain smacks his face shield and makes the pavement slick as he weaves in and out of traffic toward Cambridge.

10

Lamont's car is in the driveway of the Victorian ruin on Brattle Street, not a single light on, no sign of anyone.

Win touches the hood of her Mercedes. It's warm, and he notes the quiet clicking sound car engines usually make right after they've been turned off. He goes around to the side of the house, out of sight, waiting, listening. Nothing. Minutes pass. Every window is dark, has nothing to do with the candle he took from the room where he found the mattress, the wine. Something else is going on, he can tell by looking through the window he broke the other night. The alarm panel is dead, no green light. He walks around, looking for cut power lines, for any indication of why there might be an electrical failure. Nothing, and he returns to the back door.

It's unlocked, and he opens it, hears footsteps on the wooden flooring. The impatient flipping of switches. Someone walking room to room. Switches flipping. Win shuts the door behind him, loudly, so whoever it is—Lamont, he's sure—will know someone has just come in.

Footsteps head his way, and Lamont calls out, "Cal?"

Win walks toward her voice.

"Cal?" she calls out again. "There are no lights anywhere. What happened to the lights? Where are you?"

A switch flipping on and off in the room beyond the kitchen, what may once have been a dining room. Win turns on his tactical light and shines it obliquely so he doesn't blind her.

"It's not Cal," he says, directing the light at a wall, illuminating the two of them.

They're standing maybe six feet apart in the middle of an empty, cavernous room with old wooden flooring and ornate molding.

"What are you doing here!" she exclaims.

He turns the light off. Complete darkness.

"What are you doing!" She sounds scared.

"Shhhh," he says, moves toward her, finds her arm. "Where is he?"

"Let go of me!"

He leads her to the wall, whispers for her to stand right

there. Don't move. Don't make a sound, then he waits by the doorway, no more than ten feet from her, but it seems to be miles. He waits for Cal. Long, tense minutes, and a noise. The back door opens. The beam of a flashlight enters the room before the person does, and then confusion as Win grabs someone, a struggle, and footsteps from all directions, and Stump is yelling, and then nothing.

"Are you all right?"

"Win?"

"Win?"

He opens his eyes, and the lights are on in the house, and Raggedy Ann is standing over him. Dressed a little differently this time. In a polo shirt, cargo pants, a pistol on her hip. Stump, Lamont, and some big guy in a suit, thick, gray hair.

"It's my damn house. I have every right to be here," Lamont is saying.

Win's head hurts like hell. He touches a huge lump on it, looks at blood on his hand.

"An ambulance is on the way," Stump says, crouching next to him.

He sits up, sees black for an instant, says, "You hit me, or do I have someone else to thank."

"That would be me," Raggedy Ann says.

She introduces herself as Special Agent McClure, FBI. The big guy in the suit is New Scotland Yard's Jeremy Killien. Now that Win knows the complete cast of characters, he suggests they might want to broadcast a "Be on the Lookout," a BOLO, for Cal Tradd. Since he's probably a bank robber, and a copper thief, and his luring the district attorney here was for purposes of blackmail, bribery, threatening her. Monique and Win set the whole thing up. All part of a sting operation that just got blown to hell. Lamont watches him spin the story. Not a glint of gratitude in her eyes that he's saving her ass.

"What sting operation?" McClure asks, baffled.

Win rubs his head, says, "Monique and I have been on this guy for a while. The way he follows me around, then started following her around, not to mention his maniacal obsession with covering the very crimes we were suspicious he was committing. Typical sociopathic behavior. This seventeen-year-old whiz kid—well, actually sixteen, birthday's next month—sheltered and controlled all his life, until he finally left home for college, younger than the usual freshman."

Nothing registers on Lamont's face. But Win has no doubt she didn't know. Even she wouldn't stoop so low as to have sex with a minor, if that's what the two of them have been doing when they rendezvoused in the very house Cal probably vandalized, stripped of copper. Then photographed. For souvenirs, just as he's done at so many other places. Thrill crimes. Not because he needs the money. Imagine that. Super Thief. Reporting on your own copper thefts and bank robberies, getting chummy with the very people investigating your crimes, even screwing the district attorney. What a wunderkind.

"This is completely embarrassing," Killien says in disgust.

"Whose bright idea was it to have the power turned off?" Win looks at McClure. "Oh. You guys. The F-Big-I. Then what?" Rubbing his head. "You call the power company and have it turned back on? Pretty cool to have connections like that. No pun intended." To Stump. "I don't need an ambulance." Touching the knot on his head again. "Fact is, I feel smarter. Isn't it true some people who get hit on the head with a flashlight end up with a higher IQ?"

"What sting operation?" Stump isn't amused.

No one is. Everybody looking at him with hard faces.

"You never mentioned any sting operation to me," Stump says.

"Well, you weren't exactly forthright with me, either. At least not about Special Agent Raggedy Ann."

"It's McClure," says the FBI agent.

"A print on a Fresca can," Win says to Stump. "A print on a note delivered to my apartment. No hit in AFIS, meaning the person who left them sure as hell didn't spend time in prison for stabbing her pimp. Sure as hell has no arrest record at all. And now that I know she's FBI, some undercover whatever, I'm not surprised she has no prints on file for exclusionary purposes."

"I couldn't tell you," Stump says.

"I get it," Win says. "Of course, you couldn't tell me that this Raggedy Ann criminal was really an informant who is really an FBI agent who is spying on me because she's really spying on Lamont."

"I believe you should lie back down," Killien says to him.

Stump continues to explain. "When you were so determined to follow her, Win, I had to come up with the Filippello Park scenario, have her deliver the note and all the rest. So it would appear I had no choice but to admit she was an informant, ensuring you would back off before you figured out she's FBI. You know how it works. We don't give up our informants, and had I offered that information easily, you would have been suspicious. So I had to script something. I had to make it appear I had no choice but to blow her cover and order you to stay the hell away from her."

They hold each other's gaze for a moment.

"I'm sorry," Stump says.

"So why the party?" Win says to everyone. "Why are we here? Because it's not about Janie Brolin. And it's not about Cal Tradd."

"I believe the easy answer is we're here because of your district attorney," Killien says to Lamont. "Romanian orphans. Large transfers of cash. Which flagged you, brought you to the attention of the FBI, Homeland Security. Finally, the Yard, unfortunately."

"What I should do is sue the hell out of every last one of you," she says.

And McClure says to her, "Your electronic communications with . . ."

"With Cal." Lamont steps into a role no one plays better than she does. The DA again. "I think Investigator Garano's made it clear what we've been doing since these serial bank robberies, copper thefts began here in Middlesex County. That part of our sting operation was my communicating with Cal, who's been, to put it mildly, of interest."

"You knew she was e-mailing Cal Tradd?" Stump asks McClure.

"No. We didn't know who she was e-mailing. The IP came back to Harvard. A machine code isn't helpful unless you can find the machine to compare it . . ."

"I know how it works." The look on Stump's face.

She probably liked McClure better when she was Raggedy Ann.

"The most recent e-mail indicating you would be meeting this person of interest . . ." McClure starts to say.

"Cal," Lamont says. "Meet him in the usual place at ten. Meaning here at ten."

"He didn't turn up," Killien says.

"Probably saw a posse thundering on the horizon and scuttled away," Win says. "The kid's used to dodging cops. Has cop radar. So you guys show up and blow everything Monique and I have been working on for months. And that's the problem when you monitor electronic communications, now, isn't it? Especially when you're undercover and monitoring somebody else who's undercover, one sting operation investigating what turns out to be another sting operation, and everybody gets stung."

*

Two nights later, the Harvard Faculty Club.

Georgian Revival brick, oil portraits on mahogany-paneled walls, brass chandeliers, Persian rugs, the usual arrangement of fresh flowers in the entryway—so familiar and intended to make him feel out of place. No fault of Harvard's, just another Lamontism. She always summons him to the faculty club when she needs to feel powerful, or more powerful than usual, because she either is secretly insecure or needs him, or both.

Win sits on the same stiff antique sofa he always sits on, the tick-tock of a grandfather clock reminding him Lamont's one minute late, two minutes, three, ten. He watches people come and go, all these academicians, visiting dignitaries and lecturers, or prominent families visiting to investigate whether they should send their prominent children here. One thing he loves about Harvard, it's like a priceless work of art. You never own it. You never deserve it. You just get to visit it for a while, and are a far better person for the association, even if it doesn't remember you. Probably was never even aware of you. That's what he finds sad about Lamont, no matter how much he dislikes her at times, finds her despicable at times.

What she has will never be enough.

She walks in, furling her umbrella, shaking rain off her coat as she slips out of it, heading to the cloakroom.

"You ever notice it always rains when we meet here?" Win asks her as they walk into the dining room, sit at their usual table by a window overlooking Quincy Street.

"I need a drink," she says. "How about you?" A tight smile, scant eye contact.

This can't be easy for her, and she searches for the waiter, decides it might be nice to have a bottle of wine. White or red? Win says either.

"Why did you do it?" Smoothing her linen napkin in her lap, reaching for her water. "We both know, and for the record, this conversation not only will never happen again, but it didn't happen at all."

"Then why bother?" he says. "Why did you invite me to dinner if all you wanted was to talk about not talking and exact the promise that we'd never talk about not talking again? Or whatever you just said."

"I'm in no mood to be glib."

"Then fire away. I'm listening."

"Foundation of International Law," she says. "My father's foundation."

"I believe all of us know what FOIL is by now. Or what you turned it into. A limited liability company, a front to protect and shield the person behind the purchase of a multimillion-dollar Victorian ruin that will take years to renovate. Too bad you didn't pick some other name, can't help but wonder about the karma of using a name associated with a father who always treated you like . . ."

"I really don't think you're in a position to discuss my father."

The waiter arrives with a silver bucket of ice, a fine

bottle of Montrachet. He uncorks it. Lamont tastes it. Two glasses filled, waiter gone, and Lamont starts looking at the menu.

"I can't remember what you usually get here." She changes the subject.

Win retrieves it. "More than anyone you know, I'm in a position to discuss your father. Because at the end of the day, Monique, he's why you got yourself into a mess that could have . . ."

"I don't need to hear your version of what it could have done." Drinking her wine. "Are you really surprised I'd buy another house? Maybe not want to live in the same one? Maybe spend very little time there. Almost none. Actually, I rented an apartment at the Ritz, but driving back and forth from Boston isn't much fun."

"I understand why you bought a house. I understand why you want to get rid of the one you're in—never understood how you could spend another night there after what happened." All said carefully. "But let's look at the chain of events and how underlying emotional issues set you up for something you don't want to repeat. Ever."

She looks around, making sure no one is listening, looks out at the rain, at gaslights and slick cobblestones, her face touched by sadness for an instant.

"Your father died last year," Win continues in a quiet voice, leaning into their conversation, elbows on the white tablecloth. "Left half of everything to you. Not that you were hurting before, but now you have what most people would consider a fortune. Still doesn't account for your subsequent behavior. You've never been a have-not. So for you to become a wild, crazy spender means something else is going on. Hundreds of thousands of dollars on clothing, a car, who knows what else, all cash. Millions on a house when you already own a multimillion-dollar house, and you rent a place at the Ritz. Cash, more cash, all this cash moving from a French bank to a Boston bank, to who knows how many banks."

"My father had accounts in London, Los Angeles, New York, Paris, Switzerland. How else do you move large sums of cash if not by wire transfers? Most people don't use suitcases. And paying cash for clothing, for automobiles, is what I've always done. Never buy things on credit that begin to depreciate the minute you leave the store. As for the house on Brattle? In this dreadful market, I got it for a song compared to what it will be worth after I fix it up—if and when the day ever comes that our economy recovers. I didn't need a mortgage for deductions, and I really don't care to discuss the nuances of my financial portfolio with you."

"In point of fact. You moved huge amounts of money. Made huge purchases in cash. Went on a spending spree the likes of which I've never seen with you, and I've known you for a fairly long time. Donated to charities you didn't check out. Then you get involved with . . ."

"No names." She holds up her hand.

"Certainly convenient to own a house you don't live in and isn't in your name," Win says. "Good place to have a meeting or two. Or three or four. Bad idea to have such meetings at the Ritz. Or a house where the neighbors know you and maybe watch you out their windows. Not good to have meetings in college housing." Drinks his wine. "With a college kid." Holds up his glass. "This is pretty good."

She looks away from him. "What's going to come out in court?"

"Hard to imagine he's a juvenile. I wouldn't have guessed."

"He lied."

"You didn't check."

"Why would I?"

"You ever notice needle marks on his hands, speaking of not checking things? Fingertips, palms."

"Yes."

"You ask him?"

"Botox injections so his hands wouldn't sweat," she says. "His father's a plastic surgeon. You know that. Started giving them to him when he was performing. You know, piano recitals. So his fingers didn't slip on the keys. Now he continues the Botox because he plays keyboard, is used to it."

"And you believed that."

"Why wouldn't I?"

"I suppose," Win says. "Can't say it would enter my mind,

either. Unless I were already suspicious of the person. Not to mention, I've never heard of anybody doing that. Botox in their fingertips. Must hurt like hell."

"Wouldn't be foolproof," Lamont says.

"Nothing is. But you walk into a bank, shove a note under the glass, and your hands are clean and dry. No prints on paper."

"Good luck proving all this."

"We have his copper print, for lack of a better thing to call it. On the camera box he stupidly left in the kitchen of your new-old house. Don't worry. He's going to be locked up for quite some time," Win says.

"What's going to happen?"

"I don't understand your question," he says.

She gives him her eyes. "Of course you do."

The waiter wanders toward them, picks up her signal, and retreats.

"He's a pathological liar," Win says. "The one time there was a meeting that was witnessed by others? Well, not only was he not there but the witnesses are aware of a sting operation that explains various electronic communications that frankly the Feds and others might prefer the public didn't know about. Since the Patriot Act is about as popular as the bubonic plague."

"You were there before," she says. "At the house. And saw me return to my car. And what I was carrying. And all the rest."

"No evidence of that, and I never saw him that night. I will say, however, I don't appreciate someone wearing my skin. Part of the thrill. Stealing my stuff . . ."

"Setting you up?"

"No. Stealing me. Psychological," Win says. "Probably goes back to what his mother said about me when they were apartment shopping, which had to make him feel more inadequate and resentful than he already felt. Anyway. I guess in his own way, he put on my skin, walked around in my shoes. Overpowered me in his own weirdo way. You didn't drink the wine he stole from me."

"Wasn't in the mood," she says, giving him her eyes again. "Wasn't in the mood for any of it, to tell the truth. Had gotten out of the mood rather quickly, which didn't set well, if you understand what I mean."

"Boy toy gets boring."

"I would prefer you not make comments like that."

"So on that occasion, the one I sort of witnessed, things didn't go well. When I saw you leave the courthouse, you seemed to be arguing. Were on your cell phone. You seemed upset, and I followed you."

"Yes, arguing. I didn't want to go there. To the house. He was persuasive. Had things on me. Made it difficult for me to refuse. I'll be candid for a moment and tell you I didn't know how I was going to get out of it. And further, I have no idea how I got into it to begin with."

"I'll be candid for a moment and tell you how it all

happened. In my opinion," he says. "When we feel powerless, we do things that make us feel powerful. Our appearance. Our clothing. Our homes. Our cars. Pay cash. Do whatever we can to feel desirable. Sexy. Including, well, maybe even exhibitionism." He pauses. "Let me guess. He made those YouTube videos. But it wasn't his idea, it was yours. One more thing he had on you."

Her silence is her answer.

"Got to give it to you, Monique. I think you're the shrewdest human being I've ever met."

She drinks her wine. "What if he says something about it. To the police. Or worse, in court," Lamont says.

"You mean airs your dirty laundry, so to speak? Which you were smart enough not to leave at the scene after your . . . ?"

"If he says something about anything," she interrupts.

"He's a liar." Win shrugs.

"It's true. He is."

"The other thing when we feel powerless?" Win says. "We pick someone safe."

"Obviously not so. This was anything but safe."

"Want to feel desirable but safe," Win says. "The older, powerful woman. Adored but safe, because she's in control. What could be safer than a bright, artistic boy who follows you like a puppy."

"Do you think Stump's safe?" Lamont says, nodding at the waiter.

"By which you're implying . . . ?"

"I think you know what I'm implying."

She'll have greens with vinaigrette, and a double order of tuna carpaccio with wasabi. He orders his usual steak. A salad. No potato.

"We're close friends," Win says. "Work and play well with each other."

It's obvious Lamont wants to know two things but can't bring herself to ask. Is he in love with Stump, and did she tell him what happened long years ago when Lamont got drunk in Watertown?

"Let me ask again," Lamont says. "Is she safe?"

"Let me tell you again. We're close friends. I feel perfectly safe. How about you?"

"I expect you back in the unit on Monday," Lamont says. "So I'm not sure how much you'll be working with her anymore. Unless, of course, there's a homicide and she rolls up in that rather ridiculous truck. Which brings me to one last point. The organization she started."

"The FRONT."

"What should we do about it?"

"I don't think there's anything we can do about it," Win says. "It's moved in like a front, rather much living up to its name. You're not going to get rid of it."

"I wasn't suggesting any such thing," Lamont says. "I was wondering what we might do to help. If that would please her."

"Please Stump?"

"Yes, her. Keep her happy. And safe."

"If I were you, I would," Win says. "Safe to say, that would be a smart thing to do."